craving
MIDNIGHT

A.M. HARGROVE

CRAVING MIDNIGHT

**She's a starlet with secrets. He makes scandals go
away. Together, they'll make sparks fly…**

Midnight Drake's squeaky clean reputation has suddenly
taken a nosedive. She's horrified after she wakes up naked from
a drugged stupor, but the worst is yet to come. She just found
three sex videos on her phone of a night she can't remember.
Midnight wonders if her promising new career will go up in
smoke …

Harrison Kirkland cleans up Hollywood's sordid messes for a
living, and he's never met a scandal he couldn't contain. But

when he's assigned to fix the sultry Midnight's problems, he never expected to get dragged in after her...

Behind Midnight's diva exterior, Harrison discovers a mysterious woman with a web of secrets he can't untangle. The deeper he's pulled into her world, the stronger his desire for her grows, but can he handle the truth about her past? If he's not careful, the next heart that'll need fixing... will be his...

Craving Midnight is a red-carpet ready contemporary romance novel. If you like steamy chemistry, flawed characters with compelling secrets, then you'll love A.M. Hargrove's pulse-pounding story.

*This book contains sensitive subject matter that may not be suitable for all readers.

Cover: Letitia Hasser RBAdesigns.com
Photography: Wander Aguiar
Models: Jonny James and Desiree Crossman
Editing: Jennifer Sommersby Young— www.commanaut.com
Proofreading: Sydnee Thompson

Acknowledgements

WOW ... THIS BOOK. CAN I JUST SAY CRAZY? IF YOU'VE READ MY other stuff, you'll notice it's a bit different from the rest. Yeah, it was a stretch, but I thought it was time. Midnight's journey was not only painful for her, but for me as well. I hope you felt it in the pages as you absorbed the words.

Many thanks go out for this one. I need a wig because I pulled out too many hairs during the editing process. But thank you to all my beta readers for your awesome feedback—Terri, Ashley, Chanpreet, Kristie, Andrea, and Heather. My pestering questions on how to get this book to where I wanted it to be had to drive you all crazy. Thanks for holding my hand.

Thank you Jenn Sommersby Young for your awesome help with all your movie knowledge and your super editing skills.

Thank you to all my girls in the NCC—Angel, Terri, Michelle, MJ, Megan, Ann Marie, Kristen, Heidi Jo, Heather, Gina, T.K., and Sarah. You guys are so awesome and I love how much we are there for each other. Let's keep it rocking!

Hargrove's Hangout peeps—you guys are the best! I love hanging out with you. I'm sorry I've been MIA but you know how I disappear when it's crunch time. I'll be back with guns a blazing now that this puppy is done. Get those sexy pics ready to roll! WOOT!

For those of you who aren't members of Hargrove's Hangouts, if you want to join in on the fun, click here.

Thank you Nina, Chanpreet, and Jenn at Social Butterfly. I love you ladies, especially when I'm having a freak out.

And thank you Rick and Amy at Red Coat. Thanks for your appreciation of Walter and my use of the F-bomb (this goes to Rick-haha)!

Lastly, thank you family. I can't wait until January. Coco will be one happy lady!

To keep up to date with the latest from me, sign up for my newsletter here.

This book is dedicated to all my readers. Thank you for sticking with me. I love you guys!

"Love's a bloody river with level-five rapids. Only a catastrophic act of nature or a dam has any chance of stopping it—and then usually succeeds in diverting it. Both measures are extreme and change the terrain so much you end up wondering why you bothered."

—Jericho Barrons, *Shadowfever* by Karen Marie Moning

Playlist

"From Afar" ... Vance Joy
"Green Gloves" ... The National
"Sucker For Pain" ... Lil Wayne, Wiz Khalifa
"Say Something" ... A Great Big World
"Stay" ... Rihanna, Mikki Ekko
"Rise Up" ... Andra Day
"Til It Happens To You" ... Lady Gaga
"Words of Mine" ... Cary Brothers
"Ghost" ... Striking Matches
"Kissing Your Tattoos" ... Eli Lieb
"If You Say So" ... Lea Michele
"Over The Hills And Far Away" ... Led Zeppelin
"Seven Wonders" (remastered)... Fleetwood Mac
"Shattered (Turn The Car Around)" ... O.A.R.
"Curse + Crush" ... Dispatch
"Nothing Else Matters" ... Metallica

Chapter 1

MIDNIGHT

My life has finally turned around. Things are looking up. Coming to New York has always been a dream for me, and now here I am, on a photo shoot for my upcoming film no less. And this time, it isn't for some shit role, or a porn flick being shot in the back of a dank warehouse where I would be freezing to death because the director wanted my nipples to constantly stick out. No, I'm here because of the major new contract I recently landed for the film *Turned*. I plan on working my ass off to prove to the world that Midnight Drake has what it takes to be taken seriously as an actor.

Gazing out the window of my hotel room, the New York City skyline is even more stunning than I'd imagined. LA is great and I love it there, but nothing beats the Empire State Building. I don't care what anyone says. My phone rings, interrupting my musing.

"Hello?"

"Midnight, it's Dex McCloud. Just wanted to let you know we're all meeting downstairs in five minutes."

Dex is the photographer. "Oh, thanks. I'm on my way."

We're meeting in the lobby to take some promo shots for the

film. It'll be the lead male actor, the producer, and me. I've never been this pumped up about anything in my whole life.

Grabbing my coat, purse, and a handful of gummy bears, I head for the elevators. The last thing I want is to be late. We're supposed to meet by the huge floral arrangement and I'm the first one here. Points for Midnight. Glancing around, I notice lots of business types hurrying by, but then there are tons of elegantly dressed people meandering around. It makes me feel slightly out of place, and even happier that I wore the outfit I chose. The conservative black pants and black sweater are perfect for where we are.

The only thing that stands out is my red lipstick. It's sort of my trademark. I feel naked without it. Maybe it goes back to when I was young and remember my mom always wearing it.

Shoving those memories aside, I scan the room.

A man approaches me with a warm smile. He has a camera strapped around his neck, but I'm still wary. You never know with the paparazzi these days.

"Hi, I'm Dex McCloud," he says, extending his hand. I offer my own smile and take his hand, shaking it.

"Hi, Midnight Drake."

"Yeah, I recognized you." His friendly tone puts me even more at ease. "Glad you're here. I usually have to wait on everyone."

"Ah, I hate to be late. Is Danny here?" I ask. He's the producer.

"He should be. And so should Holt." He checks his watch, then looks back at me.

"How long do you expect this to take?"

"Not long at all. I thought we'd go across to Central Park. I usually can get what I need in about thirty minutes. And the lighting is perfect for outdoor shots today."

"Sounds great," I say.

He eyes me for a moment. "You're a lot smaller in person than on camera."

"Oh." I don't quite know how to respond to that. Does he mean I look fat on screen?

Then he shuffles his feet and adds, "What I meant is on screen you look a lot taller. You're actually quite petite."

"Yeah, I always wanted to be five ten, but only made it to five four. It's why I usually wear heels, which I didn't today." I sigh. "I had these illusions of becoming a famous model when I was a kid and you can see how well that worked out for me." A weird laugh bubbles past my lips. I ended up doing B-rated movies after porn, which isn't exactly modeling's first cousin. I leave that tiny detail out though, because no one is aware of the porn bit. Having my nose slightly altered, ditching my brown contacts along with the bleached hair helped to alter my appearance, so no one realizes I was the former Lusty Rhoades.

"I think the modeling industry is crazy. You're beautiful and would make a perfect model. They want their models to look emaciated. Consider yourself fortunate."

Raising my eyes to his, I inhale the breath of fresh air that he is. "Wow. You have a very unique opinion, you know that?"

"I spend a ton of time behind the lens and recognize what true beauty is. Those poor scarecrows are not beautiful. They're pitiful. Anyway, congrats on your upcoming movie."

"Yeah, thanks. I'm super excited about it."

Holt and Danny stroll up and our sweet conversation halts. "Hey, kids," Danny says. "Thanks for flying out here, Midnight. We were on such a tight schedule with Holt's last film, there was no way we could squeeze in a flight back to LA."

"No problem," I say. Holt zeroes his icy stare on me. He despises the fact I'm in the film. He wanted someone famous who could guarantee a box office hit, but he ended up with a girl who is almost unknown. His disdainful glare has me feeling like I'm a virus.

I sort of don't blame him. He's the sexy, hottest man of the year. He reigns as king when it comes to leading men. When I secretly inspect him, it's easy to see why. Brown hair kissed by the sun, eyes so green they look like gems, perfect teeth and a mouth to match. The man is pure sin on two legs. And he ends up with a nobody for a costar. Nope, it's hard to blame him one bit. But I'm going to win him over, little by little, even if I have to buy him a fucking puppy.

"Everybody ready to take a little walk?" Dex asks.

"Why the fuck not?" Holt says sourly.

Danny shoots him a glance but says nothing.

"Sure," I chirp. "Let's go."

We exit the hotel out the main entrance. The Plaza is gorgeous. I've never stayed anywhere this fancy. We follow Dex across the street into the park. True to his word, he's finished in thirty minutes. We return to the hotel and Dex wants to get some shots of us drinking coffee in the restaurant.

Holt grumbles and then says, "Oh, for fuck's sake. Why don't you make it tea? Don't they serve tea here? Maybe add a biscuit or something."

Dex looks extremely uncomfortable. "I'm sorry, Mr. Ward, but if I don't get enough shots, everyone will want to bring you back together. It's best we get everything now while we're here."

An impossibly long sigh roars out of him. Jeez, you'd think Dex was asking him to pull his fingernails out, one by one, with the way he's acting.

Smiling, I say, "I'm fine with whatever you decide, Dex." I decide to be the one to make his job less difficult.

"Go on there, Little Miss Sexpot, score some brownie points while you can."

What the fuck! I totally expect Danny to step up and say something, but he's such a wimp, he acts like he didn't hear a thing. Well, I won't stand for that. I've had enough of Holt's surly act.

"Holt, I'm sorry you don't like the fact I was cast in this role, but that does not give you the right to insult me."

A nasty grin curls his lip. He lowers his eyes and they skim over my body. I instantly feel dirty.

"Is that right?" Then he takes a step toward me and invades my personal space. He leans in close and whispers so that only I can hear him. "What I'd like to know is how someone like you got cast in a film with me. What did you do, Midnight? Did you put that hot mouth of yours around Danny's dick and do him a few dirty favors?"

A red ball of fury nearly blinds me. I'm not sure how to respond to this asshole without sinking to his level. I do know one thing: I haven't encountered someone this vicious in a long time. It takes me back to a time I can barely force myself to think about.

Shaking myself out of that memory, I grit out, "Step away from me, Holt." When he doesn't, I walk away, toward Dex, and ask him where he needs me.

"Why don't we get a table at the restaurant," he suggests.

On the way, I question how I am going to tolerate working closely with Holt for the duration of the film. The man is revolting.

Once seated, the three of us smile as if we're the happiest people around. I cover up my dislike for Holt by pretending I'm in a happy place. But I notice the steely glint in his green eyes, the disdain imprinted on his expression. The curl of his lip that I used to think was sexy I now only see as cruel. Dex is quick, and soon, the session is wrapped.

Danny, who finally takes his eyes off his phone, asks, "So, what are you two up to tonight?"

Holt mutters something about meeting friends. I hardly pay attention. My mission is to stay as far away from him as possible.

"Midnight? What about you? You interested in grabbing a bite to eat?"

"Sure. What time?"

"I'm all about early. Is six okay?" he asks.

When I check the time, I see it's already five thirty. "That's fine. I'll meet you back down here then. Do we need a reservation?"

"No. There's a great place right around the corner."

Dinner with Danny turns out to be great. One on one, he's very outgoing and friendly. I decide to take a chance and ask about Holt.

"It seems Holt isn't very excited about my role in the film."

Danny nods. "He wanted his main squeeze. That's how Holt is. Every time he makes a film, he pushes for his girl of the moment to be cast as the lead female actor. I keep telling him his women don't have any experience."

"I hope I'm not overstepping, but what made you choose me?" My curiosity is killing me.

"I don't mind telling you at all. Your presence on-screen is unreal. When we looked at your screen tests, we were blown away. And you were the perfect fit for Christine. Your hair, your eyes, your stature. You were born for the role. Don't worry about Holt. He does this to everyone he works with—tries to intimidate them. Don't let him. Ignore him. He'll get over it as soon as he works with you a couple of days and catches your emotion on the set."

"That's comforting, but he makes me want to punch his face."

Danny takes a sip of his bourbon. "Yeah, I get that from all the women who work with him at first. He's an asshole. What can I say? But wait until you watch the finished product. You'll be raving about him then. Especially when you see your bank account."

"Good to know." Admittedly, Danny's calmed me down about Holt. We finish dinner and he invites me to go for a drink. I'm more than a little leery about this.

"Midnight, I'm not into sleeping with my actors, if that's what's holding you back. I don't believe in that shit. It spoils a good working relationship."

"I did hear that about you." I checked him out before I agreed to take this role. After you've worked in the porn industry, you think everyone's out for one thing.

"So?"

"Sure, why not?"

We hop into a taxi and go to a really cool club. Danny grew up in Manhattan so I'm comfortable with him leading the way. We dance, have a couple more drinks, and I excuse myself to use the restroom.

When I return, I can't find Danny. Then I spy him out on the dance floor with someone. I'm alone at the bar when a nice-looking guy approaches and asks me to dance. We weave our way through the throng and claim a piece of the real estate. He's not bad, but I know how to move. I used to imitate my mom, who was a stripper, so my exotic-dancer skills are pretty damn good.

Not wanting him to get the wrong impression of me, I tone it down and move like everyone else does, swaying my hips to the beat.

A few songs later, we walk back to the bar and he leaves. Danny returns with his new friend and introduces us. She recognizes my name from some TV work I did. She gets excited and we chat. Then he leans in and asks if I mind taking a taxi back to the hotel alone. I'm cool with that. I guess he got himself a hookup for the night.

The guy I danced with, who says his name is John, returns.

"How about I buy you a drink?"

One more can't hurt. I'm only slightly buzzed. "Sure, why not?"

"So, what's your poison?"

"I'll have a vodka tonic with extra lime." I figure after this one, I'll have the guy out front grab me a cab. As I wait for my drink, I take in the scenery. John hands me the glass and I sip the tasty concoction. We chat a bit, but then halfway through, I'm not feeling so hot. The room tilts and I get dizzier by the second. I begin to sweat and feel sick.

"Hey, are you okay?" he asks.

"No. I think I need to leave." But I'm not sure I can make it to the door.

He takes my arm and says, "Don't worry, I've got you." He quickly ushers me outside as I slur the words, "The Plaza," and my mind goes blank after that.

The next thing I know, I wake up—sort of. I'm on a bed, and everything is fuzzy. When I try to get up, I can't move. My limbs are weighed down, as if I'm stuck in concrete. I hear voices, only my brain is so foggy I can't tell what they're saying or who is speaking. What the hell is going on? *Focus, Midnight. Focus.*

Blinking to clear my vision makes things worse. The room spins, so I keep my eyes closed. Maybe waiting will help. The mattress depresses next to me—someone climbs on the bed. Am I back in Phoenix? What's going on?

"She's waking up." It's a man's voice, but whose? Is it the guy from the bar? I swallow and my throat burns.

"Good. Now we can move to stage two. This is getting old."

What's getting old? I want to talk, to ask questions, but my mouth won't work.

"I'm freezing. Can I get dressed?" A woman is talking now.

"No, you can't get dressed. You still have work to do." Another man speaks, a different one this time. His voice sounds deeper and harsher than the other one's. I open my eyes again and the blurred images are a bit more distinct. My mouth and throat are dry, so dry. I lick my lips and they see it.

One of them slaps my cheek. "Hey, wake up. You need to get in the game, lover girl."

"Get her some water," someone says.

The bed moves and then I feel a bottle pressed against my mouth. I drink greedily.

"Slow down, Nelly, or you'll throw it all up."

He's right. I'm suddenly sick to my stomach as it churns with the unwelcome liquid. It soon passes and I ask for more. This time I sip.

I open my eyes again but someone blindfolds me. "What's going on? Where am I?" My voice is hoarse and I can barely speak.

"No questions. You only get to play."

"Play? John, is that you?"

He doesn't answer. Instead, he says, "Start the camera again."

Oh, fuck. As the hazy edges of my brain fade, things begin to click. Someone shoves something cold between my legs. I try to close them, but I can't because my ankles are attached to something that won't allow it. I'm so exposed and it brings back terrible memories from long ago.

"No, please don't," I beg.

"Gag her."

Something is shoved in my mouth and there's no way I can scream for help now. The scene progresses and I'm lost in a sea of hopelessness and terror. But then something stings my arm. Did they just drug me? When the rush hits, I have my answer. What the hell did they give me?

Then I'm instantly aware, floating on a cushion of tranquility, but I don't really care. They remove the gag and do all sorts of things to me. It's three-on-one and more sex than even I've experienced. Somewhere in the back of my mind, I know it's wrong, but this feels so damn good. I hear myself telling them, "More, more. Harder, yessss." Even in my drugged state, the questions are in bold italics. *Who is doing this? Who are these people? And why? What do they want?* And though it's horrific, I don't really give a fuck. All I want is for it to keep going.

"Ahhh, yesss, don't stop," I say. I whimper when something ends, but am happy when they start something else. Every part of my body is attended to and I hear one of them say, "We need to get her to do this again." I'm in the throes of an orgasm so I can't answer him.

The drugs make me lose track of time. I float above an abyss, emotionless and uncaring that people are raping me on video. My mind is present, but not. All I feel is a sense of being cradled in a cozy blanket and someone rocking me. No hallucinations, no magic, I just *am*. And it's the most wonderful sensation I've ever had.

I'm not even sure when all the sex ends because I'm high and don't really give a shit. The high is smooth, magnificent. All I want is for it to go on and on. Unfortunately, it doesn't. Reality gut punches me so hard. When I figure out that I'm free of my bonds, I take off my blindfold and crumble into a heaping pile of ragged tears.

I'm weak, shaking, and lying on a bed next to a pile of sex paraphernalia. They are not your normal, everyday toys. I never even used some of this stuff in the porn industry. A spreader bar, which was why I couldn't move my ankles, butt plug, nipple clamps, ball gag—everything imaginable. Fuck, there's even a flogger. Did they whip me? When I try to move, my limbs are so fucking sore, I can barely budge.

And then to my utter horror, my phone sits next to me. It can't be. But it is. On top of it sits a sticky note with two words: *Have fun*, followed with a smiley face. Grabbing my phone, the first thing I notice when I pick it up is a text message.

I don't waste time reading it as panic explodes in my chest. My eyes dart about the room erratically, in search of my clothing. Initially, I can't find my pants or sweater, but then I see them peeking from underneath the duvet heaped on the floor. Feeling like a drunken crab by the way my sluggish arms and legs move, I grope my way off the bed. My cute black sweater is torn in places, but my pants are okay. Luckily my coat will hide the damaged sweater.

I quickly dress and then check the room for some indication of where I am. It's a hotel in Midtown, not far from the club I went to with Danny.

Without a backward glance, I'm out of the room in search of the closest exit. It leads to a stairwell, which I'm leery of, but I rush to get out of here. I'm on the second floor, and I stumble down the steps and out of the hotel where I hail a cab back to The Plaza.

Once I'm safe in my room, I look at my phone. When I open the text message, bile rushes up my throat. It contains three video attachments. I hit the play button on the first one and throw up before I can finish watching. They recorded everything. I shake so badly, my finger can't hit the play button to resume watching. My heart fills with dread as I realize my career is ruined.

I place a call to my agent, Rita Clayton, because I don't know what else to do. Calling Danny isn't an option. What would I tell him? That I have three nice videos to show him? He'd fire me on the spot. When word gets out, my short-lived career with Alta is history.

"Hey, Midnight, what's going on?" my agent asks.

I can't even talk because I'm sobbing and hyperventilating.

"What's happening? You have to stop crying so I can understand you." Instead, my shaking hands send her the first video.

"I ... I was drugged and w-woke up in a hotel room."

She's quiet for a minute. "What do you mean?"

"I ... I just sent you a video." I try to explain the rest, only I'm sobbing too hard to go on.

"Oh, shit. Hang on." She's quiet but finally says, "This is twenty minutes long."

"Rita, th-there are three of them."

"Where are you now?"

A giant sob bursts out of me. "Back at The Plaza."

"Did you call the police?"

"No! I ran. I was afraid whoever did this would come back."

"Hang on. I know someone who can help. I'll call you right back."

I'm pacing when my phone rings. Rita says, "Someone will be there to clean up this mess."

"Who?"

"Someone who's going to help fix this shit, Midnight. Just hang tight."

Chapter 2

HARRISON

As soon as the phone rings, I'm wide awake, pulled out of the coma-like sleep.

"Kirkland," I answer, heading toward the bathroom. Any time I get a call at three thirty in the morning, it means I'm going to work.

"Harrison, it's Leland. We have an issue."

"Who is it this time?"

"Midnight Drake. You know, the sultry actor who recently signed a multimillion-dollar contract with Alta Pictures."

"Hmm. What happened?"

"Pack a bag, boss. We're flying to New York. Wheels up in one hour."

"Fuck. That bad?" I ask around my toothbrush.

"Yep. The team will be joining us. I'll give you all the details when we're together."

I'm a cleanup guy. Fixing things has always been my passion. It began when I was a kid and my dog suddenly became sick and died. We came home from the vet after he couldn't be saved, and watching my dog die at such a young age broke a piece of me. He wasn't fixable, but that didn't mean other things weren't. That's when my need to become a fixer took root and grew. Broken toys, things around the house, stuff I found on the street, you name it. I'd bring them home and do my best to restore them, and if I couldn't do it, I'd recruit my dad to help. I'd even bring injured animals home, and Mom would take them away—to the vet, she'd say—and I'd be thankful they weren't suffering anymore.

As I grew older, the fixer in me expanded to people. When I went to school, I'd find kids who were in trouble and needed friends. At Crestview Academy I met Prescott Beckham. He was in the worst shape of anyone I'd ever met. A kid from a dysfunctional family, he didn't know which way to turn. So what did I do? I brought him home, just like I used to do with those injured animals. He's still somewhat fucked up. But at least he's back on track.

The following year at Crestview, Weston Wyndham showed up. I called Dad and told him to buy a couple of cases of superglue because that's what this guy needed. Dad laughed. He knew I'd show up at home with Prescott and Weston in tow. Weston had a black eye because Prescott and I had beaten the shit out of him to teach him a lesson. He'd been picking fights and needed a good ass kicking. When he figured out we only wanted to help, the three of us became inseparable. He definitely needed that glue, though. I thought Prescott's situation was bad—Weston's brand of dysfunction made me rethink what the word meant.

I'm still fixing things and people, which is how I ended up in my current profession. Since I'm so good at it, why not make some bank doing what I do best?

In less than thirty minutes, I'm on my way to the airport from my Malibu home. At this hour, traffic poses no problem. When I arrive, I drive straight to the entrance for private jets and follow the road around after going through the designated security checkpoints. I park, and Leland is there, along with the pilot. The team is boarding the jet.

"Good morning, everyone. Pete," I say, greeting our pilot. "Is the coffee on?"

Our flight attendant pops his head out from the back and says, "It'll be ready in a moment, along with breakfast."

"Oh, hi, Mike. Didn't see you back there."

"Morning, Mr. Kirkland."

Everyone takes a seat and Leland begins.

"Midnight Drake woke up in a hotel room a few hours ago, naked and alone with three fresh videos on her phone. Apparently, while she was pumped full of what we assume to be heroin, a shitload of kinky fuckery went down, without her consent, and the videos shot of the evening have gone zooming across the internet. Her agent called—it's a freak show."

"She was raped?" I ask.

"Yes. I'm hitting you with the videos now. Be prepared. They're pretty graphic. Let's just say unfortunately, Midnight was on full display."

"Fuck."

"Exactly," Leland says. "Alta is already claiming they're dumping her because she violated her contract."

"What is she saying?" I ask.

"She was drugged and raped."

"Clearly."

"She says she remembers nothing."

"Did you watch the videos?" I ask.

"Yeah, and she was totally out of it. Completely unresponsive in the first one. Then in the second, she came around a little. The third, she was so fucked up, she wouldn't have cared if someone cut off her head. I shit you not."

"Sounds like someone roofied her drink. Has our New York team found her playmates? And have you pulled the videos?"

"The videos have been pulled and we're working on the playmates. Everything was uploaded from a cell phone."

"Track the fuckers. You know what to do. Where is Midnight now?"

"At The Plaza waiting for you with one of our reps. She's totally freaked."

"Right. Wouldn't you be?"

Leland nods. "I'd be getting the fuck out of town."

Those fucking asswipes taking advantage of people like that. They're like computer hackers, out to destroy lives, and for what purpose? Because they don't have anything better to do? "Leland, did she call the police?"

"No."

"Hmm. Did she say why?"

"Nothing other than she's waiting for you."

This is odd, but I'll get to the bottom of it when I speak to her. "Okay. What about money? Did those scumbags make any demands?"

"Not that I'm aware."

I slam my hand down on the table in front of me. "Let's get on this, people. I don't care what it takes. We need to clean this shit up."

That gets the attention of everyone sitting close. Bodies stiffen and eyes open wider. They know when I mean business, and this just hit me the wrong fucking way.

Pete's voice comes to us over the intercom to tell us we're ready to taxi. We should be cleared for takeoff momentarily.

"Buckle up, buttercups. We've got serious work ahead of us, which equates to a long day. I know I ask a lot of you and I'm sorry for the early hour, but you'll be given a bonus if we nail these fuckers. As usual, this one stays under the radar."

The jet taxis toward the runway and we're soon taking off into the dark sky. It won't be long before we fly into the sun. The team starts making calls. I have one man in particular I want to contact so I make the call myself.

"Mr. Kirkland. Are you in New York already?"

"Not yet, Rashid, but I'm on the way. I need you to do something for me." I explain the situation and tell him exactly what I need.

"I've already handled the videos. But it may take a day for me to locate the phones. It'll take some extra work, you know."

My tension lessens somewhat. "Thanks, Rashid. I'm glad Leland got in touch with you. We'll be staying at The Plaza if you can't get in touch with me by phone. But I want those people found."

"Certainly, Mr. Kirkland."

Rashid benefited from my cleaning up a while ago. He was in deep shit with his hacking skills. I took care of things for him. Now he owes me and is at my disposal one hundred percent of the time. He stays in New York because honestly, he's connected to everything. He probably has every bank and investment account number at his fingertips. But the dude knows I have him by the balls. All it would take is for me to make a phone call to the right people and he'd be back where he started.

As soon as Pete says we've cleared ten thousand feet, Mike shows up with coffee and breakfast. Emily, another team member, smiles gratefully. So do I. When she's hungry, she's a grouch and her brain isn't worth a shit. I can't have that. I need her mad skills right now.

Everyone has secrets. Even me. Granted, I'm vanilla compared to most, but when I see a broken individual, I'm a magnet for them. Emily was shattered. Her Dom threw her onto the streets, cast her aside after a few years, with no explanation. I stumbled upon her one night in a bar, drinking herself into oblivion. She told me all her dirty secrets and said she wanted to kill herself. I couldn't sit by and do nothing. She didn't want to involve her family, and who could blame her? What person wants to divulge that kind of lifestyle to Mom and Dad? So, I brought her to my place where she could sober up and we could create a plan.

Emily was an events planner for one of the movie studios, and had done a variety of things from handling the press to dealing with caterers. She could mobilize a team of five hundred and get them from point A to B in a snap. I needed those skills on my team. But she needed to get her shit straightened out first, and her issues were way beyond my fixing capabilities.

She checked into a facility and thirty days later was on my payroll. Filled with more confidence than most women I know, she found a new Dom who treats her better than the old one ever did, and Emily is pleasantly flogged on a nightly basis.

Leland declines the offer of breakfast. "Mike, can you come back in five with a coffee refill?" Leland used to work for one of the largest PR firms in Hollywood. That is, until he was caught fucking his boss's wife. His boss, one of the most powerful men in the industry, promised Leland his name would be dirt. It would've been had I not come along. I dug around a bit and found some tidbits that would tilt his boss's world. Leland separated from the company on "good terms" and I offered him a job on the condition he'd leave the wife alone, which he graciously accepted. He's been with me ever since.

I ask Mike for an extra breakfast while Misha, who appears meek, nods her thanks for the breakfast and coffee he just placed on the table before her. Appearances are oftentimes deceiving because everyone in LA knows she's one of the most vicious attorneys around. It's the reason I wanted her on my team.

Misha found herself in a bind a couple of years ago. She was happily married, or so everyone thought, until her husband stumbled upon some videos of her getting her kink on with another woman. She didn't want him to know she was bisexual, so she hid that side of her life from him. He wasn't too pleased about it and threatened to post the videos on YouTube. She freaked and they got into a huge fight, during which she punched him and broke his nose. Did I mention that Misha had anger issues? The YouTube upload threat turned into a lawsuit of abuse and assault. That's how Misha landed in my office, asking for my help.

After my intervention, Misha ended up with an amicable divorce, even though she took a hit financially. It turned out in her favor though, because she's made up for it with the salary and bonus I pay her. However, she had to agree to anger management therapy, which she happily did. I saw a sparkling star in her and knew once her issues were resolved, Misha would be an exemplary coworker.

If this jet were to crash, the Hollywood entertainment industry would be in a serious jam because there would be no one worth a shit to rectify their fuckups.

My thoughts tumble back to Midnight Drake. Usually I don't have such emotionally charged feelings, but the way this woman was exploited is a million kinds of wrong. Midnight Drake is an actor who landed a nice contract with Alta, and these fuckers are trying to ruin her chances of making it big. They won't if I can help it. This team will stop whoever did this and make them pay.

My phone beeps with a text from Leland. I open it to find all the videos have loaded. I nearly choke on my coffee when I watch the first one. Holy motherfucker. These are worse than hardcore. I feel sick knowing I just witnessed my client getting raped.

"Gather round, team. Our status has just changed to DEFCON 1." Then I press play. The women are disgusted and pissed off, even though these ladies are tough as nails. But I want them angry, and by the last video's end, my goal has been accomplished.

Misha flies out of her seat. "Harrison, I want to personally cut their balls off. Look at her! She's nearly unconscious there. That's disgusting. What's worse is I don't know how anyone would want to watch such depraved shit."

Emily takes over where Misha leaves off. "What she said. What slimy assholes! And how could that other woman have participated? Let me get my hands on them. I will personally rip their dicks off."

"Okay, ladies, let's pull it together. While I want to harness your anger, we need our best brainpower and I won't get that if you don't act rationally. Calm down and keep watching."

We focus on the videos. A necessary evil, you might say, but we have to analyze them if we're to do our jobs.

"Here's where we may have a problem," I say. In one part, Midnight is cooperating and even asking for more. "Harder. Yes, yes," she says.

Emily nods in disgust. "It's like she's dazed but wants it."

"It's the drugs," Misha says. "Look at her face."

There's no doubt. "Whatever they gave her must've been good," Emily says.

When the videos are done, I explain what Rashid said. "You both know he's a bloodhound when I put him on a task. I also want to find out where Midnight went so we can check any security tapes. They should show us something. It'll help so when Rashid finds their phones, it'll be easier to ID these guys. We can have one of the guys bring them in. We'll ... take care of them appropriately."

Misha's brows shoot up. "Does that entail being on the bottom of the East River?"

"Our role is to clean things up for Midnight and get everything back on track for her. Find out what Midnight's contract states and if Alta can drop her. She may have a morality clause or something."

Misha's chest still heaves with anger, but she nods.

Emily says, "Yeah, Midnight is our mission. We can't let our anger get in the way of that. We can worry about those dick-faces later."

Now that they're refocused, I say, "Right. So, this is what we need. Emily, work on getting her into rehab. People are very forgiving about someone with a drug problem."

Emily's brow furrows. "But that's admitting she has one when she doesn't."

"Let's take a step back a minute. Remember, we have to keep our feelings and emotions out of this. It's our job to fix this mess, to find a solution. Plan A is to get her to go to the police. If you were raped like this, wouldn't that be the first thing you did? Since she didn't do it on her own, we can only assume there's a reason for that. We'll still try to get her to go, but if she refuses, we can't force her. We'll need a back-up plan. So, then ask yourselves the question—what's the best way to clean this up? What's the best way to get her career back on track? It's not whether we agree or disagree, it's whether or not this will work."

When I see them nod in agreement, I continue.

"Let's think. We have a huge issue with the videos. Even though they were pulled, they were up long enough for people to have screenshots or GIFs of that shit. Their impressions are solid. We're going with the worst-case scenario. We can say she doesn't have a problem until we're blue-faced, but people who've seen them won't believe us and Midnight needs credibility. The best way to move forward is to ask forgiveness. But in the meantime, Misha, we need to find those men if we can. I want motive. When Midnight gets out in thirty days, we want the public dying to see her. They will hopefully crawl all over her and want her back just like they want icing on cake. If Alta drops her, our job is to get them down on their hands and knees, and beg her to come back. Oh, and Leland, get to work on her speech. Relate it somehow to her tragic childhood. Do we know anything about that? If not, dig up something. I don't care if it's about a guppy that died and she never grieved appropriately. Make it emotional as shit. We want this all in place as Plan B just in case we need to implement it."

The team goes to work, while I do a little research on Midnight. She started out in B-rated films, like most actors do, trying to get noticed. She got noticed, all right. With long black hair and unusual lavender eyes, she isn't a raving beauty but she has an exotic appeal. Her seductiveness makes her unforgettable. There's something about her that screams sex. Having been cast in the types of roles that not many mainstream actors usually want, Midnight is willing to spread her wings and try anything.

Then I stumble upon something that makes me do a double take. Born in Phoenix, her birth name was Velvet Summers.

"You have got to be kidding me," I say out loud.

"What?" All eyes are on me as they ask.

"Did you know Midnight's birth name was Velvet Summers?"

"Oh, that," Leland says.

"How did I not know this?"

Misha shrugs. "Don't know. Leland sent over a photocopy of her birth certificate. I thought you saw it."

"Who the fuck names their kid Velvet Summers?" But after I say it, I think of my best friend, Weston—his wife's name is Special. Who names a kid that?

Emily shrugs. "Yeah, people choose weird names."

I keep reading and find some interesting facts. Midnight's mother was an exotic dancer, and some reports listed her as a stripper. She also was known to have a drug problem. Midnight ended up in foster care but then fell off the radar when she was seventeen. It looks like she never even finished high school. Maybe she really did have a tragic upbringing. Her mother died ten years ago, when Midnight was only fourteen—probably why she ended up in foster care. There's no mention of a father in the picture. The plot thickens.

Emily announces she's gotten Midnight into one of the premier rehab facilities in the country. Located in Arizona, it has a spa-like atmosphere. She'll be secluded from the Hollywood gossip and the rest of the world for a minimum of thirty days.

"It's pricey, but worth it, I believe. The reviews are astounding," Emily says.

"Good. We'll drop her off on our flight back to LA," I say.

Misha announces our legal team in New York is ready for us if we need them.

"Good work," I say. "Hopefully, we'll ID these people or at

least track them with Rashid's help. They didn't show any faces in the videos, and they also wore condoms, so that cuts into our evidence. Maybe there will still be drugs left in Midnight's system."

I'm going to do my best at finding those fuckers who did this and making them pay—with or without the police.

Chapter 3

HARRISON

HER FORM HUDDLED ON THE CHAIR IN THE HOTEL ROOM'S corner doesn't surprise me. I'm surprised she's not wailing and freaking the fuck out.

I stretch out my hand. "Midnight, I'm Harrison Kirkland of The Solution. We'll be handling your case here."

A puff of air leaves her chest. "Okay." Her ice-cold, trembling hand shakes mine. She feels fragile, as though her fingers will snap if I squeeze at all. "Do you think you can help?"

"I think so."

Violet eyes dig into mine. I wonder if she wears contacts. That color looks artificial.

"First things first. I'm terribly sorry this has happened to you. It's a horrible thing, and I can't pretend to understand what you're going through. In order to help you, we're going to be asking you some pointed questions. But first, have you showered?"

"No." Her voice is so small and shaky.

In the gentlest voice possible, I say, "Good. That means there still may be evidence present. Midnight, we need to go to the police so we can report the crime."

Her eyes dart around the room, as though she's frantically searching for an escape hatch.

She rubs her arms like they're freezing. "I-I can't do that. No police."

I pull up a chair and sit down next to her. "If we don't report it, these guys may go free. My contacts here will search for them, but there are no guarantees we can find them."

"I ... I, uh, I just can't go. Okay? No police."

I quickly glance at Misha and Emily. They both shrug.

"Okay, but what if we call in one of the crime experts we deal with and see if he can get some DNA off you? Maybe under your fingernails. It might help us catch these guys."

Jerky gestures accompany her trembling chin. "N-no."

She needs to understand the importance of this. Leaning forward, I say, "Midnight, if we don't report this soon, we may miss our window."

She chews on her lip. "C-can I speak to you privately?"

"Sure. Everyone?" I flick my head toward the door. They clear the room, leaving the two of us alone.

Her voice is hesitant as she begins. "If ... if I go to the police, it will expose something. Something from my past I don't want to be revealed."

"I understand. But the police will be our best option of catching these guys, if that's what you want to have happen."

Her lids flutter. "What I want is for this to go away ... to disappear."

"Right, and we're going to help with that. But the police ..."

Her mouth hardens. "No police." She pauses. "This is hard to say ... to tell you, and it's something no one is aware of, Mr. Kirkland, but I used to work in the porn industry. If this gets out, I'm finished. Absolutely no police." She jumps out of her chair and paces.

Shit. This can be a definite game-changer. "Okay, I understand. This is totally your call. I just don't want you to regret not reporting this as a crime since you were a victim."

She only nods.

"How long ago was this?" I ask.

"A couple of years." Fuck. Not enough time for people to have forgotten her.

"How many films?"

"I don't remember. I used a different name. Lusty Rhoades. I had blond hair and wore brown contacts, and I've changed my nose since then."

"I see." *Lusty Rhoades.* "So, as I see it, we have two choices. One is the police, which you are not in favor of, and two is damage control. That was to be Plan B, but I guess we go straight into that without the benefit of the police. Are you sure that's what you want to do?"

"Yes. No police." She stresses the words.

This will have to be her best option. If the police dig into her past, the porn part would be revealed, and then what would we do? People, being what they are, would say she deserved what she got.

"Let me bring the team back in, then. They have to be informed of this. Are you okay with that?" She nods.

Once we're again assembled, I say, "Midnight has decided no police, so let's get on with it. Midnight, I want to know every single thing you did yesterday, from the time you woke up to when this happened. Don't leave out any detail, even when you urinated. Am I clear?"

Her mouth and eyes match in the way they form huge circles. "Everything?"

"Yes. It's important. Emily, you ready?"

"Ready."

Emily will record everything so we don't miss any detail. I need to know if Midnight is a drug addict, or if she's really an innocent victim.

"Start from the beginning," I say.

She begins with her flight in from LA and progresses to her photo session.

"Then I went to dinner with Danny. The producer. Then we went to a club."

"Which club?" She names the place and I tell Leland to send someone over there to check their security tapes.

Turning back to Midnight, I ask, "So, do you trust this Danny?"

"Yes. He left with another woman. I was dancing with some guy. He seemed nice enough."

"Tell me about him. I want details."

"Tall, blondish hair. I couldn't see his eye color because it was too dim in the club. His name was John. I'm sure it was bogus. He had a nice voice. He wore jeans and a button-down shirt. Light blue, I think."

"How tall?"

"I don't know. I'm not good at that since I'm so short."

"Can you try? We need a number."

She squints at me and then motions with her hand. "Stand up." I do, and so does she. "How tall are you?"

"Six two."

"He was probably six feet, then."

"Good. Was his hair thick, thin, balding?"

"Thin. Not thick like yours."

"Any marks on his skin? Tattoos, moles, scars?"

"None that I could see. His sleeves were long. Were there any on the video that you noticed?"

"Unfortunately, the video only caught him from behind."

She sits back down and I notice how she squirms and shrivels up in her chair.

I crouch down next to her. "Look, I know how uncomfortable this must be, but we're only trying to figure out who did this and why. Midnight, we do have a plan, but if we can catch these assholes, get anything that might lead us to them, we might stop this from happening again."

Her expression is horrified. "Again? They would do this to me again?"

"They could do it to someone else, if not you specifically. That's why we need to stop them. From what I saw, this doesn't look like it was their first time. They didn't leave any kind of trail. A novice would have."

It turns out that Midnight is very cooperative. When she concludes with waking up on the bed, it's my turn to go to work.

I don't dance around the issue when I ask, "Have you ever used drugs in the past?"

"No, I don't use drugs."

"Ever?"

"No! I may have an occasional drink and I've smoked weed a time or two in the past, but I don't do drugs." She bends down, digs into her purse, and pulls out a handful of gummy bears.

"Misha, get her to pee in a cup for us. We need a drug screen."

Midnight bolts out of her chair, eyes on fire. "I told you, I don't do drugs."

"Calm down. It's a matter of us figuring out what they drugged you with," I tell her.

"Oh," she says. "Sorry." Then she pops a gummy bear in her mouth.

Misha takes her to the bathroom for a urine test. When they come back a few minutes later, Leland arranges for a courier to deliver the specimen to a drug screening center with instructions for rapid results.

"I'm sure the roofies will be out of your system, but if they hit you with heroin, it should still be present," I say.

She sits back in the chair, grabs more gummy bears, and tucks her feet underneath her.

"Since you haven't showered, we're going to give you a break so you can. Does that sound okay?"

"Y-yes."

"Everybody, let's give her thirty. We'll be back."

Midnight nods her thanks.

We reconvene in my suite, which includes a room with a large table that seats six. It's time to gather my thoughts. Midnight looked like hell—rough and destroyed.

"What do you think?" I ask Leland and Emily.

"She's telling the truth. We deal with enough liars that I can spot one when I see one. A liar, she isn't. She's got a lot to deal with, but she'll have to get through this," Emily says.

"I agree," Leland says. "She has fire and spirit in her."

I saw that same fire. Plus she's too freaked to be lying. The videos were awful. No one would do that and lie about it. Sitting back, I thrum my fingers on the table. "I'm not sure she's going to like our plan, but it's the only thing I know that will save her career. I'll do my best to persuade her."

Emily laughs. "You always do."

My phone pings with a text from Misha, who remained behind with Midnight. She tells us it's fine to come back.

I shoot back, ***Would she feel more comfortable in the suite?***

A few seconds later, the response is that they're on the way.

I pick up the phone and order breakfast and coffee for everyone. We all could use a little something to eat.

Misha arrives with Midnight behind her. I have them sit at the table. Midnight's black hair is wet and she wears zero makeup, yet it doesn't deter from her appearance. She's every bit as attractive without it. Only the deep, dark crescents lurking beneath her eyes mar her perfect skin and reveal her despair.

She curls into herself as she sits. This can't happen. I need strength, not someone who appears damaged.

"I ordered some food and drink so it should arrive momentarily. I need to make a call, if you'll excuse me."

When I'm in the bedroom, I call Rashid. With his hacking skills, it shouldn't take him long to find the whereabouts of the fuckers who did this. When he tells me what he's discovered, I want to smash my fist through the wall. They used her own phone to record and upload the damn videos. We're at a dead end here.

"We know where she was when it happened. Can you somehow hack into the hotel security tapes to see who she was with?"

"If they're closed circuit, they won't be much help other than with a visual ID," he says.

"True. Maybe I can persuade the hotel to give us more information."

"If you can do that, I may be able to help you ID them."

Everyone is drinking coffee and eating when I rejoin them. Midnight pecks at a piece of toast like a bird.

"You ought to eat more than that. It'll help the drugs clear faster," I say.

"It was heroin. I'm almost positive. It was sheer euphoria that I've never felt before. I've seen others high on it before. I didn't give a damn about anything."

Resting my palms on the table, I lean close to her and softly say, "Whatever you do, don't ever do that shit again. I'm only telling you this for your protection." The addiction rate with that drug is scary.

"I told you, I don't do drugs."

"The temptation may be high since you know how it made you feel. But the next time won't make you feel that way," I say.

"Do you have a hearing problem? I. Don't. Do. Drugs," she spits out.

I smile. "Good. Now that we've cleared that up, let's continue." Taking a seat, I say, "I want every single detail of what happened after you woke up."

She talks about the feeling of panic and how she ran out of the hotel, worried they'd come back and find her again. This is where she loses it.

I give her a moment to collect herself, then start in with more questions. This is key, while things are still fresh in her mind. "You remember voices."

"Yes. A woman and two men."

"Are you sure?" I ask.

"Yes." She's adamant. "That I remember, but not much else. I couldn't move my ankles. I remember that too. When I woke up and saw the ..."—she squirms in her seat—"that spreader bar, I remembered not being able to and it made sense why."

"These people knew exactly how not to get caught. My guess is they've done this before. That's why they used your phone to upload the videos," I say.

She leans forward. "My phone? They used my phone?"

"Unfortunately, yes." I hate that look of utter despair etched in her eyes.

A hand flutters toward her face, but then drops to the table. "This keeps getting worse. It's bad enough that Alta wants to pull my contract. I'm sure Holt is happy."

"Holt Ward? You mean your costar?"

"Yeah, I'm not exactly his favorite person."

This puts a new twist on things. "Do you think he had anything to do with this?"

Her mouth skews up, then gapes open. "Oh, I don't ... well, he's been a bit nasty to me, but I doubt he'd stoop to this level. Besides, I was with Danny, not Holt."

"True, but what if he had you followed?"

"I can't believe he could hate me that much."

Leaning back in my chair, I nod to Leland. This is a lead we need to follow up on. I want Holt Ward checked out. I want his phone records examined. Leland gets up to call Rashid. Rashid will have an answer in no time. And it may lead to who did this.

"So, this is our plan, Midnight. You're going to rehab."

"Rehab? But I don't do drugs!"

"Doesn't matter. Since you don't want to report this as a crime, we don't have any other option. The world has seen you with a needle and syringe in your arm, getting nailed by two guys and a girl with all sorts of BDSM toys and enjoying it. What it looks like and what actually happened are two different things, but it's the public's perception that counts. I know this is difficult to hear, but rehab is the only plausible solution we can come up with since you don't want to go to the police. You'll announce that you've made mistakes and are now ready to address your issues. The public will really dig this. You'll have them eating out of your hand."

"But it's a lie," she insists, her eyes welling with tears. Then she wraps her arms around herself.

I wall myself off from her emotions. It's a necessary evil. It's sad, yes, but my job is not to feel sorry for her. My job is to clean up the shit pile she landed in.

"Midnight, the public has seen these horrible videos of you getting raped, except those men made it look like you were enjoying it. We pulled them as soon as we could, but that didn't prevent people from taking screenshots and posting memes or digging into your past. My question to you is do you want to remain with Alta?"

"Yes," she cries. "I was the victim. I've done nothing wrong."

"You don't seem to hear what I'm saying. People don't care about the truth. They only care about what the better story is. They don't care that you were an innocent victim taken advantage of. They believe you agreed to all of this. We're not going to change their minds since the police weren't involved, unless you decide to report the crime. And if anyone does any kind of digging, they can find you did the uploading."

"What? But I didn't do any of that!"

In a gentle voice, I say, "I know that, my team knows it, and so do you, but what we know doesn't matter. You only need to care about the public's perception because they are the ones who can make or break you. You must listen to what I'm saying, and listen carefully. You're going to make a statement. You're going to say that rehab is your destination. After coming to the realization that you need help, you believe this is the best course of action."

Then I explain we are going to bring in how foster care affected her, how she never grieved the death of her mother, and why she spiraled downward into a life of drug abuse.

She buries her face in her hands. "I can't possibly say that."

"Why not? I was under the impression you wanted to salvage your career."

"I do, but bringing in foster care ... it's too ... raw."

That's when I notice the cracks in her exterior. Midnight isn't as strong and spirited as we'd all imagined. But it doesn't matter. Now is when she needs to dig deep and find strength to get through this. "That's exactly why we're doing it."

She flies out of her chair and the pacing begins. "Do you know anything about foster care?" she asks.

"A little." The truth is I am so far removed from it, it's not even funny. My childhood was idyllic. My parents were perfect and still are. They should be placed on pedestals. Honest to God, they are the greatest human beings that ever breathed air.

Skepticism coats her voice while she rubs her eyes. "Things happened there. Bad things. I don't want that can of worms reopened."

"It's already been opened. People know."

Violet eyes latch onto mine. "What do they know?"

I pick up my phone and google her name. One click and I'm there. Her bio pops up and on the page, it talks about Phoenix, foster care, her mom's death, and so on. Handing her the phone, I say, "Here. See for yourself."

I may as well have put a fist in her face with the way she reacts. What's up with this? Why is she so afraid of the foster care thing?

"What aren't you telling us, Midnight?"

"Nothing." She stares at me but flinches after a minute. She's hiding something and I aim to find out what.

"Can we have the room, everyone? Emily, stop the camera, please."

Misha says, "Harrison, I don't advise this."

I offer her a half grin. "I knew you wouldn't. But it'll be fine."

The team files out, leaving Midnight alone with me.

"This is really a shitty time for you. I get that. But in order for me to help, I need the facts, and you're not giving them all to me. Tell me about foster care. What are you hiding?"

Her lower lip trembles slightly. "It just wasn't a great place to be. That's all."

"No, that's not all. You went there after your mom died, right?"

"Before. She was a heroin addict, which is why I'll never use. I remember her leaving me and going to work. Or that's what she'd say anyway. But I knew better. She would go out to hunt for drugs. The Department of Child Safety finally removed me from the home. I'm pretty sure one of my teachers turned her in, probably because I was showing up late or missing school altogether. I recall the two of us crying for each other as they dragged me away. I only saw her a few times after that, and then she was dead."

I pour another cup of coffee and offer her one. She declines.

"You're going to hate hearing this, but that's a story the public would eat up. They would fall right into your hands. My God, think of it."

"No! I don't want them to like me because of that."

"It may be your only option. And that's why you turned to drugs."

"I haven't turned to ..."

She stops when she sees my furrowed brow.

"Okay, I get it. They don't want the truth. They only want the latest piece of gossip they can sink their stupid teeth into."

I lean on my elbows. "Exactly. Now you're beginning to understand. So we spin it. And they'll love you more than ever. In the end, Alta may even up your contract. Who knows?"

"What if they fire me instead?"

"They won't." She keeps twisting her fingers. "Midnight, what aren't you telling me?"

She chews on her already chapped lip. "Nothing. I was abused, had an addict for a mom, did porn films, and was raped. Isn't that enough?"

"It's way more than most people ever have to deal with. But I still want you to agree to rehab for thirty days, and then make the statement. I know it'll seal the deal."

"I won't even know what to say."

"You don't have to worry about a thing. That's where my team comes in. We write it and you rehearse it, exactly like a script. Act it out like your life depends on it. In the end, you'll be thanking us for saving your career. Who knows, you might win an Oscar." It's true, but she doesn't believe me.

"Okay, I'll do it. One question though. Will I really be in rehab for thirty days?"

"Yes, maybe longer, but you'll be at the best facility. It'll be like a spa."

She nods. I call in the team, log into the computer, and run a search on Lusty Rhoades. She was certainly active, not the household name some of the major porn stars are, but she made quite a few films.

Rashid goes to work, making sure there is zero connection between Lusty and Midnight. This is going to take a while.

Chapter 4

MIDNIGHT

HARRISON KIRKLAND IS A FORCE OF NATURE. TALL AND BROAD through the shoulders, the man radiates strength. Whatever he puts in his coffee must be amazing because the energy bursting out of him is tornadic. He's so confident and sure of things, not to mention dominant and sexy. I've never encountered anyone like him before. I want to trust him, I do. But after everything I've been through, it's hard to believe this idea of his is going to work. And then there's the whole other issue of foster care. He can't dig into that. If they open up that part of my life, there's not a chance in hell I'll make it through.

Plus I'm worried about what he thinks of me. Even though I shouldn't give a damn, I don't want him to think I'm just some washed-up piece of shit. I can't end up back in the porn industry earning a living, sucking and fucking. Even though ultimately it was my choice, it certainly wouldn't have been my first. It was a dirty and disgusting way to earn a living. I won't tolerate it again, so his plan has to work. Besides, if it doesn't, I'm not sure how I'll be able to pay his hefty fee. When Rita told me how much he charged, I nearly died.

We break for lunch and then reconvene in the little confer-ence room with more questions and answers. Harrison leaves a few times, only to return with information about when I'm going to make this bogus announcement. He wants it done tomorrow. My gut cramps as dizziness nearly overcomes me.

"Are you okay?" someone asks me.

"I don't feel well."

"Did you eat?" Harrison asks, as he leans down on the table, resting his hands close to where I sit.

"Not much. It's a little difficult when my stomach is in knots."

"Emily, call the doctor. She needs something to calm her down."

"No drugs." I grit out the words. I won't take any of that shit. It's a Band-Aid for a gaping wound and solves nothing.

"Fine, but you should probably be seen anyway. At least to make sure everything is okay," Harrison says. His voice is kind, and it's the first time I've paid close attention to his face. His eyes are warm. They're dark brown, so dark it feels like I've taken a dive into an abyss. He wears a suit and is very professional looking. Handsome is what I'd call him. Not super good looking like that asshole, Holt. But he's a whole lot nicer, that's for sure. But then again, why wouldn't he be? He'll be making an assload of money off me. My bank account will be drained after this ordeal. The good thing is I won't have to pay him if his plan fails. He must be confident it won't.

"Okay. If you think so," I say. One of them calls a doctor and all I can say is they must have some serious connections. Thirty minutes later, a doctor shows up with one of those little black bags. Usually it takes forever to see a doctor where I come from.

He ushers me into the other room, probably Harrison's bedroom, and examines me. My blood pressure is low and he tells me I need to eat and drink because I'm probably dehydrated. Without the benefit of blood tests, there isn't much more he can do.

When we come back out, Harrison explains I tested positive for heroin. This is news to me as they hadn't shared this yet.

"Nice of you to tell me." My tone bears more than a hint of sourness.

"We were getting ready to, but then you became ill," Misha says.

"It's not a surprise, really. When I felt the sting of the needle hit my vein, I couldn't imagine what else it could be." Because of my mom's drug abuse, I'd read enough about it to know what the effects were.

"There were also traces of GHB present, which is what they hit your drink with. It's a date rape drug." Harrison hands me the report of my urine screening. No other drugs were present.

"I hope you believe me now that I don't use drugs," I say.

He's seated at the big table, but he rises out of his chair and stands before me. "You need to get something straight. It's not a question of whether I believe you. I'm not your judge, jury, and executioner. The public is. And for your information, I did believe you when you told me. That's why I urged you to go to the police."

Does that make me feel better? Not really.

The doctor steps forward. "Under those circumstances, you're probably still feeling the aftereffects of both drugs. I advise you to drink plenty of fluids and eat, Ms. Drake. You'll feel better tomorrow," he says.

A hysterical laugh leaks out of me but I clamp a hand over my mouth. I'm sounding a bit crazy, and feeling that way too. It's hard to believe less than twenty-four hours ago, I was on top of the world, thinking things had finally shifted in my favor. Another laugh threatens to burst past my lips, but I press them together and hold it at bay. This isn't the time to let my crazyville loose. I need to hold my shit together. The tears can flow when I get back to my own room later tonight.

"Eat. Drink. Got it. Thanks, Doctor."

He nods, and Harrison escorts him to the door. I'm sure

they have a few words about me, but who cares. I'm doing my best not to let all the pieces of me come tumbling apart.

My phone rings, sending me almost shooting to the ceiling. Snatching the thing, I check the caller ID. Unknown. I won't be answering that.

"Answer it," Harrison says harshly. "And put it on speaker."

"No. I don't know who it is."

"That's why you're going to answer it."

I pick it up. "Hello." I tap the speaker button as Harrison instructed.

"Ms. Drake?"

"Yes."

"We just wanted to see how you're feeling today."

"Who is this?"

"A friend." He chuckles. The voice sounds vaguely familiar.

Harrison, who motions to everyone as they scramble around like little mice, distracts me. I've never seen people move so fast in my life. Then the line goes dead.

"Fuck," Harrison explodes. "Why didn't you say something? It was him, wasn't it? You should've kept talking."

"I didn't know what to say. He freaked me out." My voice sounds small even to my ears. Even he's frightening me now, yelling at me like that.

"If you get a call like that again, try to keep the guy on the line. Just keep talking. Talk about anything, the weather, your cat, I don't care what. Just say something."

"I don't want to talk to him. Would you want to talk to your rapist?"

He blows out a long, frustrated breath. I know he's trying to help catch the guy, but he doesn't know what it was like. He can't possibly know. I was violated and I don't know by whom. It's disgusting, but I still want to see their faces. I want to look in their eyes and ask them if they're proud of what they've done. I also want to get back in the shower and scrub every inch of my skin until I'm raw and bleeding. Maybe then I'll feel something again. Maybe the pain will lessen the numbness that's invaded my brain cells.

"What are you thinking?" Harrison asks.

The vehemence that explodes out of me makes me step back, but I tell him.

"Anger is better than feeling sorry for yourself," Harrison says.

I lose my temper again. "Just shut up for one damn minute. You think you know everything, but you don't." And I stomp out of the room. I need space ... need to breathe, to get away for a minute. My room isn't far from his and I don't stop until I get there.

My chest heaves and my cheeks are wet with my tears. Standing in front of my room, I try unlocking the door but then I feel a presence behind me. I nearly scream.

"It's only me," Harrison says.

"Damn you!" I say, slapping at him like I would a bug. I hit anywhere I can, only I'm weak and ineffective, plus his hands lock around my wrists, bringing everything to a halt.

There's a slight upward curve to his mouth. Is he laughing at me? "You're such a jerk, laughing at me like that."

"I'm not laughing at you. I'm laughing at the way you're swatting at me. I'm not a mosquito."

"You motherfucker." I try to pry my hands loose, but he has them in a death grip.

Suddenly, I'm bawling my eyes out at the helplessness of this situation and it pisses me off. I don't want to ask *why me*, but why the fuck me?

Harrison takes the key from me and opens the door, leading me inside. Then he sits me down and stuffs a wad of tissue into my cupped hands. He's not exactly the warm-and-fuzzy type, but right now, I don't care. All I want to do is curl up in the bed and cry myself to sleep.

Next thing I know, a glass of water is shoved into my hand. "Drink this."

I don't have the strength to object.

"I said drink, not nurse the damn thing."

Lifting my eyes, I ask, "Do you have to be such an asshole?"

"Right now, I do. You've been drugged, you're probably dehydrated, and you've eaten enough for a baby bird to barely eke by on. If you don't fuel yourself, you'll have more of these breakdowns and tomorrow will be shit."

Is he for real? I sniff, and then say, "Has it occurred to you that I'm dealing with a lot right now?"

His voice softens. "Yes, and it's only going to get worse over the next twenty-four hours. That's why you need to drink and eat."

I swallow more of the liquid, but my belly rebels. "I'm nauseated. It's hard to put anything in your stomach when you feel like it's going to make a return appearance."

"It feels like that because you haven't eaten."

"Oh, are you a doctor now too?"

"No, I just happen to know you need this. Now drink."

I guzzle the damn water just to get him to shut up. Maybe I'll puke it up all over his fancy suit. Unfortunately, I don't.

I shoot him a nasty look. "Satisfied?"

"Yes. Now, tell me more about foster care."

I stiffen and look the other way. He won't get that information out of me. "There's nothing to tell other than I went and as soon as I turned eighteen, I got the hell out. End of story."

"No, it's not. There's more."

I pierce him with a glare. "Listen to me. I've bared enough to the public, no pun intended. I'm going to tell them a pack of lies, because you think it's the best thing for me to do. But what I won't do is open up my teenage life for them to dissect. You can yell, you can beg. I don't give a fuck what you do, but that book stays closed."

A tiny muscle twitches on his cheek. He's pissed, but too bad. My life is fucked anyway. If he salvages it, I'll eat my own damn underwear. But I am adamant about not sharing that part of my life.

"You obviously don't give a fuck about that contract, then."

"Yes, I do. But what I give a bigger fuck about is everyone and their brother knowing things that should never be revealed. So thank you very much, but that book will remain closed. And please don't bring this up again."

He rubs his jaw, his scruff scraping against his fingers.

"How would you react if you were in my shoes?" I ask.

He walks to the chair next to mine and takes a seat. His long legs stretch out in front of him, and then he crosses his ankles.

"I would hate every second of it, but I would listen to the experts. It's hard to eat a shit sandwich but sometimes you do what you gotta do."

Don't I know that? How many times have I dined on shit in my life? Too many to count and from the looks of it, I'll be living on it for who knows how long.

Chapter 5

HARRISON

SHE WON'T BACK DOWN. ALL I WANT IS FOR HER TO HAND US A tidbit, one tiny fucking morsel the public can latch onto and then they'll love her forever. Because they'll feel so damn sorry for her, they'll want to cuddle her like a baby. But she wants nothing to do with it.

I check the time and see it's almost six. I'm meeting Prescott in an hour, so I'd better make this the greatest show on Earth.

"You remember Marilyn Monroe?"

She squints. "Seriously?"

I ignore the question. "You remember how they found her?"

"Dead?" Sarcasm isn't her best trait. I love a little sass in a woman, but sarcasm hits me in all the wrong places. I bite my tongue.

"Not just dead. Dead from a drug overdose."

"What about it?"

"You remember all the conspiracy theories that everyone talked about?"

She purses her full lips and says, "I think I recall something about them." I want to tell her to cut the snark.

"Like it was a Mafia hit because she was too close to JFK.

Or someone high up in the government had her knocked off to keep her from running her mouth."

"So? What does that have to do with me? You think someone is trying to kill me?"

"Not in the least. If they had wanted you dead, you and I wouldn't be having this conversation. What I am saying is, Marilyn Monroe's death evoked and still evokes so much sympathy in people, they still hang posters of her everywhere. That could be you, minus the dying part, of course."

Those intensely violet-hued irises search mine for answers, and it chills me. Midnight Drake is no shallow woman. I get the feeling she would rather stand there and be whipped to death than buckle under the pressure of a few insults. This is no little kitten waiting for the first person to come along to pet and feed her. Instead, here sits a wounded tigress, willing to fight for her life. I just need to sharpen her claws because right now, they're dull and hiding.

"I am not at the mercy of my drug addiction, waiting for the first man to come along and rescue me, *Mr. President.*" She says it in the breathy tone Marilyn once used at a birthday party for JFK.

"Never did I indicate you were. All I said was that it could be a great ploy to create a sympathetic response."

"Ugh," she huffs, more to herself than me.

"Let me reiterate. Many people saw you in a seriously compromising position on YouTube. It was uploaded from your phone. Who knows how many people saw it before it was pulled. You had a syringe full of heroin stuck in your vein. What more do you need to portray to the public that you are a train wreck? I know this is terrible, worse than anything you should have to go through, and I'm terribly sorry for that. But all I'm suggesting is you give the public what they already know, except tweak it a little. Tell them the why behind it."

She stands and paces. Again. "I've spent the last few years running from this. Avoiding it. Now you want me to revisit it."

"So that's why you were a porn star. Makes perfect sense to me. And it will to them."

She tries to shove me but I grab her hand. "I won't tell them that!"

"I'm not asking you to," I say.

"Do you know how hard it is to earn an honest living?"

"And the purity of the triple X–rated entertainment industry is the way to go, isn't it?" I ask. It's time to get tough with her. This is a part of my job I don't particularly care for, but in order for me to really save her career, she needs to listen to my advice.

She clamps her jaws together and says through them, "I needed the money so I answered an ad for a film role ..."

"I know. And some dude said he could help ... and the next thing you know, you're naked with a dick, balls deep in your mouth."

She licks her lips and swallows annnd ... I get a fucking hard on. Okaaaay, Harrison, where the hell did that come from? I usually take a huge step back from my clients.

"It wasn't exactly like that," she says.

"But I'm close, aren't I?"

She shrugs. "What does it matter? You're going to believe what you want to anyway."

"And you're going to do what I tell you tomorrow or this whole deal is off, I leave, and you're left to handle the vultures on your own." We stare at one another before she gives me a slight nod.

I click my fingers. "Foster care. Give it up."

After a long sigh, she says, "I was abused."

"I'm not surprised. Is that why you left?"

"I ran away a few months shy of my eighteenth birthday." She glances at her hands, which are in her lap now that she's sitting back down.

"So we add, you turned to drugs to escape the harsh reality of abuse from when you were in foster care. That's it."

"What if he hears and comes after me?"

"Who?"

She blows out a breath. "The man who abused me."

"We'll handle him." What she doesn't know is if anyone shows up to hurt her, we'll bury the motherfucker. Not literally, but he won't ever touch her again.

Her eyes drop down, and then back up to mine. The way her hands tug on the hem of her sweater tells me she doesn't believe me. That's when I recognize it. Fear. Throughout all this —the waking up in a hotel room after she'd been drugged and raped, the potential loss of her career—I've never seen what's lurking there until now. Raw, bone-chilling terror. What the fuck happened to her back then?

I drop to one knee and take her hand, which is like a block of ice. "He won't get near you. I promise. No names, no dates, just the words, *I was abused*. That's it," I say.

Her voice shakes as she answers, "They'll hound me for more information. And I don't want to be *that girl*."

In a soft tone, I say, "You can be THE girl who rose above it and became the one who survived. Isn't that what happened?"

She nods slightly.

"Look at me, Midnight."

Large, terror-filled eyes stare back at me. Gone is that sassy-mouthed woman who wanted to punch my face moments before. "I don't know what happened, and it's your business. All I need is to arouse the sympathy of your fans and would-be fans. This will do it." I grab her other hand and add, "Let me do my job and make your name one of the top in Hollywood. Then maybe one day, you can help save others from the same fate. It's up to you. This will give you the power to do anything you want."

She glances from our hands to my face, then back to our hands. I see her nod, only slightly at first. But soon, it must sink in and she finally says, "Okay. But all I'm saying is I was abused as a teenager. That's how my drug use began."

"That's perfect. I want those exact words. We'll incorporate them in our media kit we send out to everyone, along with your videoed statement. Then we'll fly you to Arizona on our way back to LA."

"Not Arizona. There has to be somewhere else I can go."

"It has the best reputation in the country."

"It's too close to where I was raised. I need distance."

When I think about it, she's right. Maybe that's what's adding to her anxiety over this.

I call Leland and have him check around. When he texts me back, he tells me of a place in Malibu with excellent ratings that has an opening. Midnight seems more amenable to it, which I like because it won't require an extra stop on the way home.

I text him back and have him book her in.

"You live in LA, so Malibu will be more convenient since it's right there. Especially if they require any follow-up," I say.

"How am I going to pull this off?" she asks, worry lines creasing her forehead.

"Aren't you an actor?"

"Yes, but I usually follow a script. I'm not a very good liar."

"You'll have to improvise, then. This will be great for your career. But you'll have a script to practice with."

"Improvising is a far cry from lying. I feel awful about lying."

Wait until she's in this industry for a while. She'll be changing her mind when lying becomes a daily occurrence to save her career. "Consider it a catharsis. The counselors will help you with any issues you may have too."

"Issues. Great. They'll probably dig so deep, I'll be stuck there for the rest of my life."

I laugh. "You sound like my two best friends."

"Why? Are they loaded with issues?"

"You have no idea." Which reminds me, I'm supposed to meet Prescott soon. "I hate to cut out on you, but I have a dinner meeting."

"No, go."

"I'll have Emily drop by with some dinner and Leland's first draft of your speech for tomorrow."

"Okay."

"One other thing. We checked out Holt and he was clean. All of his phone records checked out. No calls were made to anyone unidentifiable. Your guy is good, so you don't have to worry about him. See you in the morning."

I head back to my room and let them all know what happened. Then I leave to meet Prescott. He's already waiting for me. It's been a while since I've seen him and he's looking a little shabby.

"Dude." We man hug. "What's going on?"

"The same old. So, Midnight Drake, huh?"

"Yeah. What's up with you?" I ask.

"What do you mean?" he asks.

"You don't look like you're on your usual Scotty game."

"Bullshit."

"No, man, I'm serious."

"Come on, Harry. Have you been talking to Weston?"

I hold both hands in the air. "No. I swear. I know you like a brother. You should know that. What's the deal here?"

"Family shit. What else? Weston didn't tell you?"

"Nah, you know how he is."

He rolls his shoulders. "You remember what happened last Christmas, right?"

"Oh, yeah, the step-cunt fucktastrophe, you mean." His stepmother accused him at Christmas dinner of hitting on her, which was completely false. The opposite happened, and besides, Prescott hates the woman. His father ended up kicking him out during dinner and they've been at odds ever since.

"Dad and I had another run-in at a company sponsored event and it got pretty nasty."

"You're joking," I say, leaning on the table.

He laughs bitterly. "Granddad stepped in and diffused the situation. Work has been a bitch since." He works at the family business with both his grandfather and father. Talk about awkward.

"Dude, you should come to LA for a visit. Get away from here. Tap into some fresh, ya know?"

The waiter shows up and hands us menus. We order appetizers and he leaves. I can't decide what to get for my entree. The food here is amazing.

"It's a damn meal. If you can't decide, order two," Prescott says.

"Do you ever do that?" I ask.

"No, but you're whining like a baby so I figured it would shut you up."

I laugh. "You're such an asshole."

"It's my middle name."

A server plunks a basket of bread on the table. I grab a slice and slather it with butter.

We talk about more shit and then I ask him a question he doesn't answer. "Well?" I prod.

"What?" He downs the rest of his drink and flags the waiter over for another and while he's here, we give him our dinner order.

After the waiter's gone, I aim my finger at my friend. "See? I was right. *You're* not right. Something is fucking with you. Prescott Beckham is all about money and finance—except when he's got his dick buried up to his balls in some woman. And right now, as far as I can tell"—I check under the table —"there's not a woman in sight. So, what's going on? Who is she?"

He has the courtesy to wear a sheepish expression.

"Okay, you'll never guess who I ran into."

"Jesus, tell me already. I hate when people fucking do this."

"Vivi Renard." He says her name like she's a goddess.

"Who the fuck is that?"

"Yeah, you wouldn't remember. She went to Crestview."

"Did you fuck her, like all the other girls there?" I laugh.

"No, I did not fuck her. Christ. I didn't fuck every single girl in school."

My brow practically hits the ceiling. Who is he kidding? "I'm not buying the Brooklyn Bridge, asshat."

"She did my homework."

"I only remember that girl you used to pay, but her name doesn't come to mind."

"She's the one," he says.

"You ran into her? The brainiac? Is she a nuclear physicist or something now?"

"Not even close. She works in a coffee shop."

I lean back and blink. "You're fucking with me. Not that girl."

The waiter chooses that moment to deliver our food.

"So, tell me about her. Other than she works at a coffee shop."

"I think she does something with their IT. But she's changed."

"Oh? What does she look like? I hate to say it, but I don't remember her face."

"Sort of average," he says in a nonchalant manner. I don't buy it for a second.

"Bull-fucking-shit. That's why you're off your usual Scotty game. It's Vivi, isn't it?"

"I don't know what you're talking about. I ran into her. That's all. But I didn't come here to discuss Vivi. I'm more interested in hearing about Midnight Drake and her video. How're you going to fix it?"

"It's fixed. Tomorrow, she'll make a statement, then we check her into rehab. They delay filming for a month or so, but it saves her career. We've built a story about how she was abused as a teen and never told anyone."

"Is it true?"

"Yeah. But she wasn't keen on talking about it. It happened in foster care. I had to wheedle it out of her."

Our plates are both polished and the waiter swoops in to clear them away.

"Harrison, what happens to the people she was with?"

"We're working on that."

"What are you going to do?"

My expression loses all signs of friendliness. "I'm not at liberty to discuss it."

"Fair enough. I don't want to know anyway."

"No, you really don't." If I tell him, that's one more person I have to worry about.

Prescott says, "Let's blow this place and go to mine. I have some great weed at home."

"Actually, I need to get back. We have an early morning call to run through her announcement and then the cleanup. Hey, come out to the West Coast. It would be a good trip for you. Get away from it all."

"Yeah, I might just do that."

He won't. He's been saying that for a while now. Something weird is going on with him. But he has to figure it out, and I have a full plate of my own, most of which is occupied by Midnight Drake.

Chapter 6

MIDNIGHT

WHEN THE DOOR CLOSES BEHIND HIM, I RUN TO THE BATHROOM, strip off my clothes, and talk myself out of throwing up. Visions of their filthy hands touching my skin keep coming back to me. It worsens by the minute, making me feel nasty and soiled, like the vile creature I am. Maybe I should forget about this ... go back to porn. Maybe that's where I belong after all.

The scalding water stings my skin as I scrub away the reminders of what they did to me. Hazy images come into view, but no faces, only hands and fingers digging into my flesh. There is no pain or pleasure, only numbness. I should be happy there is an absence of sensation, but if I felt pain, at least there would be something. It's the lack of anything that pushes me to the edge.

Grabbing chunks of my hair, I pull, trying to make myself *feel*. Only that produces memories of one of them having his hand wrapped in my hair. Hopeless ... that's what my situation is. Harrison Kirkland is confident he has the answers, only I'm not so sure.

Finishing my shower, I scrub the water droplets off with the soft towel. I'm wrapping myself in the towel when I hear a soft knock on the door. I look through the peephole to find Misha standing there.

"Hi," I say, waving her in.

"I've ordered you dinner."

"I'm not very hungry."

"I have strict orders to make sure you eat," she says with a smile.

"I'm sure you do."

"Do you want me to leave so you can dress?"

"No. You probably think I'm obsessed with showering."

"Not at all. I won't pretend to imagine how you feel."

Her sympathetic gaze gives me pause. I press my lips between my teeth because I don't want to talk about this.

"Midnight, you barely know Harrison, but when he goes after something, he gets the job done."

"I don't doubt that. It's just that it's all built on lies."

"But is it?"

The question looms before me. The foster care thing isn't a lie. That's a cold, hard fact. One I wanted buried forever.

A knock interrupts us. It must be room service.

"Go into the bathroom. I'll handle this."

I do as she says, closing the door behind me. I put on the oversized plush robe hanging on the door. It swallows me up, but it's cozy and I love that it wraps me in a cocoon of comfort —something I currently crave.

I listen for the man to leave and then I join Misha. Everything is set up on the table.

"Have you eaten?" I ask.

"No, but I'm getting ready to." She suddenly laughs and I see there are two places set.

"Good. I don't like to eat alone."

At first, my stomach rebels, so I take it slow, forcing each bite down.

"Having a hard time with that?" Misha asks.

It's chicken soup and crackers. There's a baked potato and

bread too. You'd think I'd be able to inhale this since the last meal I ate was with Danny the night before.

"A little."

"You're doing the right thing. You know, eating slowly. But you need the food. It'll make you feel better."

A frustrated huff gusts out of me. "I just want to feel something. All I am is numb."

Misha sets her fork down and leans back. "Have you stopped to think that maybe it's for the best? Maybe your brain doesn't want you to feel?"

"What do you mean?"

"Sometimes the body only deals with what it can tolerate and throws out the rest. Maybe that's what yours is doing now."

Thinking back to the other traumatic points in my life—and there have been several—maybe she's right. My brain doesn't want to go there.

"But I *want* to remember their faces," I say.

"Why?"

"Because I want to have someone to direct all this anger toward. Now it's just a blank slate."

"But then they'd haunt your dreams and who the hell wants that?"

She has no idea that my dreams have been haunted since I was fourteen. Tortured is more like it. That's a subject that I don't dare open with her. I'd rather take a dose of haunting. Anything's better than what I lived through.

Her stare is intense before she says, "Maybe after a good night's sleep, you'll feel differently."

Misha looks as though she's never had to deal with anything difficult before. Her clothes are expensive, her nails are perfectly manicured, and even though she's been eating and drinking, her lipstick still looks freshly applied. Her long, blond hair gleams in the dim light of my room and she probably spends lots of money on hair products. Just watching her throws me back to another time, a time when I could barely afford soap to take a bath.

"It's going to be okay, Midnight."

"Nothing about this is ever going to be okay. The fact that I was pumped full of heroin and felt like I was on cloud nine makes it worse. I can't even explain that part. No, wait. How's this? Imagine getting raped and knowing you're being raped, but liking it and feeling cozy while it's happening."

I've hit the mark because she can't make eye contact.

"Now I have to make up a story about being addicted to drugs, when I'm not, but was raped. Don't you see how completely wrong this is in my brain and why I'm having a difficult time with it?"

She scratches her temple and then clears her throat. "Yeah, I do. I'm sorry. It's awful. But you have to put your faith and trust in Harrison. He knows what he's doing. It's not right. But given that you didn't want to go to the police, it's the only way to salvage your career. If you don't care about that, then it's another matter entirely."

"I just don't understand why we have to lie and do this rehab thing." Frustration bleeds from my voice.

Misha sits up straighter and suddenly appears a foot taller in her chair. Her soft tone is replaced by a commanding one. There is much more to this woman than I initially believed.

"Yes, you do, Midnight. Perception is everything, and you were seen online getting fucked, high as a kite. What will people automatically think?"

She's as silent as I am.

She snaps her fingers. "Come on, I'm waiting."

Anger pools in my gut. "That I deserved it."

"And?"

"And wanted it. But—"

"I don't give a damn about your *buts*. It's what they think that counts. And even though you did nothing wrong, even though you are a victim, they're not going to believe it. No police report was filed. That was your choice. And let's not even talk about if they find out you were Lusty Rhoades in the past."

"That's unfair."

"Not everything in life is fair. Get used to it."

She's right. I learned that long ago.

"Are you done whining?" she asks.

"What?" I ask, my anger returning.

"I'm not making light of what happened to you. I'm simply trying to get you to understand what Harrison is doing. You're being hardheaded and making our jobs too difficult. We don't like dealing with clients we have to beg. Stop making us beg, Midnight."

She leans back and crosses her arms. Misha just threw down the gloves.

"Okay. I got it."

"Good. Now eat. It's the last time I'm telling you. We can't have you passing out in front of the camera tomorrow. We need you looking strong."

She's right. Several more bites in and I begin feeling much better, only I don't let her know. I'm going to give myself one more night of self-pity, and then it's onto the next stage of life for Midnight. Rehab 101. I wonder if I'll pass or fail.

Chapter 7

HARRISON

"SO YOU WERE TOUGH WITH HER?"

Misha fills me in on their dinner.

"Yeah, but I got her to commit. I have to say, I felt pretty bad about it."

"That's a first." I laugh. Misha usually isn't a softie when it comes to clients.

She flips me off.

"Keep in mind we're doing the right thing for her in the long run. I thought having it come from another woman would be helpful," I say.

"I like her, Harrison. A lot. She's genuine and not egotistical, which is rare in the film world."

"Agreed. I got that too. Maybe she'll stay that way."

After Misha leaves, I sit and think. It's difficult to find any information on Midnight. Even her foster care records are a dead end for the most part, which is unusual. It bothers me that she was so frightened. Whatever she's concealing must be some serious shit.

We're all about privacy so her location won't be revealed. Safety is a priority, and I'll have someone keep an eye out for anything unusual. Names won't be mentioned so it shouldn't pose an issue.

The next morning, we assemble in the small meeting room. Midnight looks better, though she must not have slept very well. Purple crescents still lurk beneath her eyes, casting deep shadows. She offers a weak smile.

"There's coffee and breakfast over there if you'd like," I say, pointing to the sideboard.

"That would be nice, thanks."

Emily ordered breakfast so I tell her to help herself. I watch as she puts a croissant on a plate, along with some fruit. Good. At least she's eating.

When everyone is seated, we run through the agenda. Misha explains how Emily will video Midnight's statement and then forward it to the various media outlets. It'll be just a quick testimony with a couple of staged questions.

"That's it?" Midnight asks.

"That's it. Finish your breakfast and we'll get to it."

Midnight brushes a hand through her hair and I ask if she's ready to begin.

"Yeah."

We get situated again and Misha reviews what needs to be done.

Emily moves in with her makeup and conceals the weariness that lines Midnight's face.

Misha sets up the camera on the tripod and she's ready to go. She has Midnight sit in one of the chairs and we do a run-through.

Once we're satisfied, in a breathy voice, she begins, "As many of you may be aware, an incident occurred the other night of which I'm taking responsibility for." She stops and inhales deeply. "As a result of this, I will be checking myself into rehab. Due to some issues I faced as a teenager involving abuse, I sought help in the form of drugs. Obviously, that wasn't the right choice. Now I will face the problem and rectify it. Thank you for your support and understanding in these difficult times." Then she dabs at her eye. I'm not sure if it's real, but she has me one hundred percent. I motion with a finger across my neck to Misha and she turns off the camera.

"That was perfect."

Midnight doesn't move.

"Misha, pull that up for me. I want to see the replay, just to make sure we have everything we need."

"Oh, we caught it. And she was perfection."

Everyone in the room smiles, except Midnight. Then she blurts, "Does anyone have a cigarette?"

"Uh, this is a nonsmoking hotel," Emily answers.

"I can go outside. I don't care."

There's a small balcony off the bedroom and I have cigarettes. Sometimes I smoke when I drink, a bad habit, I confess.

"Come with me."

She follows me to my room and I reach into my messenger bag to pull out a pack of Marlboros. I hand her one, along with a lighter, and we walk outside the sliding glass door.

"After everything you said yesterday, I didn't take you for a smoker."

"I don't smoke," she says.

My brows shoot up.

"My nerves are shot. I needed something."

"Technically speaking, nicotine increases anxiety levels."

She offers me a blank stare.

"If you don't believe me, google it. It's the withdrawal from it that people feel, and when they smoke, they're soothing the symptoms, so they automatically feel it calms them. It's only taking away their withdrawal symptoms. Nicotine is as addictive as heroin."

In a husky voice, the one that was so hot on her porn films

(yes, I watched a couple of them last night), she asks, "Then why do you smoke?"

The corner of my mouth lifts. "I smoke when I drink. They sort of go hand in hand for me."

She takes a long puff on the cigarette, then coughs. No, she's not a smoker.

Laughing, I say, "Feel better?"

"No."

Her pouty expression is pretty damn cute. "I'm going to ask that you let me keep your phone while you're in rehab."

"Why do you need my phone?"

She's doesn't sound keen on this idea, so I continue. "It's customary for rehab facilities to ask their patients to give up their phones and computers, and not to communicate with anyone except through written correspondence. It helps with their success rate. I'm fairly confident this place will be the same. If not, I'll give you the phone back in a week or two. I'd like one of us to have it, just in case your attacker calls again so we can maybe get a lead on him."

"Makes sense."

Her giving in means she may be seeing the light. This will make our job much easier. But in reality, our job is almost over. Once we drop her off and make sure the public sees her as the victim, we basically walk away, unless some other issue arises.

"Great." She hands me her phone and I stick it in my pocket. "I promise to return it safely."

When she's finished with her cigarette, we return to the other room. The team is wrapping up, and I ask for a progress report.

"Everything's sent. I'm sure we'll be fielding calls, but we'll forward everything to her agent," Leland says.

"Good. I need to call Rashid to see if he's found anything."

"Rashid?" Midnight asks.

With a flick of my head toward Misha, I motion for her to handle Midnight while I go to my room to make the call.

Rashid says they have the videos but the men on them aren't easily identifiable. He's working with the hotel on it.

"Do you think they know anything? Were credit cards used to pay?"

"I'm not sure. The manager wasn't very helpful," Rashid says.

"Okay. I'll handle him. You just keep working on the tech part."

"Will do."

I need to run an errand or two before we leave. There's a guy I know—Gino—who can help me, so I call and ask him to meet me at the hotel. He says he'll be over in an hour.

Pulling Leland aside, I fill him in on where I'm going. "I'll go with you."

"No, stay here. You need to make sure everyone boards the plane by noon."

"Got it."

The team finishes handling some things with Midnight's agent on a conference call while I grab a taxi.

I arrive at the hotel, closely followed by Gino. He's a burly dude, even bigger than me, and I'm not anything to sneeze at. When I'm getting ready to rough someone up, size spells comfort. This isn't the classiest hotel in the city. Only I'm in for a little surprise. The person at the front desk isn't a man. It's a woman who bears an uncanny resemblance to Harley Quinn, right down to her rainbow-colored pigtails and bright red lipstick. She's even chewing bubble gum like there's no tomorrow. The only thing missing is the smudged eye makeup.

The question flies through my mind whether she actually had plastic surgery to make this happen.

When she asks, "Hey there, puddin', what can I do for ya?" my fix-it radar starts buzzing. Dammit! Why now?

Leaning against the counter, I ask, "Is the manager here today?"

"Yeah. Hang on a sec." After she winks and blows an enormous bubble, she sashays away.

My associate mumbles, "Takes all kinds, huh?"

"I guess."

A few minutes pass when a man who seriously enjoys too many beers and sports a receding hairline approaches. "You asked for the manager?"

"I did. Is that you?"

"No, I'm Muhammad Ali. Whad'ya want?"

I flash a glance over at my sidekick and he shrugs.

"We need to ask you some questions. Who was working your front desk on Wednesday night?"

"I was. Why?"

"Perfect. Then maybe you can help us out. A friend of ours was brought in here by a couple of men, against her will. She was drugged. Do you remember that?"

"Nope, not that I recall." He looks me square in the eyes without flinching.

"Is that so? Then can I see your security tapes?"

"Don't have any."

Gino glances at me and I look pointedly toward the corner of the room at a camera mounted up high on the wall.

Gesturing toward it, I say, "What do you call that thing?"

The Harley look-alike giggles. The manager shoots her a nasty look and she quickly shuts up.

"It's fake."

"I see." Gino pulls a chair underneath it and climbs up.

The manager yells, "Hey, what're you doing?"

"He's pulling it down. If it's fake, you don't really need it, do you?"

"Okay, stop. It's real."

That was easy enough. Now that he sees we're not here for a picnic, things should progress a bit faster.

"Good. We want to have a look at your videos from Wednesday night."

He rubs his nose and answers, "Yeah, well, I don't think I have any."

"That a fact? What happened to them?"

"Yeah, about that. Someone came in here and stole 'em."

"Stole 'em?"

"Yeah. You can ask her." He gestures toward Harley.

Harley's bubble pops on her face and gum is plastered all over her nose and cheeks. She pulls it off and pops it back into her mouth.

"I don't know what you're talking about, unless you mean that dickface Trent. He came in here with his friend—"

"Shut up, you idiot."

I blink at Gino, and in a matter of a second, Mr. Manager finds himself in a chokehold. Then I smile at Harley and say, "How about you and I go for a little walk?"

Her eyes widen, but I reassure her by adding, "I'm not Trent. I'm not going to hurt you. Trent hurt a friend of mine and I want to find him."

"Oh."

Mr. Manager's eyes bulge. Maybe he's worried about what Harley is going to tell me. Or it could be that Gino is applying too much pressure. I don't really give a shit. Either way, I'm going to find out some badly needed information.

"If you help me, I can help you in return," I tell Harley.

"Look, mister, I may look like that kind of girl, but I'm not."

I smile again. "And you know what? I'm not that kind of guy. So it looks like there's a possibility we can be friends. Can I ask you what your name is?"

"Helen. Helen Reddy."

Is she shitting me? "Really? Like the singer from back in the '70s?"

"Yeah. I guess my mom really thought she was woman." She's referring to the song *I Am Woman* that made Helen Reddy famous. Then she throws back her head and laughs. It's fucking contagious.

"Did she roar?" I ask, still laughing, thinking of the lyrics *I am woman hear me roar.* My mother used to sing that song all the time.

"You bet she did. Especially when she found I discovered her weed and liquor stash when I was thirteen. Then she sent me to live with my dad."

Her face loses its softness and all signs of humor. I don't want to go down this road but I have many ideas this is why Helen needs fixing.

Out of the blue, I ask, "Helen, do you need a job?"

"I have a job."

"You won't after you help me and I leave here this morning."

She tugs on one of her pigtails, then twirls it around her finger. "Then yeah, I guess I do."

"Show me the security tapes. You know where they are, don't you?"

"Yeah. Come on." She motions with her hand, but suddenly stops. "Hey, what's your name?" She pops another bubble.

"You can call me Harry for now."

We walk down a hall and into another room. Helen likes to chat and before long, I have the video I need, along with a name. Then I ask if she can pull up all the records from Wednesday night.

"Sure."

She logs into one of the computers and there is Trent's name along with his credit card information. But I'm still unclear as to what connection Trent has with Midnight. Is it just a coincidence, or is there more behind this?

I take photos of everything and download a copy of the video to a flash drive, and then we're done.

"So, Helen, do you have family here, a dog, an aging aunt you can't possibly bear to leave behind, or a hamster that would starve to death without you?"

She lets out a bubbly laugh. "No, why?"

"There isn't a single person who would miss you if you left? Not your mom or dad?"

"Fuck, no."

"No boyfriend?"

"Look, mister. I may not be super smart, but I ain't stupid either. No means no. I don't have anyone, unless you count that asshole I work for."

Chuckling, I say, "Okay, you want to work for me?"

"Sure. You seem nice enough."

"In LA."

"What? Wait, I can't move. That'd cost a lot."

"I'd take care of it."

She pinches her lip a second, then blows out another bubble. "How would I get there? I ain't got a car."

"Better English, please. You'd leave in"—I check my watch —"an hour."

"You're a crazy fucker."

"I could send someone later to pack up your belongings. In the meantime, I'd set you up in a place to live. You'd have a job doing admin work. You have good computer skills, right?"

"Well, sure."

"You in or out?"

She's quiet, so I add, "I need an answer. I'm on a tight schedule, Helen. The plane leaves soon."

"I'm in."

"And if you don't get along with the rest of the team, that's a hard limit for all of us."

"Oh, I get along with everyone. I swear I do." Her eyes are as clear and bright blue as the sky on a spring day.

"Do you do drugs?"

"No."

"You will have to submit to a drug test when we get to LA. Are you good with that?"

"Yes, sir."

"Grab your things and let's go." I can see Misha and Emily taking this one under their wings.

"I ain't got ..." When she notices my expression, she quickly says, "I don't have noth ... anything but my purse here."

"Okay."

We walk up front where Gino still has Mr. Manager in his clutches. "Nice work, my friend," I say. Then I hand Gino a huge roll of bills. He nods as Helen and I walk past. "Oh, you can let him go. I have everything I need."

"Thanks, boss. See you next time."

I hail a cab and direct him to where the helicopter waits to take us to Westchester County Airport. It's where the jet is waiting to fly us back to LA.

By the time we arrive, everyone's on board. When we get inside, I introduce Helen around. The look on Midnight's face is priceless. I take a seat next to her.

"Who the hell is she?" she asks.

"Don't worry about her. She needed a job."

"What the hell? Do you take in strays or something?"

"Something like that. It's fine." I pat her arm. "She was very helpful in identifying the man who brought you into the hotel. Once we're on the plane, we'll get more information."

As soon as we arrive at the airport, a car drives us directly to the waiting plane. Before we know it, we're LA bound.

Chapter 8

MIDNIGHT

WHO IS THIS PERSON HARRISON DRAGGED ALONG? HELEN Reddy? Is she in costume for a *Suicide Squad* party? What the hell? Is he going to pick up the Joker and Deadshot too? Maybe I need a costume. I'm as fucked up as any of those characters, only I don't have a superpower to fit in. Wait ... I can fuck like a champ. And blow jobs ... no one can out-suck me. I probably could slide right in with that group of misfits.

"What's that look all about?" Harrison asks, still sitting next to me.

"What look?" I don't dare confess my thoughts to the man. Besides, I need to pull myself together here.

"I'm not quite sure I can put a name on it."

Switching topics, sort of, I ask, "Tell me about Helen over there." I reach in my purse for a handful of gummy bears and pop one in my mouth. He eyes me with curiosity.

"She was a huge help in getting the security tapes from the hotel. The manager was not cooperative. I had to offer her a job because after we left, I'm sure he would've fired her."

"And a move to LA comes with her employment package?"

He laughs at my question. "Yeah, it does. But we got the name and credit card info of one of the guys who hurt you.

Before the end of the week, I'll have everything I need on why they picked you."

"Will you know why he's stalking me?" I chew on another gummy bear.

"Can I have one of those?" Harrison asks. I hand him a green one, my least favorite. He holds it up and says, "Wow. You're really generous with these things."

"I don't do drugs. I do gummies. It's why I don't share them." It's not intended as a comical statement but he smiles anyway.

"So, go on," I prod.

"Yeah. I'll let you know what we find and to your question, we will find out why he targeted you. If there was some kind of deep motive, we'll figure it out."

"How?"

"I have ways."

He's not forthcoming on what his ways are and I don't really want to know. He can beat the shit out of those creeps for what they did. I would, however, want to look them in the eye and find out for myself. It doesn't look as though I'll get the chance.

He's silent for a few and then adds, "Emily says the first responses to your statement are coming in and they are more favorable than we expected. You should check your Twitter account. People are showing you all kinds of love, Midnight."

"Great. Thanks." My emotionless response has him sitting up straighter in his seat.

"You need to respond to some of them while you can. Maybe say you're flying back to the West Coast and are so humbled by all the love. Hashtag rehab so they know you're all in."

I glare at him. "I'm all in. A good way to put it."

"You should have a better attitude."

"Yeah, like I should be happy someone drugged and raped me and now I have to go to rehab."

"Damn, I'm sorry. That was insensitive of me. What I

should've said was you should be happy they're buying the story."

I huff out, "The story about being abused isn't a story. It's the truth. I don't want someone's love for what I went through." This conversation needs to end. My glass walls are about to shatter and I'm in the wrong place for that to happen.

He gives no response, of which I'm grateful. Several minutes pass before he moves to sit by Helen. She's chomping on bubble gum like I am gummy bears. I signal the flight attendant and ask for water. Since I eat so many of these things, I'm conscious of drinking lots of water to get the sugar out of my mouth. The last thing I want is a bunch of cavities. I laugh. I could be any man's dream—the toothless blow job giver.

Leaning my head back in the cushy seat, I close my eyes and am surprised when Harrison jiggles my arm.

"Hey, we're here."

"Where?"

"LA. Where else?"

"So soon?"

"You snored the whole flight."

I swipe my hand across my mouth and sure enough, it comes back wet from drool. Nice, Midnight. I'm sure it was a pretty sight.

Everyone moves to grab their belongings, except for Harley, I mean, Helen. She beebops out of her seat and practically dances to the door, acting like the happiest person on earth. And why the hell shouldn't she be? Harrison just rescued her from a shit job, gave her a new one, and is moving her to LA, all expenses paid. I'd be happy as fuck too. And she doesn't have to go to rehab.

Harrison is the last one off the plane. He stays behind, thanking everyone. It's easy to see why everyone enjoys working for him because he does show his gratitude. I'm sure they are well compensated too.

We pile into the waiting limo and everyone gets dropped off, except for Harrison and me. I guess he's my escort to the rehab facility. By this time, I want to crawl out of my skin. The dread of going to this place is unbearable.

When we arrive, they are expecting us. And this place is posh. I can't imagine how much I'll be in debt after this.

We get a brief tour, at Harrison's insistence. The take-charge guy in him emerges, and everyone jumps at his requests. When we get to my room, I realize I never went home to unpack and repack.

"What's the matter?" he asks.

"My things. We never stopped at my place for me to switch them out. I don't have any clothes, other than what I took to New York."

He slides a hand over his squared jaw, which is covered in scruff. I ignore the tightening of my stomach muscles because for once, I'm not angry or bitter as I glance at him. He exudes a raw sexuality that I respond to. Why now of all times?

"I can get Emily or Misha to run by and grab some things for you."

"Guess that'll have to do."

The person checking me in says, "You'll only need casual things while you're here. We have yoga classes and other exercise groups you can join. You'll need those types of clothes too."

"Running shoes," I say. "I don't have anything like this. Maybe I need to run home and do this and then come back."

"Um, I'm sorry. Once you're here, you're here," the check-in person says.

"Excuse me, what's your name again?" I ask.

"Melody." She smiles.

"Can't you make an exception just once?" I ask sweetly.

"I'm sorry, but we never do that here."

My temper flares and I want to punch her, but what good will that do? Probably land me in solitary confinement.

"Midnight, I promise Misha or Emily will handle this," Harrison says in a soothing voice. The problem is, I don't want two strangers rifling through the contents of my drawers, or my apartment for that matter. It's more than a little unsettling. But what other choice do I have?

"Yeah, fine."

Merry Melody chirps away about how lucky I am they had a spot open and then she talks up the room I've been assigned. It is nice, I'll grant her that. But for the undisclosed price tag, I should probably be back at The Plaza.

We tour the rest of the facility, and my knees almost buckle when we get to the group therapy room. I have no idea why this comes as such a shock, but it does. How the fuck will I get through this? Acting 510—the truest test of how good I am. Maybe it'll propel me to the top of the list of contenders for the envied Oscar. Doubtful, but a girl might as well dream.

Harrison leaves me to my new home for the next thirty days and I scurry back to my little cave. Tomorrow begins a new life for me, bright and early at 6:00 a.m. This should prove interesting, to say the least.

Chapter 9

HARRISON

THE WEEK AFTER MIDNIGHT CHECKS INTO REHAB, I'M SITTING IN my office when Misha and Leland walk in. I can tell by their frowns this won't be a happy-dance kind of visit.

Misha doesn't mince words. "Ward is filing a suit against Alta."

"Ward?"

"Holt Ward, Midnight's costar in the film," she explains.

"Why?"

"He says the delay will cost him another role in a different film."

"And what do you say?" I ask.

"I call bullshit. Midnight said he didn't want her as a costar from the beginning. He's using this as an out. The bad thing is Alta's hands are tied."

I gesture to the door, indicating for Leland to close it. I have an open-door policy here but in this case, we need privacy. When we're away from prying ears, I ask, "What do we have on him?"

Leland groans. "He's squeaky clean. I've tried to dig up something, but it's a blank slate."

"No one is a blank slate."

Misha laughs. "You are."

She's right. The only thing anyone can find on me are a few speeding tickets and that I rent the occasional porn flick. "Okay. Then we'll manufacture something."

"What do you want?" Leland asks.

"Something so damaging, it would ruin any chances of him acting again."

Leland is quiet for so long, I figure I've lost him. Then he says, "Connections to the Russian mob."

Misha's head snaps toward him. "No fucking way. If the Mafia gets wind of that, we're all six feet under."

"How would they?" Leland asks. "Why the hell would he leak that, because we certainly wouldn't?"

"What if he comes forward and says it's not true? Then we're forced to come out with more information. I'd rather do something like he's gay or into cocaine. Then if he calls us and we fire off some bogus pics, we won't have Vladimir Kolikov breathing down our necks."

"Who the hell is Vladimir Kolikov?" Leland asks.

Misha pins him with a chilling glare. "You don't want to know."

I hold up my hand. "Okay, no Russian mob. Misha's right. That's way too dangerous and someone could get killed. Personally, I think him being gay would only land him more fans and that's not an unfavorable thing anyway. We need to go with something else. Like maybe linking his name with human trafficking."

Misha snaps her fingers and a demonic glint hits her eyes. "That's it. That would put him in one fuck of a hot seat. Rashid could set up a phony website to threaten him with and if he won't back down, then we go in with the big guns. Rashid can hack into that site they've been targeting and make it look like his name is on there. It would totally put him in the spotlight."

"What's the website?" I ask.

Leland names it and I tell them it's a go. "Who wants to contact Mr. Ward?"

"I think you should do it," Misha says to me.

"Fine. I'll call Rashid and have him get everything set up, and then Mr. Holt Ward will be getting a sweet little call from me."

This Midnight Drake case is getting more complicated every day. We found Trent Dexter. Gino grabbed him and took him to an undisclosed place for *questioning*. He was very cooperative after Gino *explained* some things to him that involved more than a few jabs with Gino's oversized fists.

According to Trent, he spotted Midnight at the club that night and recognized her from her films and TV roles. He was with his friend and they'd been scouting the place for someone to persuade to spend the night with them. Their idea of persuasion, compared to everyone else's, is wildly different. Trent drugged Midnight and took her to the hotel where his friend met them out front. That's when their fun began.

The bad part is the videos they uploaded on Midnight's phone aren't the end of it. They also filmed the whole episode on camera but cropped out her face. Then they did more editing—getting rid of them shooting her up with heroin—and uploaded it to a porn site where it's been downloaded over fifty thousand times. Each time someone streams, it costs $5.99, so these fuckers cashed in on this.

We're stuck between the proverbial rock and hard place. If we report this as a crime, Midnight's career is fucked. If we sue, her career is fucked. We pulled the film, but who knows how many people have it on their hard drives and uploaded it to pirate sites? It could be in the millions. I want to cut that fucker's dick off. It was a good thing Gino went instead of me. Then again, according to Gino, after he was finished with him, Trent won't be doing this to anyone else.

My conversation with Rashid is brief. He assures me it will only take him a few minutes to give me what I need to scare the shit out of Holt Ward. He delivers it about an hour later, and it almost scares the shit out of me.

"Are you sure this is fake?" I ask.

He laughs. Rashid is the best. "Yeah, boss. When it comes to the cyber world, you can't beat me."

He's right about that. When this is all said and done, Holt Ward will be hiring me to clean the shit I stirred up. A hearty laugh roars out of me.

Misha is walking past my office and veers inside to find out what's so funny. When I tell her, she laughs right along with me.

"It'll serve the asshole right. Midnight's been through enough as it is. She doesn't need his bullshit to go along with it."

"Let's see how this pans out." I take a screenshot of the website and then make the call to Holt's agent, asking for his number. He tries to give me the runaround, but when I explain how urgent it is and that if I don't personally speak to Holt about this matter, he can expect to be fired, he rattles off the number immediately.

Holt answers his phone and I calmly say, "Mr. Ward, my name is Harrison Kirkland, and in about two seconds you will receive a photo from me via text. I hope this persuades you to drop your lawsuit against Alta and Midnight Drake regarding your contract in the film you two were cast in. If you have any questions, feel free to call me." I end the call and wait for him to call me back.

Holt Ward doesn't disappoint. When I answer, he tries to rip me a new one. I lean back in my chair and listen patiently as he rants about how I can't do this and that I'm framing him, blah, blah, blah.

When he finally runs out of steam, I say, "It took you long enough to shut your fucking mouth. One, I'm not framing you. It's not my problem you have an affinity for buying and selling women, especially those who are under eighteen. Two, if you don't drop the lawsuit, this shit will go broad, and by that, I mean my firm will release it to every media outlet in the entertainment industry. Any questions?"

"You can't do this! I haven't been involved in anything like this. I don't know where you found this, but it's phony."

"Prove it, Mr. Ward. It looks legit to me. I even clicked on the links. It's a pity too. I would've expected better from you."

"Dammit, it's not mine!" he yells. I have to hold the phone away from my ear, he's so loud.

"Sure looks like it to me. Aside from that, this trafficking site may be on the Feds' radar. Your name wouldn't be on it if you were clean. Drop the lawsuit and I can make this all go away. You can even hire me if you want. But my first priority is Midnight Drake. I want you back on the film with her, and I want Alta happy again. Am I clear?"

I hear his heavy breathing on the line. Finally, he says, "Fine. I'll make the call. But clean this shit up, will you?"

"Not a problem. Expect a bill from my firm."

It's my turn to end the call and after I do, I toss my phone on the desk and chuckle. The asshole just lost a wad of money by fucking with my client and he became my client in the process.

I buzz Helen and ask her to send Misha and Leland in. When I relay how the call went, they high-five me. I wait for the call from Alta—which comes about an hour later—to have Rashid pull the dummy site down. It was never active to begin with, so there was no concern there. If you didn't have the web address, there was no way you could've found it. When he's finished cleaning everything up, I have Helen send Holt a pricey bill.

Now we have Midnight back on board. When I'm on the phone with Alta, they tell me their fan division is fielding more correspondence than ever for her. Everyone wants to know how she's doing. It's great to hear our plan is working. Which reminds me, I need to get her phone back to her, if it's allowed.

I'd love an opportunity to talk to her. Not a day goes by that

I don't think about her. She was so worried about being stuck there for a month so I wonder how she's doing.

The next day, I check with the facility and ask about her ability to have a phone. They say she can have visitors on the weekend, but no phones are allowed until her final week. I decide to pay her a visit on Saturday to fill her in on what's happening.

But when Saturday rolls around, she refuses to see me. A crushing wave of disappointment washes over me. Where the fuck did that come from? She's a client, dammit.

I shake it off and write her a note instead, briefly explaining what's been going on. When I'm done, I give it to the front desk and ask them to deliver it to her. She's completed her second week so she's halfway through the program. I think about what she has to look forward to when she's released.

Pushing the unexpected and unfamiliar feelings of excitement down, I refuse to let myself question them. There's no way Midnight Drake has gotten under my skin. Not at all.

Chapter 10

MIDNIGHT

HARRISON CAME TO THE FACILITY. HE'S BEEN ON MY MIND constantly. I think about his strength, how his warm eyes draw me in, and that he's the only man I've ever wanted to touch, but yet I refused to see him. The last person I want seeing me like this—scraped raw and razored open from stem to stern—is him. He's the reason I'm here ... and because of this damn place, my fucking heart and soul have been ripped out of my body. I've been left a bloody mess. I knew coming here was a bad idea, but I had no idea how terrible it would be on me.

If you're an addict, they take away your drugs—drugs I don't fucking use—but they also delve into your psyche, tear it apart bit by bit, pry into things that are better left untouched. Wounds have been reopened; scars that were healed are now gaping holes with blood pulsing from them. And I'm left to deal with the consequences. My counselor is one smart fucker. She picked me apart for hours until I broke and vomited my whole fucking story. Damn Harrison Kirkland for sending me here. This is his fault.

And now I'm supposed to feel better because of this presumed catharsis. Well, I don't. My body fucking screams pain. And all I can see is his face and what he did to me ... what he forced me to do. I didn't need this reminder ... didn't want it. But I got it anyway. And to think I have two more agonizing weeks of reliving those horrors. My counselor says in time, I'll appreciate these sessions. The only thing I'll appreciate is when day thirty rolls around and I can say, "Adios, motherfucker."

They say time flies when you're having fun. Well, the opposite is true when you're not. In fact, someone has completely shut down the passage of it altogether. The last four weeks have taken about five years. Becky, my esteemed counselor, believes I may be bipolar. What she doesn't realize is my moods are so fucked up from having to carry on this charade and then revealing so much of myself on top of it, anyone would act as though they're bipolar. One minute I'm crying so hard I'm practically having a seizure, and the next I'm manic, zigzagging around her office, incapable of controlling my actions.

In my final session, the day before I'm to be set free, she says firmly, "Midnight, sit down, or I'll call someone in to tranquilize you."

That grabs my attention. I'm not about to screw up my final day here. Getting forcefully injected with a potent drug is not what I need. My ass slams down in the chair, but I can't keep my hands still. I just need to get the fuck out of here. I came in sane but will be leaving crazy as fuck.

"How are you feeling?"

Is she serious? "How do you think I'm feeling?"

She doesn't answer. I hate when she does this.

"I'm agitated today, Becky." I can't keep the snark from emerging.

"And why's that?"

"I don't know."

"Yes, you do," she says. Her calm manner irritates me.

"I want to go home."

"I don't think you're ready."

We've been through this before. I'm going whether she wants me to or not. "It doesn't matter."

"Midnight, I want you to be as strong as you possibly can. If you leave, you might start using again."

"No, I won't. I won't ever use again." *Because I've never used to begin with.*

"Then explain your agitation."

"It's my past," I say in frustration. "You already know that."

"And you know how to deal with that."

"By confronting it, but it only makes me more miserable." I wanted it to stay buried. I was much happier that way, gummy-bearing my way through life. But no, Harrison Kirkland came up with this braniac plan and ruined it.

"Midnight, it will make you stronger."

"I can't. You want me to visit him. He ... it would never work. You have to trust me for once." The last thing I will ever do in my life is visit the man who ruined me.

She holds up her hands, spreading them in the air. "It's your life."

Fucking A, it is. However, since this is my final session with her, I do want to leave her with one lasting impression.

"Let me just say this, Becky. There's not much I would like to say to the man who forcibly made me have sex with him and give his friends blow jobs for almost three years while I was a minor. Is that something you can personally relate to?"

There's a subtle change in the coloring of her face and she shifts in her seat.

"No, I didn't think so. That's the reason I will never have any contact with that man as long as there is breath in my body. I'm pretty sure this session is over."

"You could bring charges against him."

"Oh? And have all that attention focused on me? No. I don't think so."

I tremble during the long walk back to my luxurious room.

The conversation brought to mind that other piece of the puzzle —the one that always shatters me—the one Becky doesn't even know about.

I lie down on the bed and cover my face with a pillow so no one will hear the sobs as they rip from my body.

Sixteen hours later, I walk past the front desk, waving flippantly to the cheery staff people. They're the last ones I give a shit about. Those happy faces are a sham. The entire month I was here, they were never pleasant to me. Every time I asked them for something, I was denied, even if it was as small as a glass of ice. With the gigantic price tag on this place, you'd think they could afford a glass of fucking ice. I want to flip them off, but I refrain. Who knows whether they run their mouths when they're away from here? The last thing I need is more enemies than I already have. Holt Ward is enough to deal with as it is.

I'm not surprised to see Harrison walking toward me. He wouldn't have sent anyone else to pick me up. And damn, is he a sight for sore eyes. He's wearing a black shirt and dark jeans that mold to his perfect body. If he looked any better, I'd probably faint. There isn't a man alive who can hold a candle to him, dammit. Even though I'm still angry with him, it's hard to deny the happiness I feel, though I don't want to let it show.

He smiles as we meet midway in the parking lot. I want to launch myself at him and press my lips to his perfect mouth. Is this what happens when you lock someone up for thirty days and put them through intense psychotherapy? A giant lady boner nails me. "So? How are you? I stopped by to visit, but you refused to see me that day."

I swallow away the desert in my throat. "I survived. Truth is, I'm not in the mood to see you today." *Liar!*

"Then you'd miss out on all the important news I have for you."

That piques my interest, but I don't want him to know. I shrug. "I don't really care." *Liar!*

By this time, we're at his car, an old convertible red Mustang. He puts my bags into the trunk and then opens the passenger door for me. Such a gentleman.

As I'm sliding onto the seat, he says, "You should care. It's your career." He's right. I should, and I do.

When he gets into the car, he digs inside the glove compartment and hands me a baseball hat. "Here. Your hair will be in knots if you don't put this on."

"Thanks." I say it like I don't mean it. Why am I being so bitchy? I stuff my hair under the hat, grateful for it, but keeping that from him.

He doesn't let my sour mood affect his. "I'm a thoughtful guy."

"Let's dump the Mr. Jolly. While I'm glad to be out of that fucking hell, I just want to go home, okay?" I ball up my fists and rub my eyes.

"Jesus, who stole your happy?"

"You did when you sent me here. They dissected and tore me apart. Satisfied?" I cross my arms and stare into the sunny sky.

I must've hit a nerve because he puts the car in reverse and off we go. Not another word is spoken until we get to my place. He helps me to the door and that's when he says, "We have a lot to discuss."

"It can wait. I need time. Alone. In my own home." I need to get a grip on my emotions. He doesn't deserve my nasty behavior.

His eyes meet mine and then he does that thing I love. He licks his lower lip and runs a hand over his scruffy jaw. Damn his sexy self. I need to get away from him before I do something stupid … something I'll regret, like make a play for him. He's all I've thought of for the last thirty days, and I haven't been around my vibrator for that whole time. I've only had my finger to keep me company at night, and now I'm standing before the amazingly hot Harrison Kirkland and I have an unbelievable desire to drop to my knees and do the dirty, just to hear him groan with pleasure. Thinking about it, I nearly groan myself. What the hell is wrong with me?

"Fine." Then his teeth scrape over his lower lip. His chocolate irises razor straight through me and I don't like it one bit. Or maybe I like it way too much. "You've changed. What happened in there, Midnight?" His tone is soft, and it makes it even worse.

"Things you don't want to know."

"Did someone hurt you?"

A hysterical laugh bursts forth. "Of course they hurt me. That's why I didn't want to go." I turn around and close the door, leaving him with a baffled expression on his attractive face. I need to get away from him. He makes me want things I shouldn't. Men and me don't mix.

But Harrison is different. I want to hate him, only I can't. I'm angry for what happened in rehab, and he's the only one I can take it out on. But I still want to do things with him … dirty, sexy things. It's best if I keep my distance from him or things may get out of hand.

Chapter 11

HARRISON

THIS IS NOT THE SAME WOMAN I LEFT THIRTY DAYS AGO. WHAT the hell happened in there? They were supposed to help, not tear her apart. The idea of her suffering in there is a gut punch. Leaving her is the last thing I want, yet she's offered me no invitation to come inside. What do I do? I can't find anything out until I speak to her. I've no choice but to leave because I can't break down her door.

I drive to the office, my mind filled with questions. When I get back, Misha asks how it went.

"I'm not sure."

"Was she pleased with everything we did?"

"I didn't tell her." After I explain, Misha wants to go over to Midnight's apartment.

I stop her. "She wants to be alone."

"Is she suicidal?" she asks.

"I doubt they would've sent her home if she was."

But then I wonder, so I make a call. All I get is that information regarding her treatment is confidential. Even when I explain that I'm worried about her condition, they tell me nothing. They do say they'll have her therapist call. And she does.

"Mr. Kirkland, Midnight is many things, but she never

showed any suicidal tendencies while she was here. There are other issues we addressed and I did suggest she stay another thirty days to prevent her from relapsing back to using, but she refused." I know exactly why too.

"I see. Thank you for returning my call."

My thoughts are eased, but I'm still worried about her. Why wouldn't she at least talk to me? A month is a long time, but that comment about how they hurt her disturbs me. To what was she referring? Did they physically abuse her in there?

My mind won't rest until I know, so I shoot her a text.

I need to know if you're okay. Believe it or not, I'm worried about you. It wasn't my intention for you to have a terrible experience there. Please call me.

She's all I dwell on until I get home that night and the phone rings.

"What did you want to tell me?" Midnight asks.

"We actually have a lot to go over. Can we meet?" It's only about six and I offer to take her to dinner.

"I'd prefer takeout at my place."

"Are you sure?"

"I never do anything I'm not sure of. Except for one thing, and I was right on that. Massaman curry with shrimp, brown rice, and a fresh roll." She names the place and I hang up to place the order.

When I show up at her apartment, she looks like a waif. She's wearing an oversized sweatshirt and a pair of baggy pants. Her eyes look ... old. They've aged since she left.

I set the food on the kitchen counter and then stare at her as she pulls plates out of the cabinets.

"I brought some beer and wine as well," I add, not knowing if she had any beverages since she's been away for the last month.

"Thanks. I didn't think about that."

"So, what's your pleasure?"

She lets out a snicker. "Gummy bears." Then she loads up

our plates. After she hands me mine, I follow her to the living area where we sit on the sofa. I've poured us a couple of glasses of wine, after she admitted she'd prefer that over beer, and we eat.

"I love this food," she says around a mouthful of curry.

"It is good. I've never been there, but I'll definitely be going back." We eat in silence for a few until I ask, "What's up with the gummy bears?"

"They're my crack. Everyone has something, right?"

"I guess."

"Oh, come on. Name yours."

"No, I'm clean of addictions."

"Yeah, right." Her deep violet eyes fasten onto mine and their intensity has me hypnotized. I've never seen anything like them before. "Give it up."

"No, I really don't have any. Alcohol only occasionally, and a cigarette every now and then when I drink. I smoke weed once in a while, but not enough to amount to anything."

"I know." She grins like she's discovered something super important. "You have a secret addiction to porn."

I laugh. "No, porn's good—what man doesn't like it? But no addiction. Sorry, I'm clean."

She studies me for a long minute, then uses her fork as a pointer. In a sort of singsongy voice, she says, "Maybe addiction is the wrong word. Weakness is more like it. You must have some kind of weakness. What is it?"

She's touched a nerve, one that doesn't need exposing. "Everyone has weaknesses."

"So? Name your worst."

I aim my gaze at her. "Nope. Not until you share one of yours."

She sits up straighter and takes a bite of her dinner. After she swallows, she says, "Broken people are your weakness, aren't they? You saw I was broken and thought you could put me back into working order. That's why you brought in Harley, or Helen. Isn't it? Is that your addiction?"

How is she so astute? I gulp down some wine and face her. She's not going to drop this. "I don't see it as a weakness, but I do like to help others, so in a sense, I suppose you're right."

She pushes a chunk of long, shiny black strands out of her eyes. "Nah. It goes much deeper than that. You're flawed, Harrison. You see, during my stay in rehab, I had a lot of free time, more than I've had in years. I thought about a lot of things, and you were one of them."

"I'm flattered."

"You really shouldn't be. There were times I wanted to use your face as a punching bag."

"Ouch," I say, leaning back and rubbing my jaw.

"Yeah. It wasn't nice. It was so bad, in fact, that every night before I fell asleep, I'd curse your name and tell myself somehow I'd make you pay for sending me there."

This is really shocking. I'm speechless.

"Surprised by that, are you?"

"I have to admit I am." All I wanted to do was save her career. And the more I think about it, the more it pisses me off.

"I can see those little fix-it cogwheels spinning in that smart brain of yours."

A man can only take so much, and she just pushed me to the cliff's edge. "Let's get one thing straight. I was saving your sweet little ass, saving your fucking career by arranging for you to go there. That was it. There was no ulterior motive. It wasn't because of a weakness of mine. If you needed fixing, it had nothing to do with me. My goal was to clean up the shambles your damn career was in with Alta, which, by the way, you haven't even asked about. I've had to pull a couple more strings while you were unavailable. Oh, and while we're on the subject, your little friend, Trent, used the video he filmed and had it uploaded to several porn sites, which had thousands of downloads by the time we got to it. I took care of that too, you're fucking welcome. Holt Ward will no longer be a problem either. The lawsuit he filed has been dropped —the one you weren't aware of because my team took care of it in your absence. Don't mention that to him, by the way. Your career will skyrocket, thanks to that rehab stint." I stand up, with every intention of leaving.

Her words stop me. "We're not finished."

"That's where you're wrong. You can handle your own messes from now on. My work with you is through."

"I wasn't talking about that."

I'm clueless. What the hell is she referring to?

"When I was in rehab, they opened old wounds. That's what I'm blaming you for."

Patience is one of my finer attributes but currently, it seems I'm out of stock. I tilt my neck to look toward the ceiling, praying to some unknown deity for more. Then I level my gaze at her. "Seems everything's my fault and that makes an assload of sense. I think when you checked out of rehab, you left your damn brain there."

"You asshole."

"I believe you're the asshole. You need more than gummy bears, my friend. They aren't cutting it for you. Maybe you need some happy pills or something." My insult level climbs.

"Oh, that's a good one. Such a man thing. When a woman has a right to be angry at something legit, they automatically tell her she needs happy pills."

"You hit a key word, and that's *legit*. What you're saying and insinuating doesn't come close to being legit. You sound fuck-nuts. Look, whatever happened to you in your past, I'm totally sorry about. But it's not my damn fault."

She gets in my face and yells. "No, it's not. But opening up those old wounds is."

"Yeah? You wouldn't have wounds if nothing had happened, hence, not my fault."

"Ugh. You are so stupid."

"You just said I was smart."

"Oh. My. God. I can't talk to you anymore," she says.

"I was trying to leave but you wouldn't let me."

The next thing I know, she flies at me, but instead of slapping or punching me as I expect her to do, she kisses me. Angry kisses. I have zero time to react. We're suddenly bound together, and I can't determine where one of us ends and the other begins. Her teeth sink into my lower lip and I taste blood. It's hot as fuck, spurring me into action. I pick her up beneath her thighs, backing her into the closest wall and propping her up with my knee.

Her fingers tear at my shirt like she's a possessed demon, shredding the fabric with her nails. It doesn't matter because my hands are doing the same to hers. She's naked underneath her baggy sweatshirt and I know what to expect. Sick as it may sound, I've watched her porn videos, even rubbed one off to them more than I care to admit.

Her nipples point directly at me, and as I gaze down, a hand lands on my chest, shoving me away. She doesn't speak, only moves to the button and zipper of my jeans. Those actions have frozen me in place. Her experienced hands have my cock exposed in seconds and I watch, fucking mesmerized, as she sinks to her knees and takes the whole thing down the hatch.

Midnight knows how to suck a man off. The thought ekes into my brain that there's a good reason for this. She did it for a living in the triple-X film industry. Should I care? Maybe, but right now, my hands burrow into her silky hair and I let her do the job. I'm not sure if she's aware, but her moans are almost as hot as what her mouth and tongue are doing to me. When her finger rubs a tiny circle behind my balls, I don't have time to tell her my cum's about to explode into the cavern of her throat.

I growl out an orgasm that lasts way longer than usual. Then I glance down to see her wipe a dribble of my jizz from the corner of her mouth.

Plowing my hands through my hair, I wonder what the hell

just happened. One minute we were arguing, and the next she's dining on the vine. If that doesn't make me hungry for more, I don't know what could. Only she has a different idea. When I reach to pull her up, she backs away and says, "I think you should leave."

"Leave?"

"I'm pretty sure you know what the word means."

My fingers tighten around her arm and I practically drag her back to the sofa.

"Sit your ass down. Now." I slide my hand across my hair again trying to figure out what to say to her. This scene is like one out of a movie, only I'm not an actor and not sure how to deal with her. It's also beginning to freak the fuck out of me because I care about her. I don't know how or why, but I do.

Her lavender eyes darken as she glowers. At least I haven't frightened her. For a moment, I thought maybe I had.

"I'm not sitting down."

"Yes, you are. Moments ago, you kissed me like a sex-starved animal, then sucked me off, and now you tell me to leave. I want to know exactly what's playing out in that brain of yours."

"Why? So you can fix it? I'm gonna let you in on something. I'm broken, Harrison, and not fixable." She yelled at me—as in, shouting at the top of her lungs.

This time I don't ask but shove her down onto the couch. She doesn't seem to respond to nice.

"I asked, but apparently you don't like to be asked. Now sit the fuck down and stay there. When two people have sex, it usually ends up differently."

"What world are you living in? That's not the way it works for me."

"So, what next? Am I supposed to pull out a handful of bills and pay you?"

Her arm comes out, lightning fast, and strikes. Only I'm faster and catch it.

"What the fuck happened to you in there, Midnight?" I ask

her, my tone softening.

She pulls her lower lip in and bites it. It makes her look like a little kid.

"I'm not going anywhere until I have some answers."

A long sigh rolls out of her and she tries to tug her arm from my grip. "I'm not pressed for time," I tell her.

"They put me through those stupid psychobabble sessions and this is the end result. Happy now?" I get the feeling she wants to stick out her tongue at me, and I do the unthinkable: I laugh.

"You motherfucker."

"I am a lot of things, but never that."

"I went through hell in there and you have the nerve, the audacity, to laugh at me."

"I'm sorry. I wasn't laughing at what you went through. It was only that your expression had you looking like you were ready to stick your tongue out at me."

Then she does and I totally lose my shit.

Her fingers suddenly pinch the shit out of my nipple and my laughter turns to a shriek of pain.

"Not so funny now, is it?"

"You are so fucking mean. Has anybody ever told you that?" I ask.

"No, but so are you. It seems we are on equal footing."

"You're nothing but a spoiled little kid. I only tried to help you and here you are, acting like a little shit. You need to grow the fuck up."

"You know what? Why don't you get the hell out of here? I don't need to continue the hell I went through. A month was long enough and I am anything but spoiled."

"I disagree."

We glare at each other in silence. And then something comes over me as I grab and kiss her. I have no idea what the hell I'm doing, other than falling into the pit of nutsville. I am sure of one thing—this will not end well.

Chapter 12

MIDNIGHT

HE'S SO DAMN IRRESISTIBLE. I SHOULDN'T WANT HIM, BUT I DO. I shouldn't have kissed him, but I did. Even though I'm furious with him, his lips are undeniably addicting. For thirty days, I fantasized about this man and here he is, kissing me, touching me, and nothing in this universe could prevent this from happening.

Passion flares deep within me, and it's like nothing I've ever felt before. Flames lick my skin, heating me in every imaginable place. Oh, I've kissed more men than I care to count. Fucked just as many, if not more. Only they never stoked the fires like Harrison does. Kissing him empowers me, frees me, gives me back this part of my life that was so ruthlessly torn away. Vile memories are replaced with a face and body that I've dreamed of and desired for the last month. Maybe if I get him out of my system, I can get on with my life. Only I doubt that will happen. One taste of this man will probably be worse than any heroin ever could be.

Sinking my fingers into his thick hair, I kiss him back with everything I have. It's dirty, wicked, raw, but oh so good. How can I want him so much, the one I want to hate? This isn't something I ordinarily do. Even getting him off was a surprise to me. But I had to taste him, have him in my mouth. And the pleasure it gave me may have been more than what he got. The sounds he made when he came ... oh I'll never forget that.

His cock is still exposed and I wrap my hand around it, enjoying its velvety thickness. If only I could feel it pumping deep inside of me. But after our little verbal exchange, it's probably the last thing on his mind. Maybe I can change that. Making men desire me is my area of expertise.

My hand slides down to his balls, where I squeeze and massage them. Then I rub that place he was so fond of earlier. But he quickly breaks off the kiss.

"Stop. Are you gonna go psycho on me again?"

"What the hell kind of question is that?"

"Exactly what it sounds like. A few minutes ago, you told me to leave when I wanted to eat your pussy. What's it gonna be, Midnight?"

"You wanted to eat my pussy?"

"Yeah, but I never got to even try because you were shoving me out the door." He rubs his face and I hear the scratchy sound his scruff makes. God, I'd love to feel the rub of that between my thighs.

My hands slide under the waist of my pants and I push them down. I'm not in the mood for games. All I want to do is fuck. Let's get the party started.

"Follow me." I lead the way to my bedroom, where I also have some condoms stashed just in case he didn't bring any. I climb onto the bed and spread my legs. "I'm ready."

His expression registers shock. "Jesus. Is this what you usually do?"

"Why waste time is my motto."

He grimaces as his cock deflates a bit. That's not very encouraging. Maybe my attitude is too casual for someone like him. "I look at sex between two consenting partners as a very casual thing. You have to see it from my perspective, and please don't lecture me. If it bothers you, maybe you should leave."

He doesn't speak, only stalks aggressively toward me. It's both sexy and scary. My thighs automatically close.

"Nuh-uh. None of that. Don't act like some kind of tease with me. Keep 'em open."

I comply as I watch him step out of his jeans and remove the shirt I destroyed with my nails. Harrison has ink and it's sexy as fuck. It definitely amps up my horniness. In a superfast move, he snatches my ankles and drags me to the end of the bed. From between my thighs, because he's now kneeling on the floor, he says, "I'm extremely fond of casual sex, but your attitude is more of a two-dollar hooker than that of a consensual partner."

Is that how I acted? He gives me no time to ponder my harlot behavior before he dives between my legs and assaults my pussy. His tongue has me feeling like a virgin on her wedding night, and I spent two years in the porn industry, getting sucked and fucked, oftentimes by multiple partners, including women, who are supposed to know what to do with said pussy. No one has ever done to my nether region what Harrison is doing now. I'm afraid to ask or look.

There may possibly be an alien that's invaded my vagina and has taken residence down there for all I know. An enormous ripple of pleasure vibrates through me. I do know this—I am building up to an orgasm of massive proportions. And no one, at least not of the human variety, ever gives me orgasms. I am O-negative. Period. And I'm not talking about blood type.

Using his fingers and mouth, he makes me come exquisitely, but I do my best to pretend I didn't enjoy it. Only I practically meow like a fucking tomcat. I wouldn't be surprised to find a herd of feral females in heat outside my window, waiting for Mr. Feline to emerge.

I feel puffs of air on my vag. There's a possibility he may be laughing in my crotch. Jesus. This has not gone the way I'd intended. I'm supposed to be teaching him a lesson, not the other way around.

I finally brave it enough to open my eyes and find him

staring at me with the biggest smirk on his face. His sexy lips glisten with my wetness. Oh my. Before I can stop myself, I grab him by the ears and pull him up to my mouth so I can lick him clean. Without a doubt, I'm losing it.

But we don't stop at a kiss. Oh, no. I should've known better. He hikes my leg over his shoulder and commences to wrap his thick, hard cock in latex. The man's got game. In one swift move, he's covered and sliding deep inside of me. Once he's balls deep, he stops, and I catch my breath. He's thick and I have to accommodate myself to him.

Using a thumb and index finger, he takes my chin and forces me to look at him, which I'm not very willing to do. I don't usually fuck people I know. It's uncomfortable and the aftermath isn't something I care to deal with.

"What are you thinking?" he asks.

Is he kidding? Should I tell the truth? If I don't, I'm sure he'll find a way to get it out of me.

"I was thinking how I don't like to do this with people I know, and this is way too soon for us to be doing this."

"Should I stop?"

I want to say yes, but I don't. "No. Don't even think about it."

"Guess we both should've thought of that earlier, gummy bear." Then he pinches my nipple as he bites my lip. My body clenches in every place imaginable. But what's this gummy bear shit?

Before I can say anything, he pulls out and thrusts into me so hard, a long whoosh of air oomphs out of me.

"Just so you know, I'm going to fuck that sassiness out of you." Then he flips me over like a rag doll. Where's all this coming from? He slides in behind me, doggy-style, which has never been my favorite, but then he surprises me by straightening me up. We're both on our knees as his hand moves to my clit and the other steadies me under my breasts.

Bam, bam, bam, his hips bang my ass. The hand on my clit

holds me against him to meet his thrusts. Each time, I'm almost lifted off the bed. I won't last long at this pace, especially if his finger keeps up that little motion. Sure enough, a few more swirls and I'm coming like the pro I am. Only this time, I'm not faking my orgasm.

He lets me go and I land face down on the bed, where he enters me again from behind. It occurs to me he hasn't come yet. Shit. I'm going to be limping in the morning. He jams pillows under my hips, and I'm getting thoroughly fucked once again. By now, my pussy is nearly raw and sore, but also aching for more of Harrison Kirkland's dick.

How is this possible? What the hell kind of spell has he cast over me? I never respond to men like this. I always thought the only way I could come was with a vibrator. Guess I was wrong, because after several minutes of him pumping in and out of me, I have another big one. Miss O-negative has leaped over to the positive side. A tiny giggle escapes me but I quickly cover my mouth.

Knowing I won't have time to catch my breath, I'm still not ready when he flips me onto my back and puts the soles of my feet against his chest. Then he slides inside of me again, carrying on, never breaking stride.

"I want to look into your eyes while I come." His voice is gruff and it triggers an unlikely response in me. I've never wanted to look in anyone's eyes during sex. No, no, no. But with him … I do. I want to fall into those dark caverns and never leave.

I don't respond, because I'm afraid of what I'll say. The other truth I'd like to tell him: *will you let me rest then, because damn, I'm worn the fuck out.* Harrison is a fuck machine.

It doesn't take him long before he slows his thrusts and thrums my clit to one more climax. As he does, his lids half close and I watch, totally enthralled, as this gorgeous man finally explodes in his own epic orgasm.

When he finally pulls out, he scrutinizes me and announces, "Damn, your pussy is swollen."

"It ought to be. You fucked it to smithereens."

He chuckles and soon it turns into a roaring laugh. It's impossible not to laugh with him because he did indeed fuck me to pieces.

When we finally stop laughing, he asks, "Are you ever going to tell me what the hell happened to you in rehab?"

Why did he have to go and steal my fun?

Chapter 13

HARRISON

A VEIL DROPS OVER HER EYES AND THE LAUGH DISAPPEARS. Whatever happened in therapy opened up too many old wounds she won't show me. Right now, anyway. Then I think about what just took place between us, and I question my own sanity. What the fuck was I thinking? Sex and business should never mix. I broke one of my cardinal rules. I didn't just break it, I pulverized the damn thing, and it's now scattered into dust. Maybe I should pretend it didn't happen.

But I can't do that. And why? Because it was the most epic sex of my life. And it was with Midnight, someone I've developed feelings for. How the hell did that happen?

Leaning down, I take my tongue and give her pussy one last, long swipe. Then I stand and go into the bathroom to dispose of the condom. When I'm done, I pick up my discarded clothes and get dressed. Her eyes practically burn through the skin on my back, which isn't exactly the most comfortable feeling.

Before I leave, I walk next to the bed. "I'll be back tomorrow around the same time. And don't tell me you didn't like what happened between us. If you do, I'll call you a fucking liar," I say. I want to kiss her, but I don't. Instead, I tug at one of her nipples and the response is immediate. She sucks in her breath and my dick twitches in my pants. I have to get out of here before I strip off my jeans and push said dick back inside her swollen pussy. I'm pretty fucking sure she'd be willing too.

On my way out, she says, "Tomorrow, I want Italian. Make it spaghetti Bolognese. And find a place that serves the best. If you're going to fuck me like this, I need to keep up my strength."

The corners of my mouth curve up. "Yes, ma'am. Anything else?"

"Yes. A bottle of Barolo, a Caesar salad, and some great bread. You pick the bread. And butter, none of that olive oil. Bread needs butter."

"Demanding, aren't you?"

"Not at all. You have the opportunity to choose your own entrée because I never share."

I chuckle. "Dessert?"

"Surprise me."

I'd like to surprise her, but I don't think I have a single trick up my sleeve that she hasn't seen or experienced. That should bother me, but it doesn't. At least not yet.

The next afternoon I'm sitting in my office, my thoughts bouncing from last night to a new client that just hired us, when my cell phone rings. It's my dad.

"Hey, son. Your mother and I are thinking about flying out to visit. Is this a good time?"

I bolt out of my chair. "Oh, well, Dad, not now. You know I was planning on coming home for Christmas."

"Yes, but since you don't come home much, your mother has been worried silly about you. You know how she is."

"I know. I'm sorry, but now isn't such a good time. Maybe after the first of the year you two can come out."

Disappointment laces his tone. "All right. I'll let your mother know. Is everything okay out there?"

"Yeah, all is well. And you're good, right?"

"Yeah, we're fine, son. Well, you take care of yourself."

After the call ends, I let out a loud groan. Misha takes a detour into my office. "What's wrong?"

"Mom and Dad want to visit and I keep putting them off. They worry about me. But if they come, I know it'll be a little painful. Mom will be trying to shove food down my throat the entire time. And then she'll be on a mission to marry me off to someone from Virginia. Plus they have no idea I own this company."

She cackles.

I aim my finger at her. "This isn't even remotely funny."

"I don't know what the big deal is."

"They think I work in PR. They have no idea whatsoever how ruthless I can be."

Emily brings in a stack of folders and slams them on my desk. "Okay, this is what I have on—"

My hand shoots out. "Not now."

"What do you mean, not now? We have to get this done today," she argues.

Rubbing my face, I say, "Give me a minute, please."

Misha adds, "He's recovering from a parental phone call."

"Ahh."

Helen decides to join our little group. "Hey, boss, can I ask a favor?"

I look at her as she toys with one of her pigtails. Emily and Misha have been relatively successful at getting her to dump the Harley Quinn look at work, but the pigtails and hair color remain.

"What do you need?"

"Can you get tickets to Comic-Con?" Her eyes are huge circles—she looks like a five-year-old.

I want to laugh, I swear I do. But I tell her I'll work on it. She pops a bubble and waltzes out.

After Helen leaves, Emily says, "Hey, Harrison, Helen is really doing a great job for us. Her organizational skills are amazing. I have to say, I'm impressed."

"Thanks for filling me in. I'll have a talk with her to let her know how pleased we are."

Leland pops in shortly after to inform me we need to meet a potential client that evening.

"Can't you do it?" I ask.

"He specifically requested you."

"Who is it?"

"Vince LaMar." Leland grins.

Vince LaMar is one of Hollywood's biggest actors, and he's been involved in all sorts of shit from women to DUIs to drugs. It must be bad this time.

"Hell. Is his agent going to be there, because if not, neither of us is going."

"Yeah. I think the agent wants him to go to rehab," Leland says.

"Dammit. Okay. No dinner."

"Dinner. They insisted."

Better call Midnight to let her know I can't make it tonight. My dick just shed a few tears. But then my heart gives a little squeeze too. What's that all about?

Midnight answers immediately. "You miss me already?"

How am I supposed to answer that?

"Actually, I have to cancel tonight."

"Why am I not surprised?" The humor that was present in her voice before disappears.

"It's not what you think. A client called and is insisting on seeing me for dinner. I'm really sorry. I promise to make it up to you."

"We'll see."

She doesn't believe me. But I'm going to make sure I live up to this promise.

Chapter 14

MIDNIGHT

My agent, Rita, calls late the following afternoon. She wants to meet so she can bring me up to speed on everything. I agree to meet her for lunch the following day.

I take care to pick out a very conservative outfit. Although, thinking back, that's exactly what I did the last time and look where it landed me. I opt for a cute, flowery dress along with a sweater. I add ballet flats and take a quick glance in the mirror on my way out—I look like a rockabilly chick. Oh well, maybe Rita will like that look on me.

Rita's already waiting when I arrive, even though I'm early. She greets me with a huge smile. I pray that's a good sign because I need good right now.

"Midnight, you look amazing." She hugs me.

"Thank you. I feel pretty good too." I hope she can't tell I'm lying and that I'm scared shitless.

"First off, I hope the new contract meets your approval."

"Yes, I went over it and it looked the same as the old."

"It is. Only the dates were changed. Are you able to sign it today?"

"Sure. I can do it after lunch," I say.

"Great. I want you to know that we've been fielding calls for you constantly since you've been gone. This whole thing has really notched up your career."

Well, fuck me upside down. Harrison was right after all. "Really?"

"I'll have someone link you up with the fan page from the studio so you can see. Alta has a separate one as well. There's no way you can answer all the emails. It's ridiculous. But I do want you to have a look. There's a Facebook fan page, a Twitter account, an Instagram page, you name it. They even set up a special website for you. They called it Midnight's Minions. I'm positive after filming starts, your stuff will literally explode."

"I don't know what to say. Midnight's Minions? That's crazy."

"It just shows you how much people will stand up for you. And all you have to say is you're ready for the new version of the script."

"The new version?" I'm familiar with the old one. A case of anxiety rushes over me.

"Just some minor changes," she says.

"Oh, yes. Yes, I am. More than ready." My fingers itch for a gummy bear that's sitting in my purse. My mouth waters for one, but I restrain myself.

The waitress pops over and takes our order. I'm reeling with this website thing. After the waitress is gone, Rita explains where we stand. The film, *Turned*, is about a man who loses his job and is desperate for money. He ends up robbing a bank with a group of thugs to save his family from financial ruin, but of course, things don't work out like he plans. The people he robs the bank with are true criminals, unlike him, and they end up killing a bunch of innocent bystanders. He has to figure out a way to either get out of the country or turn himself in.

I'm playing the guy's wife and eventually, he ends up turning himself over to the police. But he gets killed in the final scene, where the wife watches it all unfold. It's a gritty, root-for-the-bad-guy film. In the end, the wife leaves town with her daughter, fleeing to start a new life. It's heart-rending, emotional, and moving with an all-around ugly-cry sort of ending.

"Apparently, Holt and the rest of the crew are dying to get started with you, and as soon as you learn the script, they're ready to go. They've already been filming."

"I'm ready, Rita. I just need some time to get my new lines down."

She hands me the revised screenplay and says, "Do it, then. You'll see there aren't many changes in this. Since they're filming part of it here, and then the other part in Santa Monica, they don't have to make any heavy-duty travel arrangements. How much time do you need to re-familiarize yourself with the script? I know you already have a copy, but they've actually made a few changes since you've been gone. Nothing major, though."

I look at what she hands me and take some time to thumb through it. I'm a fairly quick study. "Shouldn't take me long. If I start reading this afternoon, I should be done by tomorrow."

"Excellent. I'll let Danny and Greg know." Greg is the director, which I'm super excited about because his reputation is stellar. "They both want to do the table read ASAP. How about the day after tomorrow, then? That'll give you an extra day just in case. This shouldn't be all that different from the last time you went through it."

I nod, saying, "Yeah, I like that idea."

"Good. I think everyone else will too."

"Even Holt?"

Rita chuckles. "I don't think Danny gives a shit what he thinks. Holt will do as Danny says."

"Then everything sounds great to me."

The waitress delivers our salads. Before Rita digs into hers, she asks, "How much time afterward do you think you'll need before we go into production?"

"Honestly, I don't think I can answer that. I learn fast and am quick on my feet. Do you know if Greg minds a bit of improvising?"

Rita's brow furrows. "I'm not sure they'll want you straying off script too much."

"Oh, I won't. I just may not hit the exact words every single time."

"My suggestion would be to try your best not to do that. Is a week enough?"

"I think so."

"I'll let them know," Rita says. "Keep in mind, we're already behind thirty days. All the sets have been established. They've already shot the bank robbery scenes, and they've completed a few of the others that don't involve you. Of course, I'm not the decision-maker here. Keep that in mind."

"Thank you. I appreciate that. And Rita, I promise you, I'll work harder than anyone on this."

After lunch, we go to her office to sign the updated contract and part ways after that. For the first time since I entered that godforsaken rehab, I feel lighthearted. I owe Harrison. He was right about how the people would respond.

Wasting not even a second, I dash home and devour the screenplay. I am so immersed in it, I don't even take a break to eat. I only stop when I'm finished at four in the morning. This is epic. Tears course down my cheeks, and I have to use paper towels to dry my eyes because I'm fresh out of tissue. Each time I read this, it's more impactful than the last. Holt better play this as it's written because this is Oscar-worthy stuff. I can't remember when I've been so moved by anything.

My emotions are so raw and exposed, there's not a chance I'll be able to sleep. Looks like Netflix will be my balm tonight. I hunt for something to make me drowsy, but nothing interests me except for *Daredevil*. I turn it on and before I know it, the sun brightens my room. I'm exhausted yet jacked up at the same time. This screenplay is so dynamic and full of style, I want to shower and run to the studio right now.

But I'm not exactly thinking clearly. Padding to the kitchen to power up the Keurig, I cradle the script tightly to my chest. I'm standing there waiting for the light to turn on when there's a loud knock on the door. It's only nine in the morning. Who could that be?

Peeping out the tiny hole, I see Harrison's face.

"What are you doing here? Trying to bum some coffee?" I ask as I open the door.

"Jesus, you look like hell."

"Top of the morning to you too," I say, flipping him off.

I turn away, figuring he'll follow me into the kitchen. He does. The machine now ready, I brew a cup and hand it to him. "What's your poison?"

"As is," he says.

I make another and he asks me why I look so rough. I hold up the script. "This."

He looks at it. "Ahh. You stayed up all night?"

"Yes. This is fantastic. If Holt doesn't fuck it up, he should win an Oscar."

"That good, huh?"

"Oh my fucking hell. It's everything I've always wanted in a movie. Not even kidding one bit. I wish you could read it, Harrison."

"Damn, it must be great. I've never seen you so upbeat. You're almost giddy."

"I didn't fall asleep because I kept thinking about that damn screenplay."

"Yeah, neither did I, but for different reasons." He waggles his brows.

I shove his shoulder. "Oh, stop."

"At least we took care of the new client, but Harrison went home a lonely man when all he wanted to do was fuck Midnight."

"Poor guy." I push my index finger into his chest. "Do you

know how sorry I feel for Harrison? I bet he went home and watched one of Lusty's videos."

"Pervy bastard."

The way he says it makes me laugh.

"So, how's your ..." He aims his finger between my thighs, making a circle.

"Hmm, isn't that quite the question this morning?"

He lifts one large, muscular shoulder. I have a flashback of when one of my legs was draped over it.

"I thought so, or I wouldn't have asked. I figured gummy bear was a bit worn out." His teeth scrape over his lower lip. Harrison has a mouth that would make a nun orgasm spontaneously.

A change of subject is needed or I may find myself on my knees. "Are you hungry?"

"Of course." A hoarse laugh rolls out of him.

"Shut up." I smack him on the arm. "I'll make you breakfast if you like. I'm starving—I forgot to eat dinner last night."

"Sounds good. I'll have eggs. And why didn't you eat?"

I point to the script I set on the counter. "I got so caught up in that, I never stopped."

"Damn. You make me want to read it."

"You can't. And don't you dare touch it." I snap my fingers. He puts his hands in the air, and I pet the script where it sits on the counter. "I can't begin to explain how great this is."

"Can you tell me what it's about at least?"

"Nope. It would spoil when you see it for the first time."

The butter in the pan sizzles so I put the eggs in and pop some bread into the toaster. In no time, breakfast is ready. Harrison inhales his; I'm only a couple of bites in and his plate sparkles like it wasn't used.

"Damn. Did you even chew?"

"I was hungry, I guess."

"There's more bread if you want to toast it." He gets up and pops two more slices into the toaster. He devours those too.

"I can cook you more eggs," I offer.

"Nah, I'm good."

He makes another cup of coffee and then announces he has to leave. "Time to earn a living."

"I have to be at the studio at seven tomorrow. We're doing another table read. Since I've been gone awhile, Danny wants to do it again."

"Good idea," he says.

I watch him as he lets himself out the door. His tailored black pants look sexy as hell as they hug his hips and firm ass. I remember that ass with my hands molded around it while he did the dirty to me. Will that happen again? I sure as hell hope so. My poor vibrator doesn't stand a chance as I wait for that time to come.

Chapter 15

MIDNIGHT

THIS SCREENPLAY HITS ALL THE POINTS I LOVE IN A GREAT movie, but when we sit down to go through it again as a group at the table read, I'm blown away all over again. Even some of Holt's surliness has disappeared.

"Fantastic reading, Midnight. With a little bit of honing, you're going to kill this script," Danny says.

I beam. "Wow, I don't know what to say. I hope to make you proud, Danny."

"Just thank the man, for God's sake. Can't you recognize a flirt when you see one?" Holt stands behind Danny's shoulder bearing a sour expression. I don't know why he has to act like an ass and spoil the fun.

"Oh, come on, Holt. One, I'm not flirting. I was just complimenting her on the great job she did today," Danny says.

"Whatever." Holt walks away.

"Ignore his rude ass. I meant what I said. You're going to shine on screen."

"Thanks and I promise to work hard."

"Good. So, we'll see you in two weeks then. If you need anything, give me a call."

"Thanks, Danny."

I'm standing next to the table when Holt walks by to grab his stuff. "Hey, Holt. I was going to tell you earlier, this script is incredible, and with your talent you may end up with an Oscar next year."

Instead of a show of gratitude, he sneers. "Oh? And exactly what would you know about that?"

I'm so shocked, my tongue ends up trapped inside my mouth.

"Yeah, not much, huh?" He grabs his stuff and stomps off.

This is going to be one long haul working with that offensive prick. Why does anyone have to be such a dick? What happened to being kind to one another?

I pick up my things and go home, pushing those thoughts of Holt Ward aside.

My phone rings. "Hello."

"Hey, it's Harrison. How'd it go?"

"Ah, other than asshole Holt, it was awesome." I explain what happened. "I'll be up to my eyeballs studying, so don't think I'm ignoring you."

"Not a problem. Call if you need me. And Midnight?"

"Yeah?"

"Good luck. I'm pulling for you."

For the next two weeks, I dive into studying my lines. I'm going to memorize every letter of this story, making Holt look like an amateur in comparison. Okay, that's a stretch, but that's what I'm telling myself anyway.

My arrival time for Monday morning on my call sheet was 0600. I arrive around the same time the makeup crew shows up. We're filming several scenes today on the same set. After my makeup is finished, I arrive on set to find the lighting crew working their magic. They need to ensure the actors are lit properly on every shot. The director positions Holt and me in different spots where the scene will be taking place so the cameraman can tweak his shots. They'll film from my angle, then Holt's. It's very time intensive. We're finally ready to begin. We do a run-through to rehearse, and then it's showtime.

In the scene we're working on right now, Holt's character, Finn, and I are having marital issues because of our financial state. He's lost his job and can't find a new one. I'm working but it's not enough to support us.

Finn is overbearing and frustrated, and I'm stressed out with mounting overdue bills and a young daughter to care for. We have an argument and he storms out. Our daughter wakes up and comes into the room crying. It's a very emotional moment for me.

I'm shaken by the scene, but not because I'm acting. This isn't very far from the life I grew up in, only my mother wasn't married to the men she sometimes argued with. I wrap the young actor in my arms, soothing her, telling her it's going to be fine and that Daddy will be home soon.

The director cuts and I lean away from Sammie, the little girl I'm hugging, giving her a big smile. "You were awesome-sauce, dude." We high-five. She's so cute. At four years old, I want to steal her away. She's blond with long braids and green eyes, much like Holt's.

"Thanks, Ms. Drake. You were awesomesauce too."

Holt pops back on the set and gives me a slight nod. I'll take it. That's better than some scathing insult. The assistant director escorts Sammie off the set to her mother, who has been hanging out nearby. I wish my mom would've been around like that instead of shooting up heroin.

I wander over to the area where snacks and drinks are located and grab something as the crew prepares for the next scene. Then I take a seat in my personal chair and scan my sides (a small version of the scenes we're filming today).

The director calls for the actors so we begin the next scene, where I try to smooth things over with Holt/Finn by seducing him. I change into sexy lingerie so when he comes home, I'm ready for a little bedroom fun. Our daughter is asleep when I hear the door opening. I walk into the living room, and he has no idea what's underneath the robe I'm wearing. With all the stress in our marriage, our sex life has suffered.

I casually walk up behind him and grab his hand. "Hey. You've been gone awhile."

He doesn't look me in the eye. "Yeah. Had to clear my head."

"Why don't you come to bed?"

He shrugs my hand off. "Not tired." Then he walks to the kitchen and returns with a (fake) beer, pops the top off, and takes a long gulp.

I don't give up because my character, Christine, is a very determined woman. I turn him to face me and brush his hair off his forehead, massage the creases there, then say, "Come on, baby. I can make you feel a whole lot better than that bottle can."

He finally connects and notices me for the first time.

He knocks my hand away. "Christ, Christine. Leave me alone." He heads for the couch.

His ass plops down on it and he spreads his long, muscular legs out. But he doesn't count on me sinking to my knees between them.

"What the hell's up with you tonight?"

"I just want to be with you, baby." I rub my cheek on his thigh as I go for the button on his jeans.

He shoves my hands aside. "I'm not in the mood." His voice carries a hard edge of frustration.

"If you give me a few, I can get you in the mood."

"Oh yeah? How?"

I stand and drop the robe. His lids open slightly only he's not acting now. It's a visceral reaction.

"You think that's gonna work on me?"

I offer him my hand and smile. "Why don't we find out?"

He takes my hand and gives me a hard yank. I land on top of him and he kisses me ferociously. Then pushes me aside.

"You've been keeping this from me. Why?"

"I—I haven't. Things have been ..."

He gets up and drags me toward the bedroom.

"Cut," Greg calls out. "I can't wait to see the dailies on this."

I'll admit it was hot. Hotter than I expected from Holt.

"Nice work," Holt says.

"Thanks." It's kind of weird. He never compliments me. I wonder how tomorrow will go. That's when we do the bedroom scene.

———

0700 I show up for makeup. I wear the sexy lingerie again and I'm ready for the bedroom scene. The lighting is a pain. It takes forever to get it right today.

"His face looks too drawn," one of the crew complains.

"It's supposed to. He's stressed," Greg says.

They argue back and forth and it ends up taking until lunch before they get ready for us. They do several test shots and we're finally ready.

"Hey, let's take a short break for lunch and then run straight through," Greg says.

Sounds good to me because I'm starving. We go outside to where the catering food is and eat.

Back inside, we take our positions, and action is called.

Holt pulls off his shirt to reveal sculpted abs. I'm sure he's been preparing for this by spending time in the gym. Who wants themselves to be seen by millions of adoring fans without being in the best shape possible?

Then he lifts me up and we're in the bed, his hands roaming all over me, frantically, as though he can't possibly get enough. The camera closes in, though I'm not sure what it's getting. And then the director yells, "Cut." I want to laugh because I'm so used to porn and this is lily-white in comparison.

"That was hot," Greg, the director, says. "Now I need you naked from the waist up and under the covers, Midnight. We need the after-sex scene."

"Right." I strip off my bra, because I'm not exactly shy having had my boobs exposed for all to see so many times before. Holt tries to hold up his shirt to shield me. My contract stated it would include nudity from the waist up, but I guess Holt isn't aware of that.

"Hey, it's fine. They'll all see in a second, anyway. Besides, it's in my contract."

He lets out an awkward laugh. "Right."

We scoot under the covers and he asks if I'm comfortable. I'm more than a bit surprised he's being so considerate. Shooting begins again and we film the afterglow of our sexy time. He plays with my nipple, tickles me, and then goes in for the heated kiss, which are all actually scripted. Nevertheless, it takes me by surprise, zipping the lines from my head. My emotions are hopping all over the place, my stomach in knots.

I can't screw this up so I improvise, but the passion and tension between us produces a quality that has the scene turning out better than what was originally planned. It's gutsy, yet sweet, with Finn softening toward Christine, and Christine letting her love for him shine through her eyes.

It ends with Finn touching Christine's lips with his and Greg yelling, "Cut!" I sit up, holding the sheet against me, to see a gigantic smile spreading across Holt's face.

"That was amazing," he says.

I don't quite know what to say to that, other than, "Yeah, I think we did great."

When I get out of the bed and away from the lighting, I look across the set to see Harrison standing there, a serious expression on his face. He nods once and then walks out through the doors in the back of the studio.

Chapter 16

HARRISON

As it turns out, Midnight doesn't need me after all. Watching her the last two days were Oscar worthy performances. It's been so moving, so *real*, I felt like I was in bed with the two of them. Did they feel that passion for each other? Because it sure as hell felt like it to me. Her acting skills are better than anyone's I've seen in a long time. Move over Meryl Streep, you've got company, baby.

I have to admit, her kisses and nakedness with Holt bothered me more than a little. But why should it? It's part of the deal when you're an actor. Most roles require kissing, sex scenes, and bedroom antics, if there's any kind of relationship involved. Yet I couldn't quite help feeling they were into it a little more than the scene required. Maybe I'm just jealous it wasn't me in the scene with her. I don't know. Midnight and I are just ... what are we exactly? She was my client, but then the sex ...

And now? Now we're playing phone and text tag. But I want something more. Is she on the same page?

I'm sitting in my car, staring into space, when a tap on the window startles me. Speak of the devil.

"What are you doing here?" she asks.

"No idea whatsoever."

"Wanna grab dinner? I'm starving. We've wrapped for the day, thank God."

"Why the hell not?"

"Follow me."

We end up at an Italian place and I laugh. I owe her a dinner and she must've gotten it in her mind to collect it.

After we're seated, she goes on to tell me about her day. I'm caught up in her excitement. I needed this—this brightness tonight.

"And it's all because of you. If you hadn't pushed me into the door of that rehab center, I wouldn't be here right now."

"You ever going to tell me what happened in there?" I figure she'll give it up one of these days.

Her lips form a thin line. "What's the one thing you'd never want to share with anyone?"

"There are things associated with my business that I wouldn't want anyone to know, but they don't involve me personally," I say.

"But it would be personal to a certain degree if it involves your business."

"It would affect me, yes, but it's not directly about me."

She purses her lips and asks, "Then what's the worst thing about your business you wouldn't want to share with me?"

My tongue pokes the inside of my cheek. There are things about clients, even my employees, I can never share with anyone, not to mention the NDAs we all signed. "Nope. Can't share a thing with you."

"So, you see how I feel, then?"

"Mine is mostly from a legal standpoint. It's not the same."

"It kind of is. You still can't disclose it."

Tilting my head, I ask, "Yours is that bad, huh?"

"Worse."

We eat and she seems so ... happy. The morose, angry woman I picked up from rehab is gone and in her place is a much more lighthearted replacement. Maybe I can find my happy again too.

She's sliding a forkful of spaghetti into her mouth when I tell her, "I've missed seeing you."

The fork comes back out and she sputters, "You have?"

"Yeah." There, I said it.

"I've missed you too."

"Yeah?"

"Yeah. And that's not easy to admit." Her eyes are downcast as she speaks.

"I can sort of tell," I say.

"It stems from my background. I don't like to get close to anyone. My mother loved me. I know she did. But she was an addict who couldn't get clean, not to mention she had no education or skills. She was a stripper and lived an ugly lifestyle. Ultimately, she chose the drugs. The end result for me was catastrophic. It's made me a little leery, you might say."

The way her voice trembles and lowers may be an indication of why she didn't want to go to rehab. Maybe it circles back to her mom.

"Was the catastrophe your foster care?"

"I don't ever care to discuss that. And I would ask you never to bring it up again."

"Okay. But sometimes it's better to talk about things like that."

"Harrison, not everyone can be fixed, like you think they can. Sometimes things are better off left alone." She swirls more spaghetti on her fork and angrily shoves it into her mouth. After she chews and swallows it, she adds, "Have you ever stopped to think that maybe you're the one who needs fixing?"

"Me? How?" I'm perfectly fine just the way I am.

"This driving need of yours to patch people up is not normal. What the hell is with that anyway?"

"I only want to help."

She squints. "Nah. It's more than that. You dig into people's lives and dissect them. That's not helping. It's kinda sick. What are your triggers?"

My back stiffens at her question. There are no triggers. "Can't a person help someone without any so-called triggers?"

I finally dig into my lasagna. It needs salt, so I reach for the saltshaker, but the salt won't shake freely. I inspect the tiny openings on the top and they seem fine, but I'm getting frustrated by the fact that salt won't come out. I open the shaker and turn the lid over to see what the problem is. Midnight starts laughing.

Glancing up, I see her eyes dancing with mirth. "What?"

"I rest my case. Look at you trying to fix the saltshaker. It would be easier to flag the waiter down and ask for a different one, but no. You have to fix this one."

Shit, she's right.

"I'll concede this, but it's probably faster than waiting for another."

"Then let's have a little contest. Fix away."

She immediately gets the waiter's attention and asks for another saltshaker. Before I can unclog the tiny holes, a new shaker sits in front of me. Midnight wears a satisfied grin.

"You have to admit, our waiter is most attentive," I say.

"Oh, come on, Harrison. You need a therapist." She puts her elbows on the table and leans closer to me. "You don't like hearing this, do you? Your perfect little world isn't so perfect after all, is it? But hey, don't worry. Look around you. Everyone is fucked up to a certain degree. Join the crowd. We're a fun group." She lifts her glass of Barolo for a toast.

Midnight Drake addles me and I'm not exactly sure how to handle it. I live in a perfectly put-together world where everything has its place. She's taken that world, turned it upside down, and scattered everything about, disrupting the order of things. How will I put it back together so I can function properly?

"You're not eating," she says.

"I've lost my appetite."

"Over our conversation? You shock me."

I shrug. What can I say? She's dismantling me and it may seem absurd to her, but this shit is real to me.

"Well, I'm finished. Let's go back to my place. Maybe I can fuck some sense into you," she says.

Honestly, as good as that sounds, I'm not even sure that will work, but I'm not going to turn her down. It will distract me for a while, and maybe that's what I need.

Chapter 17

MIDNIGHT

HARRISON, THE CONTROLLING GUY WHO I MET IN NEW YORK, IS realizing his life isn't the picture-perfect existence he thought it was. It's almost laughable. One thing he is, though, is dominant in bed. As soon as we walk into my bedroom, his demeanor changes.

I'm in front of him and his hand twists my hair as he spins me around. I don't have time to blink or think before his mouth is on mine in a bruising kiss. This man may have issues, but one thing he doesn't have is an issue over his ability to fuck.

I'm wearing sexy lingerie from the last scene we filmed today. I worked out a deal with the studio on this scene beforehand. Because of my porn background I'm particular on a few things and sexy lingerie is one of them. I wanted something very tasteful and I got what I asked for. I'm wearing black thigh-high stockings, and underwear to match my sexy black bra.

His eyes rake my body from top to bottom and I feel that familiar tension in my lower belly, that burn between my thighs. His hooded gaze lands on my breasts and a finger hooks over the edge of my bra cup. He tugs it down, exposing my entire breast. My nipple hardens, as if it's reaching out to him, practically begging for him to suck it. He only brushes the back of his hand over it, torturing me.

I cross my legs and clench my thighs. The feeble attempt to ease the ache fails. My need for him is fiercer than it's ever been. He repeats the bra action on the other side, teasing my right nipple. I stare at his face as he bites down on his lower lip. Then my eyes drop to the crotch of his jeans. At least I'm not the only one who's needy right now.

My itchy fingers reach for his pants, but he pushes them aside.

"Did you tease Holt like this?" he asks, his tone harsh.

Is Harrison jealous?

"No, I teased Finn." I clear up his confusion. "The character Holt plays. I don't give a fuck about Holt."

A smile teases at the right corner of his mouth. I want to kiss it so bad, I can already taste it.

"Good. After tonight, you won't remember Holt's name." He hooks a finger in the center of my bra and jerks me up against him. Now I'll get my chance to taste his mouth. My tongue tastes the Barolo from dinner when I push past his lips. We stroke each other's lips; our teeth click together because Harrison doesn't kiss like a pansy-ass. He takes what he wants and leaves no room for any thoughts or needs.

And then I'm in his arms as he carries me to my bed. I try to get rid of my lingerie.

"No. I'm going to fuck you in that. The next time you wear it, you'll think of me."

He doesn't even take off my panties, only tugs them to the side before his mouth finds me. I'm already wet for him. He didn't have to do that, but an orgasm is always a nice perk.

I'm lying on my back for a minute or so before he flips me like a pancake. He's strong, the sinews of his biceps punctuated by this motion. He picks me up like I'm nothing more than a feather. The man has moves. His tongue tunnels into my pussy from behind as his hand, which is wrapped around me, seeks out my clit. I'm flushed with desire and need for him like I've never experienced.

When I was making smut films, I didn't think too much of sex because it was only a means to an end. I wasn't exactly ashamed of it, because I was doing it for a good reason. I desperately needed the money. The truth is it felt silly most of the time. Dressing like a hooker nurse—honestly, how many hooker nurses hang out in hospitals—and saying *yes, yes, yes*, over and over in a high-pitched, squeaky voice was enough to make anyone feel idiotic.

But with Harrison, there's this burning need, this fire in my veins that engulfs me. I only want more of him.

It doesn't take long for an orgasm to carry me off, and soon, Harrison's cock is pushing deep inside me. Slow at first, but then faster. I glance over my shoulder to watch. His eyes are closed, head thrown back, as his hands grasp my hips and he bucks into me like a wild animal. It's primal the way he fucks me, touching places inside that spark off reactions I'm unfamiliar with. My hands claw the comforter, nails almost sinking through to the down. I'm on the precipice of another climax, and when I hear him groan low and long, I follow him. He slides down to the floor and sits, panting like the animal that just spectacularly fucked me.

"I know one thing that doesn't need fixing," I say.

"What's that?"

I crawl to the end of the bed so I can see him. "The way you fuck." Then I flop onto my back and stare at the ceiling. He's quiet, and I wonder if he regrets what just happened between us. Did he feel what I did or was it just another lay for him? I'd like to ask but I don't.

"I don't think I need fixing," he suddenly says, staring off into the distance. Is he angry? It's hard to tell.

"What did you study in college?" I ask.

"Business. Why?"

"You should've been an engineer."

"Why an engineer?"

"You're OCD. Everything has to run perfectly, smoothly. If things aren't just so, you fix them. You would've loved being an engineer. Or a computer science major. Writing code and creating perfect programs. That is so you. Either way, you have OCD. Are your socks and underwear drawers perfectly arranged and is your closet color coded?"

His brows almost launch off his face. I hold my arm up and say, "See, I have you pegged. You do need a therapist. Possibly even a shrink. By the way, how's Helen Reddy?"

By now, my head's hanging off the end of the bed, resting on his shoulder. He picks up a chunk of my hair and twirls it.

"No, no, you're not getting off topic here. You can't switch to Helen. I do not need a therapist."

"Go on. Admit it. I've given you some pretty good things to roll around in that brain of yours, haven't I? Not to mention, you always think everyone has to fall into this mold. Well, look what happened to me. That mold didn't work out so well."

He sits up a little. "Your mold is fine. You're just a noncon-formist."

I chuckle. "Uh-huh. Right. Nonconformist." I'm more like a nonreformist.

"What are you hiding, Midnight?"

My thoughts tumble back to when I was a teenager. There's no stopping the shudder that rips through me. It's a horror story no one wants to hear, even me.

"Must be pretty bad. I can help, you know."

"Jesus, you can't help me. Nobody can. Besides, it's over and done. No going back so I don't want to talk about it."

He swivels on the floor to face me.

"We're friends, right?"

I nod. "Yeah, you saved my career."

His mouth curves upward. "Aha! You admit it."

"Yeah, although you put me through the damn ringer for it."

"It'll be worth it when you're up for an Academy Award."

I punch his shoulder. "Never gonna happen."

"Never say never. Anyway, if we become close, not that we aren't now, would you ever consider telling me?"

What does he mean by that? "Are we close?"

He looks me square in the eye. "I'm not sure. I get this vibe from you that you don't want to be."

"I do. It's just that it takes me a while."

"So with that, you avoided my question," he says. "Would you ever tell me?"

"I don't know. It's impossible to answer that."

"Will you answer one thing?"

"Maybe."

"Is there anyone you're close to that you've told?"

"No. No one knows the whole story. Only one person knows part of it, and it's not because I had a choice." I don't mention that several others know and it's only because they were the ones who forced me to do those awful things. "Listen, life isn't always hearts and flowers. I went through some bumps and there were a lot of rocks thrown in my path, but you know something? I figured out a way around those obstacles. And thanks to you, you pushed me through the last one and helped me navigate that shitstorm. So let's drop this. I'll never be permanently fixed. There will always be issues buried inside me. And that's okay. I've learned to live with them. If I can, you can too."

He stands and walks to the kitchen. Maybe he's thirsty. I check out his ass. It's definitely a keeper. Wicked thoughts jump into my mind, but I push them aside and follow him to the kitchen. He hands me a glass of ice water.

"Thanks." I swallow it down. "It's late and I need to get some sleep. I have to be at the studio at 5:00 a.m."

"Yeah, I know." He grabs me and pulls me into the solid wall of his chest. I run my hand over the smooth bronze skin until I get to his neck, and then up to the scruff covering his face. His hair is artfully messy, but that's because my hands were in it briefly. I run them through it again, thinking how sexy he looks standing naked in my kitchen.

"You can always stay, though you'd have to get up super early."

"Early never bothered me, but I doubt you'd get much sleep."

"Yeah, and that wouldn't do me much good for tomorrow, would it, when I'm trying to impress my director and producer?"

"And not Holt?"

"Shut up about him. I don't give a damn about him, although he did finally stop insulting me."

He only nods and walks toward the bedroom. When he comes back out, he's ready to leave.

"The ink on your stomach? Are you really *unscarred?*" I ask, referring to the large tattoo that spreads across his lower abs.

"I thought I was. Until I met you." He leans close until our lips graze. Then he walks through the door, and I have to smile at that. No one is unscarred as far as I'm concerned. If they think they are, they haven't lived.

Chapter 18

HARRISON

"Who pooped in your omelet today?"

I look up to see Emily standing in front of my desk.

"No one. Why?"

"Could've fooled me from that scowl."

Midnight has been so tied up with work, she's not getting in until eight or later every night. Then she pretty much collapses into bed. I've taken dinner to her a couple of times, but she fell asleep in the middle of it. I'm giving her space. We talk a lot on the phone but that's about it. On the weekends, she's busy brushing up on any script changes so she's on top of things for the upcoming week. I've got to give her big bonus points. She's worked harder than I ever imagined. Maybe that's why I'm scowling. I haven't gotten any lately. Now I sound like a spoiled, selfish frat boy.

And then there are my best friends. Both Prescott and Weston are giving me a hard time. They've called a few times, but I keep avoiding them. It's because they'll dig into what's going on and I don't want to discuss Midnight with them. For the first time, I'm hesitant to discuss my love interest with my best friends. It's strange because they are the two closest people in the world to me. Is it because I'm ashamed she was a former porn star? Does that part of her life bother me more than I'm admitting to myself? Or is it because I really know very little about her? She's put disorder into my orderly life and that definitely is disturbing.

"Hello, anyone in there?" Emily asks.

Shit, I forgot she's still standing here. "Yeah, sorry. My brain went to Hawaii for a minute."

She clicks her fingers. "You know what? That's what you need. A vacation."

"There's too much going on here."

"Oh, like you don't trust we can handle it?"

I need to tread carefully or feelings will get hurt.

"Not in the least. I just know things are crazy and you guys need time off too."

"Pfft. We'll get time off. Why don't you go visit your friends? Or do something fun? It's getting close to the holidays."

"Nah, I'm good. Maybe in the spring."

"You should plan a ski trip."

"Maybe." I wonder if Midnight would like to take a vacation after her filming is over.

Leland swings in and asks, "You going skiing? I was thinking about Tahoe in January. Want to go?"

Fuck. "Maybe. We'll talk."

Then he says, "We have a new client I need you to check into." Leland tells me it's a professional footballer who was caught with a minor in his hotel room after a game.

"Was it just the two of them?"

"Yeah."

"Any drugs involved?"

"Cocaine and alcohol."

"Fuck. How was he caught?"

"Her parents confiscated her phone and everything was on there. Videos, pictures, texts."

Rubbing my temple, I feel the beginnings of a headache. "Christ. When will they ever learn?"

Leland shrugs. "Never. It's why you're in business, boss."

"True. Did you tell him he fucked his career?"

"Pretty much."

"In order to do anything, we need that phone, and then God only knows who else has seen what's on it."

"Truth. Where do you want to start?"

"Get him in here and let's see if we can't get our hands on her phone."

Later that afternoon, we find that our guy picked the wrong girl to party with. She's seventeen going on thirty, a total flirt, yet completely illegal for him in the eyes of the law. And did I mention her daddy is one of LA's most famous attorneys?

When the client comes in, I sit down with him. Once he hears what we have to tell him, he freaks out.

"Are you saying this could end my career?"

"Yes. Don't you think you should've thought about that before you did cocaine with someone you knew nothing about?"

"I didn't do any. I just gave her the money to buy it." He hangs his head. What a dumbass.

"So let me clarify. You gave her the money to score the drugs?"

"Yeah. I can't do drugs. If they run a random test, I'm screwed. I only wanted to fuck her. She was hot, man!"

"And you didn't know she was filming you fucking her?"

"Yeah, I knew, but I figured if she didn't care, why should I?"

My headache starts banging out Lil Wayne and Wiz Khalifa's "Sucker for Pain." Time for a few Advil. I have to remind myself that clients like this are why I've made so much money over the years.

"Have you notified your manager and coach?"

"Yeah. I told them I was clean. They're giving me forty-eight hours to clean it up, which is why I called you guys. I hear you're the best."

I appraise the big guy and then say, "Will you excuse us for a minute?"

Leland and I move over to my office. "What's the chance of getting that phone?"

"One in a hundred thousand." Leland laughs.

"Who do we know that can steal it?"

"First, we have to figure out where it is."

"My guess is it's in Daddy's desk drawer, or a safe in his office. If not there, it's in a safe in his house."

"The cleaning service."

"And the safe?"

"Our man, Teddy. He can tap into anything."

"Security cameras?"

Leland laughs. "Rashid, who else?"

"They're closed circuit."

"You know damn well he can hack into those and send some phony video feed to the security guys. Don't ask me specifics. I'm not smart like that, but remember how he did it when we had to get into that office over in Beverly Hills? He did some magic thing that worked like a charm."

"Yeah, but maybe they all don't work like that."

"Call him. He can at least tell you what he'd need."

I call Rashid and he says he would need to hack into their system and control it from his end. How he would do it, I have no idea. I'll let him worry about that. All I care about is that there's a possibility it can work. I give him the name of the law practice and wait to hear back from him.

Motioning to Leland, I say, "Let's go tell dumbass what's going on." When we get back to the conference room, our guy looks like he's ready to cry.

"Okay, here's the deal. We can't do anything for you unless we get the phone. So give us a few days to work on it."

"Like I told you, I only got forty-eight hours."

"Then we'll work on it for forty-eight hours. If we can't

deliver, we don't charge. But if we get the phone—and don't ask us how we got it—your bill is gonna be pricey."

"I can work with that."

I stare him down. "One more thing. No more fuck-ups. I don't work with people twice for shit like this."

"You got it."

He tells us everything he possibly can about this girl. I don't care if it has to do with how many times she farted, but we need details. Believe it or not, his memory of her is pretty fucking amazing—even the non-naked parts. The girl ran her mouth. Told him all kinds of shit. Emily records everything. From what we gather, sounds like Daddy will have everything we need at his office.

Now the fun starts. The next night our guy joins their *cleaning crew*. Rashid does his thing with the security cameras. He'll run a loop that will block out what's going on while our guy is in Daddy's office, cleaning. Luck happens to be in our camp. The phone is in the drawer and not the safe, which our guy found when he picked the lock with ease. He takes the phone, and makes sure the power is off.

As soon as he has it, he cleans the office and leaves. We signal to Rashid to bring up the camera again and it's back online, with no one the wiser. We meet our guy to retrieve the phone.

Now comes the fun. We disable the tracking by putting it in airplane mode while our video/photography expert goes to work on the phone. He alters each video and photo our client is in, removes him, and inserts a different man with his face cut out or blurred to the point where he can't be recognized. Every text is also deleted. Unless the videos were uploaded to a flash drive or computer, we're good. If they were, our client is still up that shit creek.

We take the phone back to our guy who's waiting for us and call Rashid. He spins his magic again with the security cameras;

the phone is taken out of airplane mode and delivered back to Daddy's drawer.

Two days later, our client calls and says the charges against him were dropped. He's crying like a baby. I let him know to keep the tissue around because he'll be crying again when he gets my bill.

That attorney must not have been very smart. Had that been my daughter, I would've made duplicate copies of those videos and photos. But then again, I'm a suspicious fucker because of this business I'm in, so go figure.

Leland is in my office and I grab the back of my neck for a second before I ask, "You don't think he forced her to do anything she didn't want to do?"

"You're joking, right?"

"No." I look him squarely in the eye. He doesn't budge.

"This wasn't the first time that girl did this. My guess is she's been around that dog-and-pony show a few times. I'm not sure you paid attention, but it looked to me she was auditioning for a porn. She had her phone at the perfect angle, set to capture everything. Did you pay attention to what else was on her phone?"

"No, I didn't."

"Let's just say Daddy needs to keep a better handle on what she does. There were a lot of nude pictures on there, and they weren't of our guy."

I have a flashback to my days at Crestview. Some of the girls there were fairly aggressive, particularly Felicia Cunningham. She had a thing for giving blow jobs. She seemed to corner either Prescott or me all the time. I think half the guys in school were either sucked or fucked by her. But she never wanted to be videoed. Then again, we didn't have phones that could video back then, not that I can remember anyway.

"Maybe she just likes fucking. Who knows?" I ask.

"Well, we can expect a hefty bundle because of that appetite of hers."

That young girl has me thinking about the porn industry and my mind flips to Midnight. I wonder what she's up to. We haven't talked since yesterday. It's not that I don't want to see her, because that couldn't be further from the truth. I want to see her too much. But she's busy with work. That's what my brain is telling me.

But something entirely different is in my heart. And I'm ignoring it. Completely.

Chapter 19

MIDNIGHT

EXHAUSTION WEIGHS MY LIMBS DOWN, MAKING THEM FEEL leaden. Sleep has eluded me for the past couple of weeks. I haven't seen Harrison. We've only talked or texted. Normally, this lack of communication wouldn't be a problem for me. I've never given a damn about men before. Fact is, I've never really dated much or even had a boyfriend. So why him? Why now? I need to focus. My concentration needs to be razor sharp.

I stumbled through my lines today, but fortunately, Holt was on point and made it appear like I was the sad, sappy wife who was ignored while he was planning his stupid bank robbery. He and I had an argument, in character, and we had to do more than several takes because of my forgotten lines. I was angry with myself at being so invested in Harrison. I channeled that anger to Christine and the scene came out as one emotional piece of drama.

"Cut," Greg yells, and I collapse on the chair behind me.

"Hey, you okay?" Holt asks.

"Yeah. Just exhausted."

"Sit tight. I'll get you some tea."

He's been so courteous over the last few weeks, I can barely recall asshole Holt anymore. A mug of tea is shoved into my hand and I lift my eyes to see his smiling face. His eyes are kind, soft green today.

"Thanks." I sip the herbal concoction and hide my grimace. I hate tea but Holt swears by it. He doesn't drink coffee—says it decays your brain cells and prevents you from bringing out your emotions. I call huge bullshit on that but I drink tea on the set to please him. I've learned a happy Holt equates to a happy Midnight.

He takes a seat next to me and goes into a lengthy explanation about the benefits of chamomile tea and melatonin. Bless him. I want to tell him I need Harrison to lick my clit until I come and then fuck me like a wild panther, but I refrain. I wonder if that would shock him. A gigantic yawn overtakes me and Holt's eyes widen.

"Jeez, I've never seen someone yawn like that."

"Sorry. I'm glad today's Friday. I plan to spend tomorrow in bed."

A lopsided grin, the one the women love, takes away his serious expression. "You want some company?"

I'm floored. The horrible tea I just took a sip of lodges in my airway. I sputter, then it explodes out of my mouth as I erupt in a spasm of coughing.

"Christ, are you okay?"

Speech is impossible. People stare as I cough and choke. Holt stands and pounds my back.

"Say something, dammit."

My hand goes up in the air, because talking isn't possible while coughing. Finally, when the episode passes, I say, "Damn, that went down the wrong hatch."

"You scared the shit out of me."

"Scared the shit out of me too." Only I'm not referring to the tea.

His hand is still on my back, massaging it between my shoulder blades. This is totally awkward.

"So, are we on for a weekend together between the sheets?" He waggles his brows.

"Uh, yeah, about that. I'm kind of seeing someone."

He jerks back and nails me with a glare. "Nope, that definitely won't work."

"What do you mean?"

He sits back down and says, "You and me, we have this ... this chemistry going." His hand waves between us. "It's time to connect away from the set. We would be great together."

I'd like to inform him I'm the girl who used to give blow jobs on film for a living but I zip my lips. He would just die.

"Aren't you dating someone?"

He bats the air again. "Not anymore. I told her to take a hike after the first kiss you and I shared." He scoots his chair around to face me. "I felt it, Midnight. I know you did too. It was surreal."

It was part of the scene, the characters. Is it possible he's delusional?

"Holt, you're right. But we were in character, remember? We were acting."

"No, that's not true. It was the real thing."

He continues to stare, as if what I said is completely irrelevant. So I continue. "And like I said, I'm with someone."

"You'll have to dump him. We're cerebral, Midnight." Then he jumps up and is gone. What the hell does that mean?

The rest of our shooting that day is fucked. Holt is stilted and forced with all his lines. I try to overcompensate, but it's shit. Even Greg calls him out, but he tries to blame it on me, saying I'm not stepping up to the plate. It escalates into a huge fight, with Holt storming out of the studio.

Danny approaches me. "What the fuck happened between you two?"

"The truth?"

"Yes!"

"He wanted to spend the weekend in bed with me and I told him I'm seeing someone. He completely changed after that."

Danny throws his arms in the air and lets out a long, anguished sigh. "Not this again."

"What do you mean?"

"We went through this with Jennifer Arlington. When he found out she was almost engaged, he flipped. Couldn't get why she wouldn't dump her guy for him."

"Yeah, well, it's not happening in my case."

Danny flips his hand. "Don't worry about it. If he doesn't get his shit together, we'll pull the studio heads in here. That usually does the trick."

"I hope so. Things were going so well."

"You guys totally click on camera."

"Yeah, well, he confuses it with real life."

Danny taps my arm. "Do me a favor. Keep that piece of info to yourself, will you?"

"Yeah, no worries there."

And all this time I thought he was just a prick. Who knew he was a nutjob too?

Luckily, we were scheduled to shoot a scene without Holt today. It's not long and involves a phone call. It only takes a few minutes, but the director has me run through several takes. I'm off because of what happened, and I finally deliver what he wants. It should've been an easy one, but by the time we wrap up, my body is in knots.

It's after seven when I walk through the door of my apartment. All I want is a glass of wine and some relaxation out on my cute little patio. I'm standing in the kitchen when I decide to give Harrison a call. A sense of disappointment hits when it goes straight to voicemail.

"Hey, it's me, Midnight. Just giving you a call to uh ..." What exactly am I giving him a call for? "To see how you're doing, I guess. Yeah, to see how that fix-it guy who needs therapy is doing. Hope you're fine. I miss you. Maybe you'd like to come over for a little fixing. Okeydokeys, smokie pokies. See you around." I hop off the call and feel like the biggest dork. That was the stupidest message I've ever left anyone in my life. What the hell! *Okeydokeys smokie pokies. I'll see you around.* And *come over for a little fixing?* Where the hell did that come from?

I pour a glass of wine and guzzle it down. I'm going to have to get drunk to get over this one.

I'm on my way out to my patio, bottle of wine and glass in hand, when someone bangs on my door. A grin spreads across my face. I wonder how much hell he's going to give me over that dumbass message. I skip over to the door and all signs of amusement flee. Holt stands there, one arm propped on the doorjamb, and he says, "We need to talk."

He gives me zero opportunity to respond as he pushes his way past me and blasts into my apartment, leaving me standing there stunned. I'm hugging the bottle of wine like a baby when I regain my senses and find my voice.

"Holt, what's going on?"

"Like I said. We need to talk?"

"Okay, why don't you have a seat?" I extend my arm out, the one holding the empty wine glass, and add, "I'll be back in a second."

He stops me by saying, "I don't want to sit. You and I belong together, Midnight. You have to give us a chance."

Shit. This is so not cool. My phone's in the kitchen, where I put it down when I went to grab the wine.

"I thought I already explained myself."

He waves his hand. "That's a minor issue we can fix. Dump him. You can't tell me—you can't possibly admit you didn't feel what I did on the set."

He's not anywhere near joking. The man is delusional. I have to handle this in a way that won't set him off or alienate him.

"Well, yeah, I completely felt what Christine *would feel* if

Finn kissed her, you know, how their characters would feel toward each other."

He shifts back and forth. "That's not what I felt. It wasn't acting for me. I wasn't in character when I kissed you, Midnight. That was me, Holt Ward, kissing you, Midnight Drake." He pounds his chest.

Fuck, fuck, fuckery hell. Why me?

"Holt, I'm totally flattered that you felt such emotion in that particular scene."

He takes his fist and slams it into the palm of his hand. It happens so fast I flinch at the sound. Through clenched teeth, he says, "You seem to be missing my point. I wasn't in character and it wasn't in *that particular scene.*"

He's frightening me. I need to think of something to do, and fast.

I take the honesty route. "I'm honored and don't quite know what to say."

"Say you'll be with me. Or try at the very least."

His eyes look a little wild. Maybe he's drunk. I can't tell. My best course of action is to get the hell out of here, but my purse and car keys are in the kitchen with my phone. I decide to skirt around him and go in there. The kitchen is a pass-through so he can't trap me in there. If I grab my purse and run like hell, I can get away from him. There is no other choice. I refuse to give him the upper hand. No man will ever have that kind of control over me again.

I make my move toward the kitchen, only I don't get that far. His hand latches onto my wrist—the one with the wine glass—as I pass and he begs me to reconsider. I can't let him know of my intentions to leave.

"You have no idea how good we could be together. Give us a chance, Midnight. We could set the world on fire." He sounds like he truly believes this.

The only chance I want to give us is a chance for me to get the hell away from him.

"I have to think about this." Maybe this will satisfy him so he'll let me go, and I can grab my purse and run.

But he has different ideas. Whatever I said gave him the go-ahead for a relationship. "I knew you'd see things my way." A huge smile slowly spreads across his face.

Before I know it, he whips me into his arms and grabs my hair. Then his mouth crashes into mine, bruising my lips. I taste blood and this throws me into a panic. I can't allow him to see it. My heart is beating so hard, I fear he'll hear it. All I can focus on is getting away from him. I'm still holding the bottle of wine, which is smashed between us and crushing the shit out of my ribs, and the glass—which is useless as a weapon because he still grips the wrist of the hand it's in—so I'm damn helpless to fight.

Until I remember I have my legs. I lift a knee in a rapid-fire move and catch him in the groin. He groans as he releases me, allowing me to hightail it to the kitchen.

He's on my heels though, pissed off, yet begging me to stop.

I grab my purse and make it out the door, blinded by fear. I've been through too much shit with crazy, angry men to deal with another one. I don't hesitate for a half a second, but when I get through my door, I crash into the wall of someone's chest, and that's when I totally lose my composure. My fists fly out, and all I know is I have to make it to my car or shit's going down.

Then his voice breaks through my insanity, and the blood sings in my veins. Everything relaxes because I recognize the cone of safety.

Chapter 20

HARRISON

AFTER MY RUN, I HOP IN THE SHOWER AND LET THE COOL WATER sluice over me. It's heaven. When I'm dried off, I grab my phone to see I've missed a call from Midnight. Her quirky message puts a needed smile on my face. I decide to take a chance and pay her a surprise visit. Maybe she's up for dinner tonight. I've purposely given her a wide berth because she needs to stay centered on her film, and any distraction could be a bad thing for her.

I park out front but when I get to her door, she flies out right into me, and on her heels is Holt Ward. Talk about chaos. I'm not sure she knows it's me at first but when recognition hits, she sags against me. I have to catch her to keep her from falling.

"What's going on? Are you okay?" I ask. My gaze pings between the two of them.

"Thank God you're here," she breathes, panic edging her tone.

I tip her face so I can get a solid look at her and see her lip is swollen. She's holding a wine bottle and her purse, which is a little weird. "What happened to your lip?"

She sniffs back tears and says, "He cut it when he kissed me."

I look at him and ask, "Did you kiss her?"

"That's none of your business." Defiance bleeds out of Holt.

"Midnight, did you want him to kiss you?" Her answer could knife me, but I need to know.

"No!" She starts to sob.

I set her aside, even though I don't want to, and without a word, without thinking of the consequences, I ball my hand into a fist and punch Holt Ward in the jaw.

"You punched me," he whines.

"You sexually assaulted her."

He rubs his jaw. "You'll hear from my attorney."

"You'll hear from hers."

We stare each other down for a minute. "I can tell you this. You. Won't. Win. No one beats Harrison Kirkland. You just fucked with the wrong woman, Mr. Ward."

Then I turn to Midnight, wrap an arm around her, and escort her back inside. I say to her, "I'm calling the police to file a report against him." I say this for his benefit.

"Wait! I won't file charges against you," he yells. I knew the slimy fucker would back down. If anything like this got out, his career would be in the sewer.

"You also will cease any contact with Ms. Drake, except for your role on the film. Is that clear? If you ever come to this apartment again, or try to contact her outside of the studio, she will file a restraining order and this crime will be reported."

He rubs his jaw again.

"Mr. Ward. I will end your career. I am fully capable of it."

We stare at each other for a long minute, and then he leaves.

When I get Midnight inside, I snap some pictures of her face and ask if she was harmed anywhere else. She explains about the wine bottle and lifts up her shirt. She's beginning to bruise there, so I take a couple of pictures of that too.

"These are in case Holt doesn't do as he says."

"Thanks." She tells me the ugly story of his infatuation with her and how he wants a relationship. "I tried to be nice but he wouldn't take no for an answer. Thank God you came when you did."

I go to her kitchen and get some ice in a plastic bag for her lip. "Here."

"Is it bad?"

"Not too," I say. "I got your message. It was cute."

She makes a funny face and tries to laugh.

"Midnight, are you okay?"

Her head bobs. "I'll be fine. Just a little shaken up."

Then in an attempt to cheer her, I say, "Okeydokeys smokie pokies. See you around." I chuckle. "I've been giving you time. You know, so you don't have any distractions."

"Is that what it is?"

"Yeah."

"Or are you afraid of me?"

"Why would I be afraid of you?" I ask.

"Oh, because maybe I've touched on some things that make you uncomfortable."

"Why do you think that if someone has a need to fix things, there's an issue there?"

"I don't. But with you, you have to fix everything and everyone."

"I don't want to fix you. You're perfect just the way you are." The truth is she's more than perfect, and that bothers me more than I care to admit.

Her brow wrinkles. "You didn't at first."

"Why do you say that?"

"You were harsh."

Another chuckle rumbles out of me. "That was to get your attention. You were a total mess and had every right to be. We needed to work fast. But our plan came off better than I could ever have hoped. Your social media hits are through the roof. From what I understand, the dailies are incredible, you are shining like a diamond, and this film will make you one of

Hollywood's most wanted. I can't wait to see your success soar. So I'm sorry I was harsh, but I had my reasons for being so."

"Do you think Holt will fuck up the film?"

"Not in a million years. His career is on the line and he understands what that means. You need to let your producer know what happened here, though."

"I know. I can't believe how he totally freaked out on me." She wraps her arms around herself so I pull her into mine.

"Why'd you let him in?"

She glances up at me. "I opened the door because I thought it was you. He came right after I left you that dumb message."

"I liked that message. When I saw that fucker standing there, I wanted to beat him to a pulp."

"I'm glad you didn't, only because it would've delayed filming. I want to get this shit over now. Fast. Earlier today he pulled this crap and I told him I was seeing someone."

"You did?" I ask. I'm surprised, but I have to admit, elated.

"Yeah. Now he knows who I was referring to."

"Good. I'm glad you did."

"You are?"

"Yeah."

"Does this mean we're dating or something?" she asks. She looks kind of shy and it reminds me of the Midnight I first met in New York.

"How do you feel about that?"

She lifts and lowers a shoulder. "It's a foreign concept to me. I never date."

"Why's that?"

She lowers then lifts her eyes. "Why do you think?" she asks in a saucy tone.

"I don't know, which is why I asked."

"Come on, Harrison. You're a relatively bright guy."

"Relatively?"

"I said that because you asked a stupid question."

"I didn't think it was stupid. If I had, I wouldn't have asked it."

"I worked in porn. I had my fill of men on those disgusting sets. In the past, they usually only wanted one thing from me."

"Hmm. If I recall, you're the one who instigated things with that hot-as-fuck kiss."

A flush spreads from her neck to her cheeks. She's embarrassed? What a nice surprise. I tip her chin up and plant a loud, smacking kiss on the part of her mouth that isn't injured. She giggles. That's another surprise. Midnight isn't the giggling type.

"So, I was originally coming here to surprise you and ask if you wanted to go to dinner."

She sinks back into the curve of my body. "Would you be upset if I said no? I was so looking forward to chilling at home. I'm tapped out after this week and especially after crazy dude."

"I will be happy to chill at home with you. Can I call in dinner? Delivery, or I can get takeout from anywhere you'd like."

"Ahh, that sounds wonderful."

"Hey, are you sure you're okay? After what just happened?"

"Yeah. He only kissed me. I'm not gonna lie. For a minute there, I was pretty scared, but when I realized it was you, I knew I was safe."

"You're always safe with me." *But I'm the one in danger.* My heart gives a squeeze as I hold her against me. I can feel her inhale deeply. It makes me want to keep her safe, and I wonder how it got to this point. What would my parents think? And what about Weston and Prescott? Does it matter?

"You know, Christmas is in what, a couple of weeks? What are you doing?" I ask.

"No plans. Danny said we'd be working straight through, much to everyone's groaning and moaning. But the good thing is we are keeping to schedule. He said Greg, our director, was raving about me. I don't like to toot my own horn, but you're the only one I can tell this to. After Christmas we move to Santa Monica and start shooting on location."

"That'll be pretty cool for you, right? Have you ever shot on location before?"

"Only if you count beds and such." She laughs.

"Ha, ha."

"Does it bother you? That I made porn flicks?"

"I'd be a liar to say it didn't."

"But you're still here."

"Yeah. It was your job. At least that's what I tell myself. Were you ever involved with any of them? Beyond the camera?"

"Didn't you hear what I said earlier?"

When she notices my furrowed brow, she goes on. "I don't date and didn't back then, including the guys from the industry."

"Good to know."

"Let's clear the air on this because I don't want this to come up later or create walls between us. I was never with"—and she air quotes with her fingers—"any of them other than in the films. I know this sounds stupid and cliché, but none of it meant anything. It was all part of the industry. Now can I ask you something?"

"Yeah."

"Have you ever been in love or in a relationship?"

"Yeah."

"Then you were in way deeper than I've ever been, no pun intended." She smirks. Then she turns serious again. "My heart's only been affected by one thing ever. And it wasn't a man."

"What was it?"

"Maybe I'll tell you another time."

"Why do I get the feeling you won't?"

"No idea. But how about Indian food?"

"You love ethnic food, don't you?"

"I love the explosion of flavor in my mouth. It's scintillating."

"Let me give you scintillating." I plant another kiss on her lips and then let her order the food. Since the restaurant she chose doesn't deliver, I have to run out to pick it up. "While I'm gone, why don't you give Danny a call?"

When I get back, she has the little bistro table on her patio set, with candles lit and wine poured. It looks quite romantic. We eat to soft music, and she says Danny will take care of Holt. He'll talk to him and involve the CEO of Alta. That should put more pressure on him to leave Midnight alone.

Before we're finished eating, I notice her eyelids drooping. I carry our empty plates to the kitchen, clean up, and by the time I get back outside, she's drifting to sleep.

I lift her in my arms and carry her to bed. It's still early, too early for me to sleep, so I decide to watch TV in the other room.

I'm watching some snorendous movie but I've been nodding off so I don't even know what's going on when a series of gunshots goes off, shooting out the living room windows. I hit the floor, covering my head. It ends as quickly as it starts. I dial 911 and crawl to the bedroom to see if Midnight is okay. She's on the floor, fumbling around in the dark.

"Are you okay? Were you hit?" I ask.

"No. I only heard shots and rolled out of bed to the floor."

"Stay down until the police arrive. I've already called 911."

It takes them about eight minutes to get here, which feels like a lifetime. By this time, the shooter is long gone and there's no chance of us finding him or her. But I have a good idea who did this. There's too much coincidence for it to be anyone else besides the crazy Holt Ward.

The officers ask me questions, but there isn't much to go on. I don't want to tell them about Holt. It would trigger an investigation and then could impact Midnight's career. I have other ways to deal with him. They're on the unsavory side, but definitely more effective than going through the proper channels of the law.

The neighbors come out, I guess after they deem it safe, and see the blue lights flashing. The police question everyone they can. Unfortunately, they come up dry. No one saw a thing. The neighbors were watching TV, out on their patios, or asleep.

After all the excitement dies down, and the police finish gathering what little evidence there is, everyone wanders back to their respective homes. The officers tell us if they hear anything, they'll give Midnight a call. The windows are a mess—broken shards everywhere. The police found the bullet casings so we're good on sweeping everything up. But the windows need replacing. Midnight's already called her landlord and he's on the way to board it up until he can get the things fixed.

"You can't stay here tonight. Why don't you pack a bag and stay with me this weekend?"

"Oh, this is fine. Once they put the boards up ..."

"I would feel better with you away from here. What if he comes back?"

"You think it was Holt, don't you?"

"If it wasn't him, I think he had something to do with it. That's why I didn't mention what happened earlier. Well, that, and I didn't want it to fuck up the movie."

"Yeah, that's exactly why I kept my mouth shut too. Why do I attract all the mystic knights of the psych unit? And believe me, I've been there."

"Because you're beautiful and men want a woman like you."

"Okay, Boy Scout, thank you very much."

"I'm serious. You asked, I told."

She blows out a breath.

"Go pack a bag. This weekend's on me. Relaxation's the word for you."

She chews on her lip for a second and then agrees. "Okay, but I'm greedy when it comes to being spoiled."

"Not a problem. I like a greedy woman."

She elbows me in the ribs. "You may regret saying that." Then she saunters away to pack a bag while I think about how I'm going to handle Mr. Ward. He's in for a world of surprise. I can't damage his reputation ... yet. But I can make him fucking squirm.

And after the film is done, that slimy bastard is history.

Chapter 21

MIDNIGHT

Since I've known Harrison, the topic of where he lives has never come up. So when I follow him into his driveway in Malibu, and not just Malibu, but on the beach, my tongue nearly scrapes the pavement as I get out of the car. The house is no less than magnificent. It's ultramodern and chic, but not sterile. As we walk in, he flips a switch and lights glow everywhere. I can't wait to see this place in the daylight.

He holds my bag in one hand and takes my hand in the other. The long hall that leads from the entrance opens into a huge, open-concept living space. The kitchen is to the left, and it's a dream world. I would love to spend a whole day in there piddling around. It has an enormous island that seats eight. Off the kitchen to the left is a dining area with a gigantic table. I don't have time to count the chairs there. To the right of the kitchen is the living room. Oh my goodness. There are four plush couches that look so cozy, I want to plop right down on one. They circle around an enormous fireplace, above which hangs one of the biggest TVs I've ever seen. Doors open out to what must be a deck or terrace, but it's too dark to tell.

I follow him along, humming my pleasure, until we get to a massive bedroom. Who is this man again? There is an expansive king-sized bed and another fireplace in here, and lots of built-in cabinets. I see several doors, which I'm sure are the closet and bathroom. He points to one and says, "The bath is through there if you'd like to check it out. I'm going to grab us something to drink from the kitchen. What would you like?"

"Some water would be nice."

"I'll be right back."

I wander into the bath and it feels like I've entered a spa. There's a fancy jetted tub, a luxurious shower, and everything a girl could possibly want. I will be spending plenty of time in here tomorrow.

Harrison set my bag in the bedroom, so I grab my toiletries and take them into the bathroom, taking over one of the sinks. I brush my teeth and change into my sleeping attire. By this time, he's returned with some water.

"Your bathroom is really something."

"Yeah, my mom likes to hang out in here when she visits." He smiles.

"I'm super tired after all this shit tonight. Let's get some sleep."

I scoot under the sumptuous linens, which are much better than mine.

Harrison gets in on his side of the bed and says, "This switch here controls the blinds. Make sure they're down at night if, for some reason, you're ever here without me. That entire wall is nothing but glass and in the morning, it can be pretty bright in here."

"Good to know."

I don't remember closing my eyes, but the next thing I know, I wake up to the smell of bacon. And damn, it smells good. After my teeth are brushed, I trudge into the kitchen and see Harrison fixing breakfast.

He glances up, saying, "Aw, you beat me. I was going to feed you breakfast in bed."

"How sweet."

Then he looks at me again and lets out a belly laugh.

"What's so funny?"

"Someone had a party in their hair last night."

"Eek. That bad, huh?"

"Go check it out."

He points to a door off the hall in the foyer. There's a powder room down there. When I go and look, I'm appalled. I come back saying, "What the hell did I do last night?"

"Beats the hell out of me, but it must've been fun." He holds up the coffee pot. "Coffee?"

"Sure."

I take a seat at the large island and we chat while he cooks. He's making omelets. "I could never master the art of flipping those things," I say.

"It's all in the wrist."

"Uh-huh. I've heard that before, but when I try they either stay in the pan or end up on the stove, making a huge mess."

He laughs. When he's done cooking, he plates everything up. "Follow me."

We go outside onto the terrace. It overlooks the beach. Gorgeous.

"Did you build this place?"

"No. Someone only had it for about a year when it went into foreclosure. I was lucky enough to snag it. I love it here."

"It's the most beautiful home I've ever been in."

"Thanks. I thought so too when I found it. I just had to have it."

I breathe in the tangy salt air and feel refreshed as we eat. The breakfast is delicious and when we're finished, Harrison suggests I take a bath.

"Am I that dirty?"

"I actually like dirty. I thought you knew that."

"You're forgetting who you're talking to, Harrison."

"No, I am not." He brushes the plates aside, to the point where I think they're going to crash off the table, and then he pulls my chair around so it faces his. "I could never forget who you are."

His fingers slip under the waistband of my shorts and he pulls them off. I quickly look around to see if anyone is in sight.

"No one can see us. Not a chance of it."

In a couple of tugs, I'm bare from the waist down and he has my pussy spread wide open for him.

"Hmm, isn't this a pretty sight?"

The chairs are large, the kind with arms on them, and he lifts me high, draping my legs over the sides of the arms.

"But not exactly what I was going for."

He loops his arms under me and lifts me on the table. Under his intense scrutiny, I suddenly feel shy. I want this man to like me—really like me—and not find any faults in me. I don't want to be that girl who needs fixing. I want to be the one who kicks ass. Only under the warmth of those dark-chocolate eyes that are inspecting the most private parts of me, I'm not feeling very kick-assy right now.

If I could squeeze my legs together and put my hand over my vag, I would. But wouldn't I look stupid? Me, the ex-B-rated porn star who many a man—and maybe even Harrison—has jacked off to while watching me get fucked like a rabbit. Shit. Why did I have to go there?

"What's wrong?"

"Nothing." My squeaky answer tells him I'm a terrible liar.

"Are you going to tell me or do I have to lick it out of you?"

Busted.

"Do I have to?" I ask.

"Yes. I'll find out one way or another. I'm very persuasive, you know."

I do know.

"I want you to see me as someone who's strong. And for whatever dumbass reason, I just got a big case of the nerves that you think I'm a crazy wimp."

"That's it?"

I screw up my mouth and nod.

He doesn't acknowledge it one way or another, but pries my legs apart and dives down onto my bare pussy. Spreading my lips, he doesn't mess around. Going directly for my clit, he tongues me until I forget that my real name is Velvet. Then he stops, leans back, and picks up a glass of ice water. What the hell. Did that make him thirsty? Oh, hell no. He holds it over my slit and pours a long, cold stream over me.

"Christ," I say, twitching. The water trickles between my heated lips. The contrast is indescribable.

Flashing me a wicked grin, he says, "It felt like you needed a little cooling off. But I'm going to heat you up again." His mouth is a flame to that ice water. When his tongue touches me again, I'm ready for it. He pushes the tip firmly against my clit, licking and flicking hard. I'm not sure how many fingers he slides inside of me, but it's damn good. There's a rhythm to his game, the tongue and the hand, and my body hums harmony in response. I want more ... him. I don't want to just climax. Well, I do. But I want to do it with him inside me. And it scares the crap out of me.

His damn tongue is relentless to the point where I come, even though I didn't really want to. Then I reach for his neck, wrapping my hand around it, and I look into his eyes. The sun dances in them, bringing out the dark gold tones hidden within their depths.

My breath comes in uneven puffs and I pull him to me so our mouths connect. Breathing in his scent almost makes me dizzy. There's nothing but the warm sinew of muscle beneath my hand and it reminds me of his strength—that same strength I felt when I crashed into him outside my door.

Our kiss is wild, deep, with tongues dancing. His hand is in my messy hair, twisting it, pulling it. My hand is on the waist of his sweatpants, tugging, reaching for him. I need him. Inside me. We're nothing but hands all over, grabbing each other. His are on my breasts now and mine are in his pants, closing around his cock, hard and smooth.

"I need a condom."

"Yeah, yeah," I breathe.

"Inside."

My hand won't release him. There's a tiny drop of pre-ejaculate on the tip of him, and I rub it all over. He sucks in air.

"I need to go ..."

"Yeah. Inside."

I'm pulling him toward me, because I'm clean and on the pill. I don't give a fuck right now about a condom. I only give a fuck about him. I *need* him. My thighs are spread and I touch his tip to my slick, wet opening.

"Ah, Midnight."

One hand pushes on his ass, and the other has his cock. My need is so great, so urgent, I can't think straight. He bends forward and presses his lips to my temple, my neck, my mouth, and then he plunges all the way inside. I lock my ankles behind him as he fucks me, kisses me, holds my neck, and locks gazes with me. It's the headiest sensation imaginable.

My stomach tightens in a weird way, like I've never felt before. Everything inside me flutters and I'm caught in a hurricane of Harrison, swept away by an emotional tide I didn't think was possible. He takes my hand and links our fingers together. Never did I think such a gesture was intimate, until now. I kiss his chest, shoulder, anywhere my mouth can touch, until we both feel that flame igniting inside us as we orgasm together.

What the fuck just happened?

Finally, he says, "We just had sex without a condom."

"Uh, yeah."

"Are you on the pill?"

"Yeah. Are you clean?"

"Yeah. I never have sex without protection. What about you?"

"Yeah. I've been tested repeatedly. My last test was after New York and I'm still good."

Then he lets out a raspy chuckle. "That was some heavy shit, right?"

"Yeah." My belly clenches again as I think of it.

His dark brown eyes seek out my own as his lips brush over mine. "Regretting what just happened?"

I slowly nod. "Not at all. Are you?"

He kisses me again, and this time it's slow and sensual, stealing the air from me. He reminds me that his kisses make me forget about everything else.

"Does that answer your question?"

My smile is my answer.

Chapter 22

HARRISON

She's a tumbled mess beneath me, but a potent thing just passed between us. I don't know what to call it because it doesn't have a name. For a minute there, I was worried she'd run. She was shy—innocent, even. And it was sexy as hell. Her hair gleams as the sun's rays touch upon the long strands, and I can't stop touching her soft skin. My fingers rest on the curve of her cheekbone as my thumb follows the plump lines of her slightly parted lips. Her tongue peeks out to touch the tip of my thumb, so I push it in deeper and feel the heat of her as she puckers her lips and sucks. Her teeth bite down—not too hard or soft—and it makes me want to feel her around my cock again.

Pulling her into a sitting position, I lift her into my arms and carry her inside. "While I enjoy being outside, the bed is much more comfortable."

The sheets are still rumpled from when we got up and I lay her down on top of them.

"Harrison, what we did out there. I know you probably think I do this a lot, but I don't. The truth is I never do this."

"You don't owe me any explanations."

"I know, but I wanted to tell you that."

There are so many questions I want to ask, but I don't. Porn was a business for her so I leave it at that. If I let it mind fuck with me, I'll be the broken one for sure. Besides, there's a double standard. If I were the man who made my living doing it, no one would care.

She draws a circle on my chest. "What's the kinkiest thing you've ever done?"

"Seriously? You want to know that?"

"Yeah."

I rub my face, then roll on my side and prop myself on my elbow. "I guess I'm pretty vanilla. Spanking and anal is about the kinkiest I've ever gotten."

"You like anal?"

I shrug. "It's fine. I just like to fuck." I grin. "What about you?"

Her eyes shutter. "I've only fucked in films and it's all been pretty basic. No BDSM or anything like that." Her mouth turns down. "Other than what went down in New York."

I smooth her hair. "That doesn't count." My tone is soft and I pull her on top of me.

"You watched it, didn't you?"

"I had to."

She buries her face on my chest. Her voice is muffled when she says, "I hate that."

"Don't. Besides, they won't ever do it to anyone again."

"How can you be so sure?"

"I can. And they won't. You'll just have to trust me on this."

She lifts up to look at me. "What did you do?"

"I made sure they won't bother anyone ever again, especially you. But don't ask me what I did."

Her lips purse and that very look, the way her mouth puckers, has me pulling her in to kiss them. I tell myself it's to get her mind off topic, but that's not the real reason. The truth is I can't possibly keep my hands and mouth off her. I thought once would be enough to get her out of my system. It wasn't. She's irresistible. I'm tied up in knots.

My hand reaches behind her to find her pussy because I'm already growing hard again. She's still on top of me, lying on my dick, but it's not very comfortable, as it needs a little more room. I shift her to the right and open her thighs. What I really want is to see her ride me. I want to watch her come on top of me with her head thrown back, her nipples hard, and all that gorgeous hair hanging down.

Midnight's name suits her because her hair is dark as the color of night. But her birth name suited her as well. Her skin is as soft as velvet and I can't keep my hands off her.

Her mouth moves to my nipple and she tightens her teeth around it while her tongue flicks back and forth. My heart picks up as I watch and forget myself for a moment. She outlines my nipple with her tongue while her fingers sink into the muscles of my pecs. Even though it's not as sexual as her sucking me off, it's so intimate to watch, it makes me want to kiss every inch of her perfect skin. At that exact moment, she lifts her head, our gazes connect, and I grab her, pulling her up so I can taste her mouth.

"I want to be inside of you." Reaching for the drawer, I grab a condom.

"Do you think that's really necessary?" Her smirk puts a smile on my face.

"If you're okay with it ..."

"If we're exclusive ..."

"Yes." The word is spoken forcefully. It occurs to me I wouldn't want it any other way. Is she the one? Am I in love with her? This is way too fast. My mom always said I'd know and that it wouldn't take me long. But this ... this is crazy. But isn't love crazy? Nah, I'm not in love. This is only lust. I want her all the time. I think about her all the time. When I thought she was in danger, I almost lost my shit. I want exclusivity with her. So, is it love?

She grabs my face and kisses me.

I lie back down and say, "Ride me."

She straddles me and I swear to God, I could watch this

show all day. Except I can't because I'm an inept man. And I come exactly like a teenager. You'd think I hadn't had sex in ages. She unravels me so quickly, it's almost disturbing.

"Jesus. I'm sorry." I'm sort of embarrassed.

"For what?"

I scrub my face. "Thought I had a little more staying power than that."

"It must be my amazing talent."

It has nothing to do with talent. It's much more than that, but I don't know how to respond. She's gotten to me, only I'm not sure I'm ready for this. Pulling her down, I say, "It's your amazing beauty." That part's true. There's a certain quality about her, an air that's unusual. She's exotic, not the typical California blond you see everywhere, tanned with blue eyes. Midnight is dark and mysterious. And she definitely has secrets, which add to her mystique.

"What?" she asks.

I've been fixated on her, burning her with my gaze. "You're unlike anyone I've ever known."

"I can say the same thing. And to your point, I hope it's a good thing."

"It is." I kiss her. Changing the topic, I ask, "How would you like a bath?"

"I'd love one."

We soak in the jetted tub and when the water turns chilly, I hand her a fluffy towel and dry myself off as well.

"Is there anything in particular you want to do today?"

"Just chill."

"You can hang by the pool while I run some errands, if that's okay."

"Sure. I'd love that. I didn't know you had one."

"It's down below. You can access it from the lower level," I say.

"Of course. Why didn't I think of that?" She slaps her forehead and laughs.

"There's a media room down there too, if you'd care to watch a movie."

"Don't say that nasty word," she teases. "That's the last thing I want to do. I'd rather waste away on a beach chair or by the pool."

She situates herself by the pool, where she's only steps away from the beach if she decides to take a dip in the chilly Pacific Ocean. I go to my home office and make a few calls. The incident last night has disturbed me more than I let on.

"What's up, boss?" Leland answers.

I explain the details of the shooting. "See if you can dig into anything."

"Hmm. With what you just gave me, I doubt it. Sounds like whoever was responsible did some surveillance before the actual shooting. My guess it was a scare tactic."

"Mine too. The bullets hit too high up for it to be anything else. It's what the cops said last night too."

"Does her parking lot have security cameras?"

"No, dammit. The place is quiet, in a safe neighborhood. Her landlord probably never felt the need. I want to talk to him today."

"I hate to even tell you this, but I have nothing to go on."

My fingers thrum a rhythm on the desk. "I figured that's what you'd say. Looks like I'm going to have to have another talk with Mr. Ward."

"Before you do that, why don't we get someone to keep a close eye on him?"

"How close are you thinking?"

"Real close."

I grab a pen and start making swirls on a pad of sticky notes. Nodding, I say, "Yeah, I like that idea. Do it. Monday."

"I'll let you know when everything's set."

"Thanks, Leland."

My next call is to Misha. She has some contacts at the

LAPD who might be able to help. I quickly fill her in and she says she'll call if she hears anything.

The landlord gets a call next. He assures me the window will be repaired by the end of the day and I discuss the advantage of installing security cameras in the parking lot. He agrees to look into it. The guy sounds truly overwhelmed by this turn of events. In the twenty years since he's owned the six buildings making up the complex, he's never had so much as an attempted break-in or an incidence of vandalism in the parking lot. To have something this severe has really shaken him. I'd like to ease his mind about it, but I can't.

Onto the next item on my list. Midnight has no interest in doing anything away from the house, so I call Emily. She knows every caterer in LA.

"Hey, I need a hand. Who can I get to come over and cook a dinner here tonight? I know it's short notice, but ..."

"I'll say. Let me think. Oh, what about that new Argentinian chef who's trying to break into the scene here?"

"See what you can work up for me, will you? I'll owe you."

"What time do you want him there?"

"Whatever time it would take for him to prepare something really great."

"Got it."

I turn on the computer, take care of a few things, and notice that all my billing is up to date. Helen really is doing a fantastic job. I make a note to have a chat with her on Monday, to check and see how she's acclimating to her new home.

I'm on my way out to check on Midnight when my phone buzzes.

"Hey, Mom. What's going on?"

"We're just calling to check in."

"Great. Everything okay back home?"

"Fine, son, just fine," Dad chimes in.

"Harrison, are you coming home for the holidays?"

"Yes, Mom. I'll be there for Christmas."

"Oh, that's just wonderful," she says. I immediately feel guilty for having stayed away so long. She fills me in with what's happening back home and then concludes with telling me that Missy Truluck is still single. "I think she'll be around on Christmas. Should I invite her over?"

"Oh God, Mom, no!"

"Laura, leave the poor man alone. He can find his own dates," Dad says.

"Thanks, Dad."

"Just trying to help."

"Mom, Missy Truluck hasn't had a date since high school."

"Oh, Harrison, that isn't true."

"Yes, I think it is."

"She came to the Garden Party Tea last week and brought the latest doilies she made and they were beautiful. I almost asked her to make some for your end tables."

"Mom!" I'm so horrified, I don't know what to say.

"Well, I didn't because I knew you wouldn't display them."

My mother keeps talking, but I'm mostly silent. I think about what Mom would say if she met Midnight. The truth is she would probably love anyone I dated.

"We'll talk soon, honey." And they end the call.

I finally get back to Midnight and find her sleeping in the sun. I take a moment to appreciate the view. She's naked, lying on her back, one arm stretched over her head. It's all I can do not to run my finger across her nipple and tease its perfect peak. I'm glad the terrace around the pool is completely private, allowing her to relax like this.

My thoughts take a detour, however, when they veer to others seeing her naked. Many have, and it's something I'm going to have to learn to deal with. I can't let it drive me crazy, but dammit, thoughts of other men jerking off to her don't sit well with me. And then I remember that I'm one of those men. That makes me just as bad as they are. But how the hell was I to know this would happen?

Son of a bitch.

"What? What's wrong?"

I hadn't meant to speak those words out loud, but she sits up in the chair, waiting for an answer. What the hell am I supposed to say?

Chapter 23

MIDNIGHT

Harrison wakes me up, yelling. I have no idea what's going on because I'm napping. And when I ask him, he stares at me like I should know the answer.

"Well? Is something wrong?"

He opens, then closes his mouth, and stomps away. What am I supposed to do with that? I throw on my cami and bottoms and trail behind him. This won't work. He can't come outside, yell, then leave without an explanation.

I find him in the bedroom, staring out the window.

"You were naked."

"And?"

"What if someone saw you?" He turns and drills me with those cocoa irises. He's angry! This is absurd.

"How could they? You told me at breakfast no one could see us."

He stutters, "You were at the pool."

"What's the difference?"

The muscles in his jaw twitch. If he's not careful, they're going to twitch right off his face. I don't understand his logic ... but then my gears switch and dumbass here finally gets it.

"It bothers you that I did porn, doesn't it?"

"No." He sounds like a pouty kid. I want to laugh, but I can't. That would be disastrous.

"Tell the truth, Harrison, so we can deal with it."

"Okay." His arms fly out. "It bugs the shit out of me. To think men jack off as they watch you get fucked."

"Is that what you did?"

"I, uh ..."

"It's okay. In fact, out of everyone, I hope you did."

"Then yes. Guilty as charged." The words rush out of him.

Pointing to the bed, I say, "Please sit."

I'm a little surprised he does. "I can understand how hard it is. I'll be honest. If it were you, I'd have a hard time too. But the fact is there isn't a darn thing I can do about it. It was in the past and I can't change it. So, we can either move forward and deal with it the best we can, or we can part ways. I'll leave this decision up to you. But what I can't do is have you freaking out over it and then withdrawing from me."

"Why were you naked?"

"You mean just now?"

He nods.

"One, I don't have a bathing suit with me. And two, I've never sunbathed naked before. You have the perfect place for it. I figured what the hell. It was either naked or in my underwear. So I chose naked."

"That's it?"

"What? You think I'm some kind of perv and want people to see me?" That thought pisses me off.

"No! I just thought maybe you were used to walking around naked."

"Jesus. Okay, let's pull back a little. The movie scenes were nude, but immediately after, I would robe up. I didn't walk around naked all day, if that's what you're wondering."

When my words register, his posture droops. "Really?"

"Yes, really. Does that make you feel better?" I ask.

"Somewhat."

A. M. HARGROVE

I sit down next to him. "Go on. I know you have more questions. Ask away."

"Did you orgasm on film?"

Laughing, I say, "Seriously? I'm a really good fake. Wanna see?"

That was definitely the wrong answer.

"What?"

"Whoa. Hold your horses, slick. This was in reference to *on film*. This has nothing to do with you. The truth is until you, I didn't think I could orgasm through sex. Understand?"

"So you never climaxed during those films?"

"Never."

"Hmm."

"Happy now?"

"Not exactly."

I'm not sure if this is fixable. "Maybe it's time for me to leave."

"You can't. I won't risk your safety. Holt could come back."

"I refuse to stay here with you acting like this."

"I can't help the way I feel."

"Then we're deadlocked."

I'm at a loss. I can't redo my past. And if he knew the other part of it, he'd toss me in the trash because that's what I am. That thought makes my decision. Moments later I'm dressed, carrying my bag, as he trails me to the car, arguing the stupidity of my decision.

"I disagree. You've made me feel cheap and I don't need a constant reminder of what I did in order to—" I clamp my mouth shut. I almost told him something I never intend to share with anyone. Ever.

"In order to what?"

"Nothing. I'm leaving. The window will be fixed today. You know where to find me. But don't call until you can deal with my past, Harrison."

I climb behind the wheel and circle around his driveway.

172

This house is like a resort, but it's suddenly left a bitter taste in my mouth. Tears blur my vision as I drive down the highway, so I pull off the road until they pass. This emotional journey called life is getting to be a giant pain in my ass. When I think back to all my problems, every single one of them leads directly back to men. Dammit, why do they cause so much trouble? Why can't they be uncomplicated creatures, like women? That thought at least makes me laugh.

I arrive home to find contractors at my place installing the new windows. I'm not gonna lie—it'll be a little freaky staying here tonight. But I'm going to have to do it sooner or later.

What a freak show Holt turned out to be. Soon after I unpack my bag, Danny calls.

"Midnight, how are you?"

"I'm fine. They're fixing my windows now."

"Good. I talked to Holt."

"And?"

"He's claiming he's under a lot of stress."

I let out a laugh. "Aren't we all?"

"I told him he has to stay away from you, except during filming. He says you invited him over and that you wanted to spend the weekend with him."

"Oh my God. That is such bullshit. He's the one who suggested it to me and I said no."

"Yeah, I hit him back with that, because that's what you told me. He stammered a bit and then I hit him with some other stuff. We're going to get this film wrapped up as quickly as we can, Midnight. I promise."

"Thank you."

"Next week is Christmas and we're only giving everyone Christmas Eve and Christmas Day off. The same for New Year's. My guess is we'll be wrapped by the second week of January at the very latest."

"You think?"

"Yeah, I do."

"That's wonderful."

"And then we go into postproduction. But Midnight, the dailies are still so fucking amazing, I can't even tell you how great they are."

"I hope you're pleased with my work."

"Very. So don't spend too much time worrying about Holt."

"Um, I'll try not to. I just want someone to be present at all times when I'm around him."

"We can handle that."

"Good. Then I'll see you Monday," I say.

I feel a little better, as long as that idiot doesn't show up on my doorstep again.

Later that afternoon, I get a surprising phone call. It's from Helen Reddy.

"Hey, I hope you don't mind me calling. I snagged your number from the office. You up to going to dinner tonight?" she asks.

"I don't mind at all, and dinner sounds great."

"There's this great place near my house." She tells me where she lives so I leave for her place around six. When she answers, I'm a little surprised. Gone is the Harley look. She still has blond hair, but it's solidly blond now. Her lips are still red, but no pigtails anymore. She's wearing jeans and a cute cream-colored top with lace trim.

"Hiya, puddin'," comes out of her mouth and normal flies out the window. Nevertheless, the corners of my mouth tip upward because Helen is cute. Really cute. Her crystal-blue eyes sparkle and she holds out her hand, so I take it and we shake. It's a firm grip, not a squishy one that women sometimes offer. "Come on in. This isn't really my place, but I wish it were. Harrison has been awful nice to me since I moved here. For some reason, I'm having a terrible time finding my way around. New York is so easy because most all the streets are numbers, you know. It's not like that here. I'm constantly getting lost."

"Don't you ever use maps on your phone?"

"Well, yeah, I do. But I usually go the wrong way. That little man they have should be pointed in the direction you're supposed to walk."

"Just check the distance. If it's decreasing, you're good."

She points at me. "You're pretty smart, aren't you?"

"I don't know about that."

"Want a beer?"

"Sure."

We sit and chat while we drink our beers. She's very engaging. She chews bubblegum like I eat gummies. I like Helen more and more.

She cocks her head and stares at me. Hard. "Do I have something on my face?"

"Yeah. Pain. You try to hide it but I see through you. You know why?"

I hope she's not one of those creepy clairvoyant types. "No."

"I have it too. You and me, we're sisters. I've been there, you know. I'm not asking for your secrets and I'm not going to give you mine. I'm only saying I can read between the lines," she says.

The air I'm holding wheezes out of me, making me sound like an asthmatic. "For a minute there, I thought you wanted to play true confessions."

"Hell to the fucking no on that. There will be no confessions shooting out of this mouth, puddin'."

"Can I ask you something—and you don't have to answer if you don't want?"

"Sure."

"Have you ever thought of changing your name to Harley?"

The biggest smile I've ever seen on another human being stretches across her lovely face. Then she aims her index finger at me and says, "You get me, Midnight. You really get me."

"No, it's just ..." What is it exactly?

"I know. And you wanna know why?" she asks.

I lean forward, dropping my elbows to my knees.

"At first, Harley was just a plain girl until she got fucked up. Then she got those superpowers. I wanna be smart, but I wanna be strong too. Not psycho strong. I know people think I'm crazy and all, but I'm not. I'm just a girl who doesn't want to be taken advantage of ever again. When people look at me all dressed up like her, they don't mess with me. I think you can understand that, can't you?"

"I totally get you."

"Yah, I knew you would. That day I climbed into the helicopter, I thought you had your claws into Harrison. I wanted to let you know then he was all yours. I sort of bat for the other team now. Girls don't hurt you. Physically, that is."

A veil drops over her, and I see it. I know where she's coming from.

"No men at all? Ever?"

She shrugs. "I'm not gonna say never. But for right now, I'm staying away from them, unless it's a threesome." She pops a bubble and giggles. "Too bad God gave men all the dicks."

We laugh.

"So, you wanna go eat?" she asks.

"Yeah. I'm a little hungry."

We take the elevator down and I ask her where we're going. She tells me it's this Vietnamese restaurant and I nearly get giddy. My ethnic food fondness is going to be fed tonight. Helen just scored another point in my book.

Over dinner, we talk about a ton of stuff. I ask her if she misses New York and she almost chokes on her Bánh xèo.

"Oh, hell no. I wouldn't miss that place in a million years. Bad memories. I'm sure you get that."

And do I ever. "That's Phoenix for me. I don't ever want to have to go back there again."

She holds out her fist for me to bump it. "See. Sisters, right?"

"I guess we are."

"So, you and Harrison? Are you two ..." And she motions

using her index finger sliding in and out of a circle she's made with her other finger and thumb.

Laughing, I set my chopsticks down and then sigh. "Well ... sort of, but now I'm not so sure. At least not after today. Oh, fuck, who knows."

"I figured you were. He mentions your name a fair amount in the office. And I only want to say this—he's one of the good guys. There aren't many, not that I have to tell you that."

"Why would he mention my name at all? Is it in passing or what?" I ask.

"There was that thing with Holt while you were at the health spa. That's what we call it."

"That thing?"

"You know, where Holt tried to say he was missing out on some roles because of the delay."

Oh yeah. I'd forgotten about that.

"Harrison was not about to let anything affect your career. You're in good hands with him."

"He certainly likes to fix things."

She perks up in her chair. "He fixed me. Well, sort of. I would've been fired and probably more. That Trent, the one who did all that stuff to you, more than likely would've come after me. I didn't tell that to Harrison. I would've had to lay low for a while, which meant I wouldn't have been able to pay my rent. It would've been a bad scene for me all around."

Her hand is on the table so I grab it. "Helen, I had no idea how much you went out on a limb to help me. That was damn brave of you."

"I wasn't working that night. But that dickhead I worked for didn't give a damn. Trent was a nasty shit and would give him a percentage of what his take was on those movies. That's how it worked. At the time, I didn't realize he was selling videos online. I put two and two together after you. Had I known, I could've done something about it."

"No. What would you have done?"

"Turned them both into the police. I used to think the girls were drunk or high. But now I know they were drugged. Those assholes."

"I still want to look into their faces and ask them if it makes them feel big, feel proud to do that."

She presses her hands together. "But see, those types of people have no conscience. Confronting him wouldn't serve a purpose. It would only upset you more."

"You're right. But logic won't listen to my heart."

"I think you just have to FIDO it—fuck it and drive on. There have been so many times in my life where I spend way too much time being upset or pissed off about stuff I can't do anything about. It's a waste of energy. Spend your time on meaningful things. After you finish this film, take a little time off for Midnight. Pamper yourself and get revived. I've never been able to do that so consider yourself lucky."

"Believe me, I've never been able to either. It's always been worrying about where my next meal is coming from or how I'm going to pay my rent."

"Life sucks sometimes, doesn't it?"

"Yeah."

She holds up her beer bottle and we toast to sucky lives.

"So, tell me what you've been doing since you've moved here," I say.

"Mostly working. Misha's been the most helpful." Two spots of color appear high on her cheekbones. I wonder what that's all about.

"She seemed so—oh, I don't know, a little scary when I first met her. Then again, I didn't spend a whole lot of time with her and it was under fucked-up circumstances," I say.

"Oh, she's a bulldog when she goes after something. I'd hate to be a guy and piss her off. She'd pinch the nuts off anyone."

"Yeah, that's the perfect description of her."

Helen scoops up the last of her food, and after she swallows it says, "But you know something? If she's on your side, she totally has your back. Like Harrison."

"How many other people work there?"

"Well, there's Emily, Misha, of course, then Leland, and they have other contacts that don't work full-time but are on contract. I guess they're like consultants or something."

"I see."

"You've never been to the office?"

"Nope."

"Hmm. I do all the billing. Man, do they ever charge a lot. I'm not at liberty to discuss it, though. I signed an NDA."

"I imagine you did." Now that I think of it, I never got a bill from them. There are so many questions I want to ask her about Harrison, but I don't want to sound super nosy or like I'm taking advantage of a friendship. Helen is nice, and she's the first person I've met in LA who I want to be friends with. My agent, Rita, is kind and considerate, but we have a business relationship only. I prefer to keep it that way. Mixing business and friendship sometimes isn't such a good idea. Helen, even though she works for Harrison, is far enough removed that I don't consider her part of the business deal.

After dinner, she invites me to go to one of her favorite hangouts.

"I think I'm going to go home. I'm pretty tired." I haven't shared with her what happened the night before.

"Okay, that's cool. Wanna go back to my place, then?"

"No, you go on. I'll find the way back. Don't let my wimpiness cripple your night."

She tilts her head and her eyes drill mine. I get the odd feeling she's reading my mind. "You sure?"

"Yeah. I'm good."

Then her arms are squeezing me in a tight hug, and while she holds me, she says, "I hope we're good friends, Midnight, 'cuz I really like you."

"Yeah, I feel the same, Helen."

I watch her waltz down the street and I turn toward my car. I'm driving home when my phone buzzes. I don't answer because I don't have a hands-free Bluetooth. My car is old and although I need a new one, it'll have to wait until I catch up on my bills. Maybe if this movie does well, I'll land another deal and I can do it then.

When I get home, I check my phone to find it was Harrison. I'm not going to call him back. We need a little distance. Christmas is next week. He'll probably spend it with his parents and either way, I need to think this shit out between us, and so docs hc. I can't be on edge because of how he feels.

I inspect the new window, making sure it's locked and no one can jimmy it open.

It's only around nine, but I decide to turn in and read for the night. My phone rings again, but this time it's Danny.

"Midnight, am I disturbing you?"

"Not at all."

"I have bad news. Holt is threatening to put a hold on the picture. He's claiming he needs a break. He says he's depressed and can't film for the next month."

"What?"

"I know, I know. We're working with his agent, trying to get him back on set."

"Yeah, well, he's going to ruin my career."

"It won't come to that. We'll keep you busy. That's something else I wanted to talk to you about. We want you to do a screen test for another role."

It's hard to contemplate another film when I'm facing a potential train wreck with this one, not to mention I've barely had time to breathe with the schedule we've been keeping. Working six, sometimes seven days a week and twelve-hour days hasn't left much time for anything else. This weekend was the first little break I've had in ages.

"Who's the lead?" I ask.

"It's not been determined yet."

I'm stunned. I would possibly be cast before the lead male? I'm a nobody.

"The person we have in mind is great. You two would be great together. I'll send everything to your agent."

"Well, you know I'll audition. But I want to finish this one too."

"Yeah, same here. Let us handle Holt. Plan on coming in Monday anyway."

After I end the call, I contemplate our conversation about Holt. I hate to even go down this road, but what if? What if Harrison could help? There's only one way to find out.

Chapter 24

HARRISON

WHEN MY PHONE RINGS, I'M SURPRISED TO SEE IT'S MIDNIGHT. She didn't answer earlier and I assumed it was because she wasn't taking my calls.

"Hey. How are you?"

"I'm fine. Well, sort of. I went to dinner with Helen."

"Helen Reddy?" I ask, surprised.

"Yeah, that Helen. So the reason I'm calling … you're gonna love this. Danny called tonight. Holt is threatening to suspend filming. He's claiming he's depressed."

My molars are about to crack by the time she finishes telling me about this. We need to pay Holt a little visit. I'll be damned if he's going to fuck up this film for her, and that's exactly what he's trying to do.

"What's Alta doing about this?"

"Danny said they'll handle him."

"Do you know how?"

"No, but they want me to audition for another film. They're sending everything over to my agent."

"That's great." And it is. But she will finish this one. I'll make sure of it.

"Harrison, is there any way you can help? With Holt, I mean."

"Let me see what I can do. And Midnight, do you feel safe over there? I'm ... sorry for the way I acted."

"It's fine. I need to get used to being here. And the window's been fixed so I'm good."

"If you need me, you know where to find me."

I make a phone call because it doesn't sit well that asshole Ward is playing these games. I want someone watching over her place. It's early enough for Leland to get in touch with one of our agencies so they can send someone over. Once that's taken care of, I can rest easier.

The next morning is Sunday. Leland calls to set up a plan for Holt.

"His place will be locked up so there's no way we can just knock on his door," I say.

"Let's put someone outside the gates and when he leaves, we follow. As soon as he gets somewhere approachable, we can make a move."

"Why not just call again and use our human trafficking threat? I can have Rashid reactivate the website and do what we did before."

"Harrison, if he's really the whack job you say he is, he might not give a shit about that now."

"True, but why not test it?"

"What if he forces our hand? Then we're stuck with our thumbs up our asses."

Leland makes a good point. "Okay, call our guy and let's tail him. I hope to fuck he hasn't turned into Howard Hughes."

"What does that mean?"

"Don't you know who that is?"

"Of course. But I still don't know what that means."

"Howard Hughes was a recluse and never left his house."

Leland sighs. "Shit. That would be bad."

By midmorning, we have eyes on the Ward estate. Too bad it's gated. I'd like to be at his door, breaking the fucker down. Sometimes a man has to learn to be patient.

One piece of good news is no one bothered Midnight the night before. Our guy said her parking lot was dead—just the way I want it.

Unfortunately, Ward doesn't make a move all day. Monday morning, at four thirty, my phone rings. I'm told his gates have opened and he's driven to Santa Monica. Midnight did mention they were filming on location from now until they were finished.

"Do not let him out of your sight. At the end of the day, we need to run him off the road, without causing a wreck."

"I'll need help. I haven't slept all night."

"Don't worry about that. You'll be relieved by then and we'll have a plan in place. Just stay on him so we know where he parks." My instructions are clear. "Oh, and since it's so early, don't be obvious."

He laughs. "Mr. Kirkland, I'm no novice at this."

"Good. Thanks for the call."

My next call is to Leland. "Who do we know at the LAPD that owes us a favor?"

"About twenty people. Why?"

"I have an idea."

Later that day, when Holt is leaving the set, our guy and Leland pull behind him at a discreet distance. When the timing is right, exactly as we planned, an unmarked police car pulls him over into a vacant parking lot. Enter me. I get out of the police car and walk up to Holt's car.

Leaning into his window, which he's already rolled down, I grab his shirt and say, "Hello, Holt."

I have to hand it to him. He must be shocked to see me, but he hides it well. "What do you want?" he snarls.

"You know perfectly well what I want."

His car is penned in with the unmarked car blocking him from behind and my guy in the front. He can't go anywhere, which doesn't add to his rotten disposition.

I jam my face into his. "Since you don't seem to be very talk-ative, let me spell it out for you. You will finish this film. On schedule. No delays. No time off for … stress or whatever the fuck you said you needed. You have two weeks left and then you can have all the damn time you need. Do I make myself clear?" I'd like to mar that pretty little mug of his, but doing so would fuck things up for Midnight.

"You have no right to dictate what I need to do."

"On the contrary. I have every right."

He finally looks me in the eye. "Who do you think you are?"

Instead of raising my voice, I do the opposite. In a menacing tone, I say, "I'm the man who will ruin your life and will love doing it. You'll never get another role in any kind of film again. Not even a shitty one. That nice little house you live in? You can kiss it goodbye. You'll be selling it in order to pay off your debts. Don't fuck with Midnight or me. Do your job, Holt. And do it well. Two weeks. Understand?"

"You think you can push people around. I won't tolerate it."

"You will. I won't tolerate you ruining this film. Do not fuck this up. This isn't a warning, Holt. It's a fucking threat. If you value your career, I would strongly urge you to take this serious-ly." I glance at Leland, who's in the car, and nod. Then I look back at Holt, whose shirt I'm still fisting. "You might want to check your phone." I release him then.

His brows wrinkle as a puzzled expression forms on his face. He reaches for his phone and there are two texts that I can see on his notifications. When he reads them, he says, "You son of a bitch."

"Actually, my mother is a gem. Like I said, this isn't a warn-ing. I can make those go away, but it'll depend on your cooperation over the next two weeks. Don't fuck up your life, Holt." I straighten and then lightly pound my fists on his roof. I saunter back to the car where Leland waits.

The unmarked car leaves and we follow it.

"Well?" Leland asks.

"I think he'll behave. I owe Mike a huge debt."

"Yeah, you do. But don't worry. He's always fucking up." Mike is the studio exec who texted Holt. He was a little leery at first, but I told him the shit he pulled and then he was all in. I also guaranteed that he would straighten his ass out too. I hope that promise holds.

We're on the way back to the office when my phone rings. It's Weston.

"What's up, man?"

"You. Where have you dropped off to?"

"Yeah, about that. I've been really busy," I say, trying to wheedle out of an explanation of why I haven't returned any of his calls lately.

"Right. So, the reason I'm calling. You know Prescott is seeing Vivi Renard from Crestview, right?"

"Kind of. I had dinner with him the last time I was in New York and he was into her, but was pretty cryptic about it."

"Well, he is. Balls deep, I would imagine."

"No shit."

"She wants to get us all together for New Year's as a surprise for him. It's part of her Christmas gift. I'm the one she's designated as the call guy."

"Lucky you."

"So?"

"So what?"

"Be there. New Year's Eve. His place. No later than three. No fucking excuses, Harrison."

"Oh, man. I'm so swamped here and there's this client."

"I call bullshit on that. It's all you ever say anymore. You own the fucking company. You can get away for two goddamn days. Don't fuck this up for him. Or her, for that matter."

"Westie, come on."

"I'm not kidding at all. Special will be on your ass over this. It's two fucking days, man."

"Okay. I'll be there." A groan rushes out of me. Leland makes a funny face.

"I'll send you the particulars," Weston says.

"The particulars. Who the fuck talks like that?"

"Me. Shut up. Be there, 3:00 p.m. East Coast time at Scotty's, or you'll be facing an ass-kicking like no other."

"Got it."

I drop the phone in my lap.

"Looks like you're going away for New Year's," Leland says, laughing.

"Shut up." Now I sound like Weston.

"What? You don't want to hang with your friends over the holiday? What the hell, Harrison?"

I can see the guy's shoulders shaking. I cut Leland a look to let him know he needs to shut his mouth. I don't want every person who works for me to know what my social life entails. Christ.

"I wanted to stay here to make sure our little buddy didn't cause any more issues for Midnight. That's all."

"Harrison, you have several people who can hold the fort down while you're gone."

He's right, but that's only half of it. I was hoping to be around so Midnight didn't have to be alone on New Year's Eve. Now, thanks to my friends, that's been tossed out the window.

"True. I just wanted you all to have some time off too."

"Hey, when was the last time you took a day off?" he asks.

Shrugging, I say, "No idea."

"See? You need this. Besides, you'll have a great time catching up."

"Maybe."

Enough of this topic. "So, back to Holt. Stay on top of him. If he so much as steps one inch out of line, we need to hit him with more texts. I want to scare the shit out of him. In two weeks, I don't care if he goes to Tahiti for a year, but until then, he's all mine. And get someone to keep an eye on Midnight for me. I don't want anything happening over there."

Chapter 25

MIDNIGHT

MONDAY AT WORK, HOLT IS SURLY AS HELL. HE ACTS OUT HIS scenes but it's a stretch. Greg has to cut repeatedly because of it. But Tuesday, he shows up a new person. He must've taken a handful of happy pills. Damn, I want some of those. The dude is all sunshine and daisies. Even Danny comments on it.

"I don't know what happened overnight, but whatever it was, I want it to keep happening."

"Me too. And can I drink some of that fairy juice?"

Danny laughs.

We're shooting outside, and the weather has been gorgeous. Holt's on top of his game and things are back to the way they were a couple of weeks ago. It's as though we were both made for this—to work together. Why can't he always be like this?

Thursday is Christmas Eve. We're off Thursday and Friday for the holidays. Holt is fine the remainder of the week. I worry how he'll be when we resume after Christmas. These are the most crucial, poignant scenes. Whatever he does for Christmas, I hope it involves dipping into his happy juice.

Harrison calls on Wednesday night and says he's on a plane, flying to Virginia. I'm a bit disappointed, but I expected as much. His parents seem like great people and he should spend time with them. It would be nice to have that in my life. I haven't talked to him since our disagreement, so I was surprised he even called. We don't linger on the phone, and the truth is I miss him, so it makes it a little awkward.

"Have a great time. Merry Christmas, Harrison."

"You too, Midnight. I'll call when I get back."

Guess it'll be Netflix and me.

But I'm happy when Helen calls.

"Hiya, movie star. Whatcha doin' tomorrow?"

"Ha. Funny. I have zero plans, other than a date with my TV."

"Good. Let's cook. My place or yours?"

"Yours," I say.

We plan our dinner and I run out to the store to get what's needed. I take the time to stuff my hair under a baseball cap and throw on some sunglasses. You never know when someone with a camera will be around.

Helen and I decide turkey's out and opt for something a bit more glamorous. I'm taking a stab at beef Wellington, which I've never done before. I'm praying I don't annihilate it. She's doing some fancy French potato dish and a salad, plus cheese-cake for dessert. Turns out Helen loves to cook.

Christmas Eve, I sleep in and it's wonderful. When I'm getting out of the shower and toweling off, my phone rings. I see it's Harrison Facetiming me.

"Uh, hi."

"Merry Christmas. Did you just get out of the shower?"

"Yeah, my towel must've clued you in."

He flashes a sexy grin and my heart thumps. I hope the towel doesn't fall off.

"Uh, it might have. I wanted to call before we left."

"Left? Where are you going?"

"To Aunt Edith's. We're eating lunch with her at her retire-ment village."

"Hmm. Sounds like fun."

"Yeah. She has it bad for Ralph, the sexy magician. He likes to pull quarters out of the ladies' bras, or so Mom says. They like that better than the traditional bunny out of a hat."

"Is that so?"

"Uh-huh. And he also serenades everyone. Evidently, he's rather handy with his maracas too. Tosses them around, but he didn't catch one once and it hit Aunt Edith's friend Hattie in the back of the head. It knocked her wig off kilter and her false teeth popped out so they've asked him to stop juggling."

"You're joking." I'm dying.

"No, it's a true story." He's laughing now. "Apparently Hattie's teeth landed in her chicken noodle soup and she had to spoon around for them. Luckily, she found them with all the teeth intact."

"Oh my God. What else does Ralph do?"

"Mom says he's a master bingo player. He can play ten cards at once."

"I need to meet this Ralph. Sounds like a real charmer. Does he snore?"

"Now that's a question for Aunt Edith. I believe he's a two-timer though."

"Did Aunt Edith catch him cheating on her?"

"Oh, yeah. She called him out in front of the whole dining room. He had to do the walk of shame carrying his plate of roast beef and mashed potatoes. Hazel was there, the woman he was two-timing with, and she was none too happy about it. He's straightened up since then. You can't pull one over on Aunt Edith."

The thought of Ralph and Aunt Edith in a shouting match really gets me laughing. "That place sounds like a soap opera. Anything else happening at the village?"

"Evidently one of the men gave a couple of the ladies gonorrhea. It started a small riot."

"Jeez. Is this place some sort of hedonistic, elderly, sexcapade village?"

"That's what I asked Mom. I'm going to give Aunt Edith a box of condoms for Christmas."

After I stop laughing, I ask, "What's after lunch?"

"Just the usual. Dinner reservations and then some party. In the morning, we'll have our traditional Christmas breakfast, after which we'll open presents."

My voice takes on a dreamy quality. "Sounds perfect." I'm so envious of what he has. I wonder if he knows how lucky he is.

"What about you?"

"I'm cooking with Helen tonight. We're doing up a fancy meal. I wasn't aware how fond of cooking she is."

"Hmm, neither was I. What are you cooking?"

When I tell him, his eyes widen. "Wow, I'm impressed. Can't wait to hear about it."

"I'm sure your day will be awesome."

"And what about Christmas?"

"No plans. Probably watch Netflix or something."

"I'm sorry."

I look closely and notice his knitted brows.

"Why? Because you still don't like my jaded past?" I say it as a joke, but now that it's out, the truth hits him hard.

He brushes a hand over his face, top to bottom, then says, "I ... I'm just sorry, Midnight."

"Me too, Harrison. Look, I have to go. Have a Merry Christmas." I hit the red button before I do something stupid like cry. Life's a bowl of fucking cherries, isn't it?

I dress and hunt down my beef Wellington recipe to get my mind off this shit. This better be good because it's the most diffi-cult thing I've ever tried to cook. I prep the mushroom layer and prepare everything else. Then I sear the beef, let it rest, then layer everything on it and stick it in the refrigerator. Now all I have to do is the last part, which is wrap the whole thing in puff pastry. I'll do that at Helen's.

I pack everything up and set out for her place.

When I arrive, her apartment smells delish.

I breathe in the aromas. "Oh gosh, this is gonna get real, and soon. It's like a restaurant in here."

We hug and she says, "Yeah, it's good, right? How about a glass of wine?"

"Sounds great."

As we drink, I take a peek at her made from scratch cheesecake that looks divine. "How did you know how to make this?"

She grins and says, "It's my specialty. Check these out." She opens the oven door to reveal a dish of bubbly potatoes that make me drool.

"Oh, God, I'm starving."

"Well, get that beef prepped so we can eat."

I do the final assembly, pop it into the oven, and we wait.

Dinner turns out scrumptious. Our bellies are about to burst and we both swear we can't eat another bite. Afterward, we watch *National Lampoon's Christmas Vacation* and get drunk together. We don't have any eggnog to drink, but we make up for it in wine. I end up spending the night in the extra bedroom. It beats going home to my empty apartment. It would've been nice if Harrison had been here. But that's not gonna happen.

Sleep eludes me for more than one reason. You'd think after all this time, I'd be used to spending holidays alone. I'm not. There's a huge piece of my heart that stopped beating when I was nineteen and no matter what I do, I'll never be okay with holidays. They fucking suck. I can't wait to go back to work, even if Holt is pouting again. It beats this any day of the week.

Chapter 26

HARRISON

CHRISTMAS MORNING, MOM HUSTLES AROUND THE KITCHEN, humming carols and cooking her usual gigantic breakfast of bacon, eggs, some fancy casserole, and biscuits—and that doesn't include the cinnamon coffee cake she already made. My mouth waters as I sit at the counter, sipping coffee, watching her. I'd offer to help, but it's pointless. She'd only take her spatula and aim it at me, and tell me to sit my rear end down.

"Mom, can I have a piece of that coffee cake?"

"That's what it's there for."

"I need a little starter, you know."

She chuckles. She knows how my little starters are usually huge chunks of the thing. I slice off an enormous wedge as Dad walks in. The kitchen smells so good. It's one of the things I love best about Christmas.

"Son, when are you leaving?" Dad asks.

"Early tomorrow."

His eyes light up. I had mentioned something about going home tonight, but then I figured what's the point in that? Even though I'm itching to get back to LA, back to Midnight, I would get home late so why not leave in the morning?

"Great. We can watch some football together."

"Yeah."

Mom smiles. She's already put the turkey in the oven so I know she's happy she doesn't have to rush our Christmas meal.

When we're done with breakfast, I offer to clean up, but Mom tries to argue. I insist and she finally takes a seat. Dad builds a fire and when I'm done, I run upstairs to fetch their gifts.

"You ready?" I ask.

"Yeah. But I wanted to give you yours first," Mom says.

"Nope. I'm first."

I hand them each a bag. Inside are a couple of hats. They give me a strange look and I chuckle. The next bag holds a small travel portfolio where they can keep credit cards and a passport. They still aren't connecting the dots. The next bags are large because they contain comfortable shoes for walking.

"These are nice, Harrison," Mom says. Dad looks on curiously.

The final bag will explain it all. It's their itinerary. They will be going on a two-month trip to the Far East, starting with Japan, then Vietnam, on to Thailand, Malaysia, Tahiti, Hawaii, and ending up at my place.

"I don't understand," Mom says.

Laughing, I ask, "What don't you understand?"

"What does it mean?"

"Mom, this means you and Dad will be going on a two-month second honeymoon. You'll be traveling to some very exclusive places, complete with your own personal tour guide, and staying at some very swanky resorts."

The circle her mouth forms is so huge I might be able to stick a golf ball in it. I laugh.

"Harrison, you can't afford this," Mom says.

"Of course I can afford this, or I wouldn't be doing it."

"But ... but ... two months?" she asks.

"Yes, two months. You've never done anything like this and you deserve it. We can tweak this if you want. On that paper is the travel agent's name. All you have to do is give her a call. She'll take good care of you."

"Two months?" Dad asks.

"Why not?"

"Who will water the plants?" Mom wants to know.

"Your housekeeper. Just have her come in once a week and check on things. Stop your mail and paper. All your utilities, forward to me, and I'll handle them until you get back. It's that simple."

"We can't possibly do that."

Dad grabs Mom and says, "Yes, we can. It's going to be amazing. I was trying to come up with an idea, but this ... this is better than Europe for two weeks any day of the year. Start packing, Laura, we're going to Asia."

Mom's hands fly to her face. "Oh, my, God. I can't believe this." Then she jumps out of her seat and throws her arms around me. "Thank you, thank you."

"It's not even close to what you and Dad deserve."

She steps back and asks, "But how can you afford this?"

It's time for them to know the truth. Inhaling, I say, "Mom, Dad, you know that company I work for?"

"Yeah." They both chime in.

"I own it. It's my company."

Mom and Dad both fish mouth.

"The Solution is yours? I don't understand. Why didn't you tell us, son?" Dad asks, his frown and voice letting me know of his hurt and disappointment.

"It sort of just happened and when the business took off, I didn't want you worrying about how hard I was working."

"So that's why you never come home," Mom says.

"Yeah, that's why. Work is sometimes a bit overwhelming."

"Well, at least now we know it's that and not because you don't like us anymore."

Dad grabs Mom's hand and says, "Honey, don't you think Harrison should open his gifts now?"

"I almost forgot. Can you get them, please?"

Dad hands me a pile of boxes, which I'm sure are clothes. I unwrap a pair of jeans, some pants, a shirt, sweaters, and some socks. None of them are my style so I'll be donating them to the homeless shelter, but my parents don't have to know that.

"Thanks, Mom, Dad."

"I'm almost sure they're your size, but I'm not sure if they're the brands you prefer."

Most of my clothes are tailor-made, and she'd have a heart attack if she saw the price of my jeans. I'm not saying that what they bought me is cheap; they're just not my style. But I love them all the same for the thought behind it.

"You guys are the greatest, you know?"

"So are you."

Dad and I settle in for some football and dozing, a perfectly great way to spend Christmas Day. Except for one thing. I wish Midnight were here spending it with me. Holidays have taken on a hollow feeling lately.

The next morning, I leave for the airport, and it's a relief to finally tell my parents the company owns its own plane. They never knew. I have no idea how I pulled that one off, but I did.

The next few days crawl by. Midnight is back at work and I'm holding my breath on what that asshole Holt is going to do. I can't believe I have to leave town again for a couple of days, but if I don't go, the guys will kill me.

Wednesday evening gets here and I'm getting ready to fly to New York. This better be worth it. If things go wrong while I'm gone, I don't know what I'll do. Being almost three thousand miles away isn't exactly comforting.

"Have a great time," Leland says. "I have you booked at The Plaza. You'll need the few hours' sleep."

"Yeah. That and I can't exactly barge into Prescott's place.

That would ruin the surprise. You know what to do if anything happens. And don't forget to keep an eye out on Midnight."

"Don't worry. I've got it handled."

"Peace out, man."

Grabbing my bag, I'm out the door. But my gut isn't right with leaving. Something nags at me during the flight, but I'm sure it's just that I don't want to leave again. I should've listened to my intuition, stopped the plane, and driven straight to Midnight's.

Chapter 27

MIDNIGHT

CHRISTMAS FELL ON A FRIDAY SO GREG WANTS US IN ON Saturday. I don't mind and it's my fault the schedule got pushed back to begin with. Besides, it gets my mind off the depressing holiday. We are so close to finishing. Only a couple more scenes and we'll be through. Then maybe I'll celebrate. I'm not sure how, because it's still unclear to me if this film will be a success or a flop. Its success will have an impact on what kind of future roles I'll be offered.

Holt comes in looking hungover as hell. He reeks of alcohol. Greg pulls him aside and has a few words with him. Then he comes over to me.

"I've decided to start the final scene today. The set is the same, only your lines will change."

"Today? But I haven't studied my lines." I reel in astonishment.

He lightly taps my arm. "Yeah, well, Holt is a little under the weather as you probably noticed. We need to do the final bit where he doesn't have to say much, other than lie there after he's been shot. It's all on you, baby. I'm sorry."

He hands me my sides so I can get to work. I'm familiar

with the lines, but this may not go as well as I want. Better start studying.

Once everything is in position, they call for Holt and me. He's been identified as one of the bank robbers and is wanted by the police. We've driven to the station and I'm begging him not to turn himself in. He gets out of the car and two police officers recognize him. They call out and tell him to put his hands in the air. I hear and run out. He yells, "Get back in the car, Christine." But I don't listen. He doesn't want me to get hurt, so he's not paying attention to the officers. I am, though. They repeatedly tell him to get on the ground, but he won't because he's still telling me to get in the car. Then I scream as he reaches inside his jacket. But this time, tears gush down my face. I shout, "Listen to the cops, Finn. Do as they say."

"I have a letter for Sammie and you." By this time, the cops are swarming. They have no idea what he's reaching for. All they know is he's wanted for armed robbery and murder. Suddenly, shots ring out. Holt's body jolts with the impact, then hits the ground. We're shrouded in silence for a couple of moments. Then I scream. And scream. My shock dissolves as I run to him, where he lies, his life bleeding away. Glazed eyes meet mine, only no life remains in them. I break down on top of him, holding him. My body trembles as violent sobs take over, and the best thing about this particular scene is with him supposedly dead, he can't hug me back.

"Cut."

Leaning back on my knees, I look down at myself and say, "I hope that was good because I'm a fucking mess with all that fake blood."

Holt groans and says, "Your fucking screaming killed my head."

"Maybe you shouldn't drink so much when you know you have to be at work at 5:00 a.m."

"Fuck you."

"Fuck you back."

"That's all I've been trying to do, Midnight."

The asshole actually smirks at me, which I find funny. I knock his shoulder before getting to my feet and striding away. Danny taps my arm and says, "That was perfect."

"Yeah?"

"Yeah."

I move over to Greg for confirmation. "We don't need another take on that?"

"Fuck no. It was great."

He runs over to check out the replay on it. About thirty minutes later he's back telling me we're good.

Holt hasn't been allowed to get up yet, because we have one more scene to shoot. It's me pulling the letter out of his jacket, the one the police thought was a gun. Then I go ballistic on the cops. That's where the scene ends.

The final scene in the movie is when I read the letter from him. We're filming that today too. Christine's heart is torn to pieces when she finds that her husband saved all his money for them to have a clean getaway. But first we have to film them taking Holt's body away in the ambulance.

I have to admit, when the cops try to drag me off his body, I'm pretty damn convincing as I yell at them.

"He didn't have a gun! He came here to turn himself in! You murdered my husband! You shot a defenseless man!" Tears still gush down my cheeks.

"He was reaching for a weapon," one argues.

"He was reaching for this!" And I pull out the letter and shake it in front of him. It has some of the fake blood on it. "How is this possibly a weapon?"

My face feels swollen from my tears. I hope it looks that way as well, because now I have a headache too.

A female cop helps me up as the ambulance arrives. I stand and watch as they put Holt's body in one of those bags. As an actor, I'm not sure I could stand that. It's completely gruesome to me and let's not mention the claustrophobia. I have to hand it to Holt. He doesn't flinch. Once the ambulance doors close, the scene cuts.

Greg and Danny seem almost giddy.

"Midnight, we want you to try for the final. Do you think you can do it? If not, that's fine. The thing is, your face is perfect. It's a fucked-up mess," Greg says.

Ordinarily, I might be insulted, but he's right. I check the sides and there's nothing there, other than what's in the letter. All I have to do is check it out and act like I'm reading it. They'll do a voiceover with Holt and me actually reading it later in the studio.

"Yeah, since I don't really have any lines, I don't see why not."

"That's right," Danny says. "All of that will be done in the studio. The thing is, we need you to look utterly grief stricken. Remember, the letter tells you of his rock bottom depression, how he never thought he could manage without the money, but how he saved the small nest egg for you. So you have to look shocked when you get to that part."

"Got it."

It takes what seems like an eternity to clear everything away from the car, so it's just me sitting in it for the final scene. All I do is pull the letter out, stare at the bloodstained envelope for a few minutes, and then with trembling hands, pull the pages out.

I open them carefully, as though they mean the world to me, and slowly read them to myself, keeping in mind what it'll sound like when the voiceover happens on film. Tears stream down my cheeks, which is getting old because all this crying has made me borderline migraine-ish, but I power through. The camera behind me zooms in over my shoulder to his written words, *I will always love you and be with you forever, if not in this world, then the next. Your Finn.*

The thought of losing a loved one nails me and I sob. Literally lose it. I hear Greg yell *cut* and a loud commotion behind me. Danny comes up to the car, but I can't move.

"Hey, Midnight, you okay?" he asks.

I hold my hand in the air, asking for a moment. I need to pull my shit together or they'll all think I've jumped into the crazy pool.

I snort back the tears and finally say, "Yeah. Yeah. Damn, I got into character on that one."

Danny chuckles. "You got into character in every scene. It was phenomenal. And I mean that."

I stand but my legs wobble. He doesn't notice because of the happy cloud he's on.

"That's it for the day. You can go change out of that mess you're wearing."

I'd actually forgotten, given my headspace. "Good. Great. So, what happens next?"

"We wrap up Holt's scene, and when he's finished, the two of you can record the letter reading in the studio. And then we go into postproduction. But after Wednesday, you're done filming *Turned*."

"That sounds really weird."

"It should feel good. But don't get too cozy with the idea. Now that you have a break in your schedule, your agent can set up that audition for the screenplay I told you about. Rita has everything on it. It was only a matter of freeing up the time for you to do it."

"Great. Thanks, Danny. For taking a chance on me."

The letter reading doesn't go as well as I'd hoped. Even though we're just standing in front of a mic with headsets on, the emotions aren't there. It's set up where I begin the letter and then Holt takes over. My tone is appropriate, serious with as many sad elements as possible, but I end up having to do several takes because I stumble. I find this harder to do than acting on set. I have greater admiration for the people who do animation. I can't imagine how difficult that would be.

Reading is hard. The damn letter is only two pages. Finn tells Christine how hard he tried over the last couple of years, but the darkness of depression got a hold of him and dragged him into a hole. He didn't have the energy to pull himself out. Even though he tried, he saw how our lives would be better without him. He was afraid Sammie would grow up in a house with her mom and dad always arguing and that was the last thing he wanted. The money seemed a good way out. He figured he would give us half and we could make a new start somewhere. His intention was to leave us be, so we could be happy.

"You may think I left you without a dime, but that's not true. I had a plan if things went south. I took out a life insurance policy six months ago. You and Sammie will be fine. Take the money and leave this town. Find somewhere nice, where she can grow up and have a good home. You know, a place where she'll be happy and safe. Don't wait, Christine. Do it now. Tomorrow at the latest."

The letter ends with Finn telling Christine he'll love her forever and beyond.

After we finish, I set the headset on the podium and smile at Holt. Then I walk out of the soundproof room we're in. I want to shout at the top of my lungs, scream for joy. But there are only a couple of people here. It's totally anticlimactic. And so will tonight be. Unless I call Helen.

On the way to my car I shoot her a text.

Guess who wrapped today?

She hits me back with **Minnie Mouse?**

How did you guess? I add a couple of laughing emojis.

So where are we celebrating tonight?

You pick.

Cool. Be at my place at seven.

I'm pretty sure I'll be spending the night there. Tomorrow is

New Year's Eve. I wonder if she's thought about that. She may have to work. Maybe we should postpone our celebration for a night. But when I think about it, no way will we find a place for dinner without a reservation with such short notice. Best we stick to our plan for tonight.

At seven, I roll into her parking lot. She's all dressed up, and I'm in jeans.

"What the hell, Helen?"

"You said celebration, so I figured …"

"But damn. You look like you're going to a premiere."

"Yeah, about that. Can I get tickets to yours?"

"Uh, I don't know. I'm not even sure how that works."

She hooks her arm through mine because she says our Uber is here, and we're out the door. On the way to the car, she says, "You'll figure it out. You're a big star now. I know *Turned* is going to be the film of the year. You watch."

"I don't know why you're saying that, but if it is, I'm taking us on a trip somewhere."

"Where?" Her eyes turn into circles reminding me of the moon. Helen had it rough growing up, though I don't know the entire story. That's the thing I adore about her. She's not nosy and doesn't dig at all. But I recognize things in her, the way her voice changes, the way her eyes dart around, and the way she pretends not to care about things when she does. She's never traveled, like me. So who else would I want to take on a trip?

"I don't know. Maybe Hawaii?" I say.

"What about Cabo? I'd like that too."

"Why not both?"

She sucks in so much air, I'm afraid there won't be any left for me.

"Really? You'd take me somewhere like that?"

"Yeah. What fun is there in going on a trip like that alone?"

"Well, none, I suppose."

"So, that's why you're coming with me. Makes total sense, right?" I ask.

"Yeah, yeah, it does."

We bump fists as we get in the car. Helen made reservations at a swanky restaurant. After, we hit one of her favorite clubs. I'm super leery because the last time I was in a club, it didn't turn out so great.

"You know how uncomfortable I am with this, right?"

She slants a look at me. "I do. But you have to get over that. Here's how it goes. You watch the bartender like a hawk when he makes your drink. Never take your eyes off it. Ever. If you set that sucker down, do not drink from it again. When you hold it, keep it in front of you so no one can slip something in it. If we dance, you don't drink out of that drink again. We get new ones. Sometimes I hold my drink with one hand and cover it with the other."

"You're smarter than I am."

"No, I have more street smarts."

"You've been date-raped before."

She squirms, looks away, then back at me. After one curt nod, she says, "Just remember what I told you."

We dance and have a great time. I watch my alcohol consumption, because I'm extra cautious with my drinks. Little by little I find I'm enjoying myself. On the way back to Helen's, she wants to know what's going on with Harrison.

"I don't know. Haven't talked to him in a few days."

"You should call him."

"That's not going to happen anytime soon."

"He likes you. "

"That's nice."

"Really likes you."

"And how would you know?"

"I just do. I can tell," she says.

"Hmmph." If he liked me, then he'd call me, he wouldn't be freaked out about my past, and I wouldn't be alone on Christmas and New Year's. "He doesn't like me. Besides, that sounds so juvenile."

"He went to New York. I overheard him talking. Something about his friends there. Men are juvenile anyway. Haven't you figured that out yet?"

"I haven't figured out a lot of stuff yet."

"I've noticed. But don't worry. It'll happen."

I'm too tired to argue. I only want to put my head on a pillow and dream about the sexy Harrison and what he used to do to my body.

The Uber driver drops us off and I climb into my car and drive home. I didn't drink enough to inebriate a flea. When I get home, I'm unlocking my door when I hear footsteps behind me.

I pull my pepper spray out, ready to shower whoever it is coming behind me.

"Hey, stranger."

"Jesus, Holt, you're not supposed to be here." He holds his hands in the air as I aim my pepper spray at him.

"Whoa, there. I'm not here to cause you any trouble. I'm sober, I swear. I just stopped by to say I'm glad we wrapped today, and also to say thank you."

"Thank me? At, what, two in the morning? Are you crazy?" What the hell is wrong with him?

"Yeah, sorry about the time, but I wanted to personally thank you for being so professional. You were really great, Midnight. Thanks for everything. And sorry for being such an ass to you. I got totally carried away." He turns and jogs away. Just like that, he's gone.

That was so strange, but I don't stand there and analyze it. I scurry inside and deadbolt my door. I still don't trust the lunatic. I decide to sleep with my pepper spray next to me. Turns out I was worried about nothing.

Chapter 28

MIDNIGHT

NEW YEAR'S EVE. ONE MORE YEAR SPENT ALONE. HELEN AND I decide to forego all the club stuff and hit the movies instead. Popcorn and gummy bears are my dinner. Afterward we get pizza for dessert. Then she ends up spending the night at my place. My terrace is perfect for viewing the fireworks display that the city puts on. It's magnificent. We watch it after the ball drops, then hit the hay.

In the morning, I make pancakes.

"I love pancakes. I remember my mom making pancakes when I was a little kid. That was before she kicked my dad out and things got crazy," Helen says.

"I never knew who my dad was."

"Lucky you. I wish I'd never known mine. He beat the shit out of me for shits and giggles."

I almost drop the spatula. She never talks about her parents. I run to her side and hug her. "I'm sorry. I can totally relate."

"Yeah, I could tell. We're alike, you and me. Same shit, different house."

"It sucks, doesn't it?"

I go back to the pancakes. Then Helen shocks me for the second time that day.

"Were you raped too?" she asks.

My lips press together for a second. "Yeah. When I was in foster care. Tell me your asshole dad didn't do that to you."

"No, not him, but his friends did. He let them. Said I deserved it."

"Fucker." My gut twists.

The sparkle leaves her blue eyes. "That's when I ran. After I cut one of them."

"What?"

She swipes her cheek, like there's a tear there, only there isn't. "It was during one of those rape sessions. At times I would vanish. Dive deep inside myself and disappear. But not that day. I got his pocketknife when he didn't notice. And while he held me down, I worked my hand between us. Stupid fuck thought I was getting into it. Until that knife ripped his balls open."

I gawk at her. "Holy shit."

In a dead calm voice, she says, "He was screaming up a bloody storm. I threw on my clothes as Dad broke down the door. The knife was still in my hand and I told him if he touched me, he'd get it too. I reached for the phone to dial 911."

"No shit."

"Dad stopped me. Said he and his buddy would pay me to keep my mouth shut."

"Why'd you do it?"

She shrugs. "I guess I was afraid no one would believe me. It was stupid, but I knew if the police showed up, I'd end up in foster care. I didn't want that."

"It was the smartest thing you ever did. Trust me."

"Right. It's brutal. I've had friends there."

"So, did you get the money?" I ask.

Her rueful smile is answer enough. But she goes on to say, "Yeah, but it wasn't enough to pay for a year's rent. I did okay though. I got a job and managed. Got my high school education, then was trained on computers. Made enough money to eke by. I wasn't starving, you know. Anything was better than life with Daddy."

I've made enough pancakes to feed the entire building. I stack them up between us and sit across from her after pouring each of us another cup of coffee.

When I get settled, napkin on lap, she asks, "So, what's your story? You don't have to tell me if you don't want to."

"No. It's fine. We've been around each other enough. It's pretty much the same, except I wish I'd had that damn pocketknife."

"I've never been one to hurt others, but that was the sweetest feeling."

"I can only imagine. Mine was the foster dad. Like I said, you did the right thing. My experience pretty much sucked."

"No shit. A fucking nightmare."

It's more like a night terror. As I stare at the pancakes, my appetite flies away. "He would beat the shit out of me. Raped me too. But I ran away and they never found me. I made sure of that. When I turned eighteen I reported him. Ratted him out but didn't leave my name or any contact information. By then my name was changed anyway."

Helen eats, and I pick at my food. I can barely swallow. All I can think about is that bastard who stole my innocence. Even my mother, who wasn't the greatest mom in the world, didn't do what he did to me.

"And your mom?" It's like she read my mind.

That brings a smile for a moment, but then it flies away too. "Ha. She was a stripper. But she got messed up with drugs. It's how I ended up in foster care." I shudder with the memory. "I wouldn't go to school and I guess the teacher finally turned me in. They showed up at my house one day, and Mom was totally strung out. She could barely talk. I didn't want to leave her like that, but those awful people made me. I was twelve. They dragged me out of her arms as she cried. She died two years later. I wanted to kill them for taking me from her. I was sure she would still be alive if they hadn't. She made bad choices, but you know in all the shit she did and ended up in, I was never really scared in her care. She'd bring men home and I could hear them in her room, but they were never mean or bad to me. She'd get in arguments with them, but they'd always leave me alone. She just couldn't stop using. I'll never, ever try drugs."

"It's how I ended up at my dad's. I stole Mom's weed. She beat the shit out of me and dragged my ass to Dad's."

I reach across the table for Helen's hand. "Aren't we two sad saps?"

"Not anymore."

She laughs and makes a muscle with her arm. "We're phoenixes. We have risen above the crap."

"Yeah, we have."

After breakfast, I drive Helen home. We agree to hang out later today, possibly taking a trip to Venice Beach to people watch.

When I get back, my phone rings. It's Harrison. Always the gentleman, I'm sure he wants to wish me a Happy New Year.

"Happy New Year, Harrison."

"Ughhh."

"You don't sound very chipper this morning."

"I'm blaming it on Weston and Prescott. They made me do it."

"Sure, they did. You're a grown man so you couldn't say no. Is that it?"

A long groan hits my ear.

"I think somebody needs to exhibit a little more self-control."

"I think you need to be here with me."

Seriously? "Hmm."

"Midnight, we need to talk."

"I thought we did. I can't change my past. What's done is done. I don't have a magic time machine to go back for a redo, Harrison."

Another groan comes out of him and dammit, it reminds me of the sound he makes when he comes.

"I know. I still want to talk to you about us. But in person. After I get back. Can we do that?"

"I suppose. When are you coming home?"

"Tomorrow. Vivi has breakfast planned and then I'm flying out late morning. I'll probably take off around noon or one. That'll put me home around eight or nine."

"Okay. Let's just plan on Sunday, then."

"Until Sunday."

New Year's Day is pretty boring. Helen and I laugh about it, as we watch all the couples jog, skateboard, and bike by.

"Aren't we the lucky ones?" she asks.

"Maybe. Better to be single and happy than in a sucky relationship."

"But I want to be in a *good* relationship." She wears a droopy frown.

"You'll find the perfect one someday. I'm surprised you haven't already." She's beautiful, even when she wore her Harley Quinn pigtails, which she rarely does these days. Her clothes still border on the quirky side—striped leggings and polka-dotted skirts—but she pulls it off madly. "One day your she or he knight in shining armor will sweep you off your feet."

"You think?" she asks as she blows a bubble.

"Yeah, I do." I pop a gummy bear in my mouth.

Saturday morning, I check my mail. I forgot to do it the last few days. I also need to check my email. My agent has sent over some enticing offers that we'd talked about, so I'm eager to check them out. We'd already discussed my audition that Danny wanted me to do. If the other offers are better, I can hedge them against what Alta's contract is.

As I scan the mail, an odd letter stands out. My address is handwritten, scribbled almost, but when I notice the postage mark, it's from Las Vegas. I don't know anyone there, but I open the envelope anyway. That's a mistake I'll regret for a very long time.

Chapter 29

HARRISON

THE SAYING *THERE'S NO PLACE LIKE HOME* IS THE DAMN TRUTH. When I walk inside my house, I instantly relax. It's after ten. We didn't leave Prescott's until late morning, and then the helicopter was late arriving because of a mix-up. We finally got to Westchester County Airport, but weather caused delays for planes taking off. Fog set in overnight so the earlier flights had to be pushed back.

I crash on the bed and the streaming sun wakes me in the morning. I was so tired, I forgot to close the damn blinds last night. It's still early, only seven, so I go for a run on the beach. After my shower and a quick breakfast, I take a chance and call Midnight. She doesn't answer so I figure she's still asleep.

When I don't hear from her by ten, I call again. And again. We left things on a positive note, so I know she's expecting my call. Alarm bells go off. It's noon now, so I take off for her place. Her car is gone and when I look in her windows, everything seems fine.

The only person I know to call is Helen. She may know something.

"Harrison? What's up?"

"Have you talked to Midnight today?"

"Not today. She seemed fine yesterday though. Why?"

"I was supposed to see her today and she's not here. She won't answer her phone either."

"Hmm. That's weird. She did mention that Holt what's-his-name came by her place the other night, but was super nice. She was a little freaked by it. Do you think he might've done something?"

"I don't know, but I'm about to find out. If you hear from her, will you call me?"

"Sure thing."

I drive straight to Holt Ward's estate. The gate keeps me from entering but I press the call button. A voice comes on and asks who I am. I give my name and am told Mr. Ward isn't at home. When I ask when he'll return, they won't say.

"Tell him to call Harrison Kirkland immediately."

My next call is to Leland. He was supposed to be keeping an eye on her. We agree to meet at the office. I need access to our computer where I can begin my search.

"What the hell happened to her? Weren't you watching her?" Anger bleeds into my tone, even though I try to restrain myself.

"Yes, or rather, I hired someone to. She's been around spending time with Helen. He's been checking on her and saw her pick up the mail yesterday morning. Let me call him." Leland places the call and I'm not happy with his expression.

"What?"

"When she went to pick up the mail, he left to go get something to eat. When he returned, her car was gone."

"Why the hell didn't he call you?" My voice is raised.

"He said he figured I knew."

"But that was yesterday. And now she's gone and won't answer the phone. I need to start a search."

"What are you going to search for?"

"How the fuck do I know?"

"Maybe she went shopping and her phone died. Don't you think you're jumping to conclusions here?"

"And what if I'm not? What if I wait and something terrible has happened?"

Leland squints at me. "You've got it bad for her, don't you?"

I don't bother answering that. Instead, I call Rashid.

"Is there a way you can ping a cell phone?" I ask.

"Depends on whose phone and what you need."

I tell him the issue I'm facing.

"No problem. When we had her phone, I installed a few things and never took them off, just in case something happened later. Give me a few minutes and I'll call you back."

Leland says, "Don't be surprised if she's at the mall."

"She's not. I know it. Don't ask me how, I just do." My gut tells me something is terribly wrong.

Rashid hits us back about fifteen minutes later. "She's in Phoenix. Actually, she's in an area north of Phoenix, a town called Black Canyon City."

Why the fuck would she be there?

"Can you tell me anything else?"

"Yeah. She was at LAX so she must've flown. I'll text you the location I have and if anything changes."

"Thanks, Rashid."

"Anytime."

I drag my lower lip into my mouth as I chew on it. What the hell is up?

"Leland? Any ideas here?"

"Vacation?"

"Fuck no. We just talked and were supposed to meet today. Pull up Black Canyon City and see what it says."

"It doesn't say much. It's sort of out in the middle of nowhere."

"Get the plane ready. I'm flying to Phoenix."

"You can't just fly off to do what ... drag her back here. What if she doesn't want to come back?"

He's right. What if she left and isn't coming back? But that's ridiculous.

"Look, don't ask me why, but I know something is wrong." I place my fist over my stomach. "I feel it here. She's in trouble, Leland, and if I don't do something, this may not end well."

Leland is already pulling his phone out and notifying the pilot. He knows me too well and realizes there is no dissuading me from this.

"The plane will be ready in an hour. Do you want me to come with you?"

"Yeah, but stay with the flight crew. I have a totally bad vibe about this."

"You don't look so good."

"See you at the airport."

I hurry home and throw some things in a duffel bag, including my Glock and an extra mag and ammunition ... just in case. I hope I'm not walking into the O.K. Corral, but I need to protect myself, as well as Midnight. I hope to fuck she's okay. If anything's happened to her, I don't know what the hell I'm going to do.

Leland's changed into jeans and hiking boots.

"You're not going out there with me," I say.

"You're not going alone. I'll stay in the car, but if something happens to you, you'll need backup."

Now's not the time to argue. Pete lets us know we're cleared for takeoff. During the flight, Rashid sends us a list of several places Midnight visited. They were a hospital, a cemetery, and a neighborhood in Phoenix. I wonder if this has anything to do with her upbringing. Maybe she came here for closure and she's not in danger after all.

But then again, what if she is? All this time I've wasted because I couldn't ... wouldn't put my petty, absurd issues aside regarding her past. And who gives a shit that she even did it? She can't take it back or change it, so why can't I be the bigger man and go forward? She's not that person today. We all make mistakes in life.

As I ponder these things, I know one thing: Midnight was right about me. I'm the one who needs fixing. I need to understand, to recognize, that not everyone is perfect and that some flaws are what make each person unique ... make them more beautiful.

The trip is short and it's not too long before we land. We pick up our SUV rental and Leland books us rooms in a hotel, just in case, before we drive out to the location Rashid provided. Weaving our way through the little bit of traffic, my phone rings. Midnight.

As soon as I answer, I almost run off the fucking road. It's not what she says, but it's the way her voice shakes and the depth of her tone. I pull the car to the side so Leland can drive. I'm suddenly ice cold, even though the heat is on in the car. Why the fuck did she come out here alone?

Chapter 30
VELVET SUMMERS–TEN YEARS AGO

WHEN THEY TORE ME AWAY FROM MY MOTHER'S ARMS AS SHE begged them not to, I cried, screaming that I didn't want to leave. A deep ache developed behind my breastbone. It lodged there and wouldn't budge, no matter how hard I rubbed and massaged it. The way her watery gaze dug into my own and her thin arms reached for me haunted me for nights on end. Without me to care for her, I knew it wouldn't be long before I'd be standing in this very spot.

The sun's scorching heat beats down upon my back, though I couldn't care less about the burning rays singeing my skin. Nor does the sweat trickling down my neck bother me. All I can focus on is that my mother died alone, with no one to hold her hand, no one to brush the hair from her forehead, and it was because of people like these. The ones who pretended to care, when all they wanted was the stupid blood money.

A seed was planted the day I left her. It took root. Those roots spread deep. It didn't take much. No nourishment. Not even any attention. Just day-to-day living. That tiny seed festered and from it grew hate. Hate for the vile man who called himself my foster father.

The preacher says some dumb crap, things he probably feels obligated to say. It doesn't matter. The only people at Mom's funeral are the foster family and me. He drones on about Mom like he knew her. My mother was a hooker, a stripper, and a drug addict. She never stepped foot in any church that I am aware of. But she was my mother and did the best she could. She showed me love and cared for me the only way she knew how. I had a place to sleep, clothes to wear, food to eat, and even though none of it was great, it was a helluva lot better than what I have now. I may not have shown up for school every day, but life with her was a fucking bowl of cherries compared to this shit hole I'm currently living in.

When the preacher finishes speaking, my foster dad steers me out of the graveyard. I want to linger, to run my hands over Mom's casket one more time. This goodbye is so final, so absolute, I don't want it to be over this quickly. The vise around my heart clamps down so I turn to run back to her, to at least let her know how much I'll always love her, that she was my number one. But that bastard clasps the back of my arm in a bruising pinch, leaving me with no choice but to stumble forward.

The hate flourishes. At night, when I'm alone, I lie in bed and devise all kinds of horrific deaths for him—a mutilating car accident, death by some terrible illness, or getting pulverized by an eighteen-wheeler. But sadly, none of those happen. He's still here, alive and breathing, unlike Mom. I'd poison the fucker if I could get away with it. But life in prison doesn't fire me up much. Nor does going to juvie, which he threatens me with all the time. I'm only biding my time. Four more years of hell—one thousand three hundred and thirty-nine days—until my eighteenth birthday. Freedom. That's what it means to me.

We get in the car and drive home.

"Nothing more than she deserved," the fucker snarls. "You do drugs, you die. Simple as that. Just remember, Velvet, if I ever catch you with any of that crap, you'll regret it. Got that, miss?" I stare at the back of his greasy brown hair and want to smash his head in.

"Yes, sir." There's not a chance in this hell I'd do drugs. I'm sure he'd whip me within an inch of my life if he ever caught me, but that's not the reason. I never want to end up like Mom.

Rusty, the son, sits next to me and sneaks a glance out of the corner of his eye. He hates his own father as much as I do. He's forced to watch as I receive routine beatings, meant to be warnings so he'll stay in line. That's what the sadistic creep says anyway. I think he just likes to see me in pain. Rusty constantly mouths "I'm sorry" to me. But it's not his fault. Foster Mom should do something other than pour liquor down her throat. But I guess she's too afraid. She so scrawny, that asshole would probably beat her right along with me if she tried to intervene.

On my fifteenth birthday, I get a chocolate cake. The first cake ever. Seriously? It's so fucking stupid I almost laugh. He beats the shit out of me to the point where I can hardly stand up straight because my ribs are probably fractured, and then turns around and gives me a fucking cake. I want to grind his face in it.

Rusty offers a pitiful smile as his mom cuts us all slices. When she hands me mine, I walk it straight to the trash, knowing it'll earn me another beating.

But I'm wrong. It earns me something even worse. That night, Foster Dad slips into my room where he binds and gags me. That's when shit turns real.

After he leaves, I throw up in the wastebasket. Good thing I didn't bother with the stupid cake. Foster Mom doesn't make me go to school the next day nor does she question the blood on my sheets. I stay huddled in my room all day. When I emerge the next morning for school, the pervert's eyes roam my body and I just about puke again. Only I can't because I haven't eaten for a day. The light is slowly dying inside of me.

Rusty looks at me with questions in his eyes. I can't answer him. He probably has an idea of what happened. The muffled screams coming from the room next to his weren't the usual ones he's used to.

My sixteenth birthday is less than stellar. They left out the cake this year. Rusty gives me a card though. Poor guy. It must be beyond disgusting knowing what a sick fuck your dad is. He has difficulty looking me in the eye anymore. This place is the house of fucking horrors. It's been a year since FD, my name for Foster Daddy—only it's really Fucking Daddy, in the literal sense too—started his nighttime visits. Every day I pray he'll die, have a heart attack ... something. He doesn't. The guy is strong as hell too.

One night, dear old FD takes me shopping, supposedly, only we end up at the house of one of his friends. Turns out to be a real treat for me. I'm forced to give his friend oral while FD does the nasty to me. My hatred festers as I think of more gruesome ways for him to die. Only I'm not a killer. I wish I were.

On the way home, he says, "You've been a good girl to me lately. I should get you something special." Then he pulls off the road. His large hand clamps down on my thigh, just above the knee, and squeezes until I whimper. His fevered glare nails me as he says in a deadly tone, "If you ever breathe a word of this to anyone, I'll kill you, Velvet, I swear I will. You understand me?"

I have no reason to doubt him. And I never so much as utter a word to anyone.

Right after I turn seventeen, I talk with Rusty at school one day.

"I can't take it anymore. We need to run away, get out of there," I whisper.

"How?" he asks, his body already trembling. "He'll kill us if he catches us."

"Then let's not get caught. Besides, being dead is better than living like this."

"Where would we go?"

"I don't know. We could hide. I'll figure something out." The burn of tears threatens, but I push it back. "I can't continue like this ... being constantly raped." I grab Rusty's arm and squeeze.

He flinches and tries to pull away, only I don't let him.

"I'm so sorry."

"Sorry isn't enough, Rusty. Your dad is a criminal." My harsh words stun him. He knows what's been happening, but there's always been this silent ignorance about him.

"Then let's go to the police," he says.

"Oh, and do what? Get put into another foster home? No thanks. Once is enough for me."

I walk away, leaving Rusty alone. At least now I know there'll be no help from him. I should've done what he suggested and gone to the police then. It might've gone a lot better for me.

Five months before I turn eighteen, before I gain my coveted freedom, I realize my period's late. It's never late. My world stops. If I'm pregnant, he'll kill me if he finds out. There's no doubt he will. He'd never want *that* getting out. And it's definitely his. He's the only one who's ever touched me. Yeah, he's made me suck off his friends, but never have they done anything else. Only him. He's kept that part of me all to himself. And boyfriends? Yeah, like I ever had an opportunity for that.

I have to escape. He takes us to school every morning, and

Foster Mom picks us up every afternoon. We're never allowed to have any friends over or go anywhere after school. He basically cuts us off from everything. My only option is when he drops us off at school. I'll go inside, hang out, and then slip out another door, before they're locked down for the day. I'll lie and tell him I have to be at school early because I'm on some dumbass committee. Rusty won't know, but he won't say anything either. This has to work. I'll stuff some clothes and other things I'll need in my backpack, along with all the money I've squirreled away, which isn't much.

Then I'll find somewhere to hide. I've overheard kids at school talking about a place where homeless people live. Maybe I'll make it there and get lost in the crowd. If I can manage it until I turn eighteen, I'll be free then. After that, he can't touch me.

It takes me about a week to build up the courage, but I go for it. I can't wait any longer than that because he keeps track of my periods and I've lied about it. Turns out, it's easier to break away than I thought. When I get to school, I hang out in the stairwell, and wait. Then, when kids are streaming in, I hit the street. FD is long gone, at work I imagine, and I am in the wind. My first stop is a Walmart close to school, where I buy hair bleach, a pregnancy test, and a baseball cap. Then I hit the restroom at a city park and do my worst.

When I walk out, I have short blond hair and know for sure I'm pregnant. Next, I find the closest Goodwill. I beg them to exchange all my clothes for some different ones.

"We're not supposed to do that," the young man says.

"Please. I, uh, I really need to. Badly." I blink a few times, then add, "Besides, I'll pick out cheaper-looking ones."

"Okay, but don't tell anyone I let you."

"No worries on that."

I scrounge through the store until I find something that looks completely unlike me. I also trade in my backpack for a different color one. Then I'm off and running again.

Four months. That's all I need are four months. One hundred and twenty days. But now I need a job. After checking out a couple of cheap motels, I get up the courage to go in and apply to one. I've heard FD complain about how they hire illegals, so maybe they'll hire me, seeing as I don't have any ID.

When I go in, I ask to fill out an application.

"Here you go. What position are you interested in?"

Not knowing what else to say, I quickly blurt out, "Um, maid service?"

"Okay."

I sit and do my best lying, making up the name Millie Drake. I pulled that one out of my ass.

When I hand in my application, a man comes out and calls me back.

"Do you have any ID?"

"No, sir." I look him square in the eye.

"Hmm."

Then I quickly add, "I don't drive."

He frowns. "What about a Social Security number?"

Fuck me.

"No, my mom died and never told me if I had one of those."

"Were you born here?"

"Oh, yes, sir. In Phoenix."

"Hmm." He eyes me for a second. "Would you take cash for payment?"

Hell, yeah. "Uh, I guess."

"We can only pay minimum wage."

"That's fine."

This is way too easy. He starts rambling on about not being late and working hard, blah, blah, blah. If he had any idea of the situation I've been living in—hard work will be a breeze in comparison.

"I'm not afraid of hard work, sir. I'll be here bright and early. Will I need to get a uniform or something?"

"No, we'll give you one in the morning."

This may be perfect. Maybe I can even shower in one of the rooms I'll be cleaning.

That night, I find a truck stop off the interstate—I'll spend the night in the bathroom. I'm lucky until about four in the morning when I get kicked out by an employee.

"Please. I'm not looking for drugs and I'm not a hooker or anything. I just need a place to sleep."

She narrows her eyes and says, "Get out. We don't allow loitering or bums here."

"I only want to stay a couple of hours or until it gets light."

"Look, if you don't get out, I'll call the cops."

That gets me sprinting for the door with my heart about to beat me to it. The last thing I need are the cops checking into my identity.

I sneak into the woods behind the place and hide until the sun comes up. Then I walk to work. The incident scared me something terrible, and hiding in the woods was just as bad, but I didn't know where else to go.

The next night, I sleep in the motel. I end up staying there every night. I find an empty room each day, and pretend I'm leaving work. I have a master key, so once I've gotten some food, I come back after dark, and slip inside. That works great until one night while I'm there, someone checks in. It freaks the hell out of me and I beg them not to go to the front desk, but they do anyway.

In the morning, I have a ton of explaining to do. My boss turns out to be a nice guy though. Instead of firing me, he tells me of a place nearby where I can stay. A lot of the employees at the hotel live there.

"Why didn't you tell me this before?" he asks.

"I was afraid to," I say.

He shakes his head. "Don't worry. This place is safe. A friend of mine runs it."

It's a big shelter with two rooms, one for men, and one for women. They are filled with cots for sleeping and then there is a dining area where they supply meals. There are separate showers for the men and women, and I'm told I can stay there indefinitely, as long as I pay the weekly fee.

The best thing of all is it's supervised to prevent crime.

"Thank you. This is great." I smile for the first time in I can't remember how long. My face aches from it.

The man and woman, who check me in, take me to my cot, and at the end of it is a small locker with a lock on it. They give me a key.

"You can keep your things in here if you'd like. We don't put up with any drugs or alcohol, so if you feel the need, we'll ask you not to stay."

"Oh, I don't do drugs. My mom, she died from that stuff so I'll never do them."

The woman offers me a kind smile and pats my shoulder.

"Honey, you need to eat. Why, you're nothing but skin and bones."

I shrug. "It's been a little tight, you know." The truth is, food hasn't been at the top of my list.

But her eyes glance down. "Well, you're not just eating for you now, are you?"

"No, ma'am, I'm not." My cheeks heat because she's the first person who's noticed I'm pregnant.

"Come with me." I follow her to the kitchen where she makes me a turkey sandwich and gives me a glass of ice-cold milk. "Now, I want you to eat every bite of this." She puts a hand on her hip, giving me the idea it's not up for discussion.

"Thank you." I wolf the sandwich and milk down. Then she gives me three Oreos.

"May I have some more milk, please?"

"I think you may." She grins as she refills my glass. "Nothing like Oreos and milk, is there?"

"No, ma'am. My mom used to give me these. I haven't had any since she passed."

The taste, the texture, and the fact that I'm sitting at a table with a woman my mom's age makes me happy for the first time since that horrible day they stole me away from her.

"So, when's your little one due?"

My happy moment is gone. "I'm not really sure."

"Haven't you seen a doctor?"

"No, ma'am."

"You have to."

I lower my eyes. "I ... I can't. Not yet." I'm not eighteen yet. Until I turn legal age, they would send me back to Hell, and he would kill me and the baby. Less than three weeks is all I have. Surely, I can make it until then.

"Does your father know?"

I wipe my mouth and say, "I don't have a father, ma'am."

"I see. And the baby's father?"

"Uh, he doesn't know. He wouldn't want it anyway."

"How old are you, honey?"

I stiffen. "I'm eighteen."

"Okay. Well, if you want me to go to the doctor with you, just let me know." She pats my back again.

"I will. And thank you."

I need to get out of here. She's only trying to help, but I can't have her snooping into my business. What if she finds out I'm not eighteen yet and tries to find the father of my baby?

I spend one night, fill my belly with as much food as I can, and leave money for them under my pillow in the morning when I go to work. I won't take any chances and come back here.

Parking lots turn out to be my friends. I discover that sleeping under cars is especially useful. No one sees you, and they're great shelter from rain, which Phoenix rarely gets. But even dew can be bothersome. They also protect you from chilly breezes. It's not summer, so the temperature drops at night.

On my eighteenth birthday, I buy myself a cupcake. It's the first time I've eaten cake since Mom left this earth. It's a sad day because it brings back all those memories, but it's a cause for celebration too. FD is no longer a threat to me.

I waltz into work, with a smile for the first time ever. My boss notices it and asks what the occasion is.

"Today is my birthday."

"Happy birthday, Millie."

"Thank you."

"How old?"

"I'm eighteen."

His jaw drops.

"I'm sorry. I only did it to protect myself."

He stares at my pregnant belly and asks, "Does it have anything to do with that?"

"It has everything to do with this."

He scratches his chin. "Well, I have to say you're one of the best workers we've ever had. You'll get no complaints from me."

"Thanks."

My boss tells me about a cheap place where I can live. It's a room with a kitchenette, but it's safe. I also go to the doctor. Since I don't have insurance, I have to file for Medicaid. It takes a little while, but I eventually get it. Since my boss is essentially paying me under the table, I have no income to claim, which helps.

My boss figures out there's more to my story than meets the eye, but he doesn't pressure me for details. I work at the motel until I go into labor. It happens while I'm at work. One of the other employees drives me to the hospital. I walk in holding my belly because I never imagined it would hurt so bad.

"Don't worry, it'll be better when we give you an epidural," the nurse explains.

"I hope so because this is awful." I've taken a lot of beatings in my day, but this is pretty bad. What's worse is I'm alone and scared to death. Turns out, the delivery is full of complications, or that's what they tell me. But what happens afterward is even more horrible. My baby is born with a critical congenital heart defect, specifically pulmonary atresia. He has to have surgery immediately.

As I'm lying there after the delivery, I hear the doctor ask, "What are the Apgars?" There's a sudden scrambling. A few minutes pass and then they tell me the bad news.

The doctor pats my arm. "I'm sorry, but we really need to get him to surgery. Fast."

I barely have time to hold my tiny boy, to love him, before they carry him off.

All the feelings of being torn away from my mom slam back into me. My chest explodes with searing pain. All the beatings I endured, the abuse, the molestation I endured, don't compare to the emotions I'm experiencing. And I have no one to talk to about it. I never cultivated any friendships in school. Rusty left home from what I saw on Facebook and joined the Navy. I've kept to myself at work, not getting involved with any of the others to keep my identity a secret, so there isn't a soul or a shoulder to lean on. I'm lying on that stupid bed, my legs still in the stirrups, without a clue of what to do.

Except for one thing. I talk to Mom. I don't know if she hears me, but I talk anyway. I tell her everything—how I hate that she used drugs and couldn't give them up. How my life turned rotten on account of it. How all I want is for her to be here right now and tell me what to do and how to handle this. I imagine her sitting next to me, giving me advice.

"Honey, I'm sorry, so sorry for the way things turned out. I was weak and never deserved a beautiful daughter like you. But right now, you have to have faith in something. It's out of your hands now. You must believe that your baby boy is going to be fine."

I latch onto those words with everything I have and when they tell me he made it through, tears course down my cheeks like an overflowing creek.

They finally let me see him and I weep for him all night.

He's so tiny with so many tubes and wires attached to him, I don't know where they end and he begins. I touch his itty-bitty finger and stroke it with my much larger one, letting him know I'm here with him. I don't want to leave, but they make me, telling me I need to rest.

For a week, it's touch and go, but he ends up pulling through. Only the doctors say it won't last. My baby will soon require a heart transplant. How in the world will I ever be able to afford the bills for that? I can scarcely keep food on the table and a roof over my head as is.

Two months later, desperate for money, I see an ad about auditions for a film. It doesn't give much more information other than that. I need a job, because my funds are gone. I'm eking by on saltines and water. My breast milk is long gone so my baby's on formula now, which is pricey. I'll be skin and bones before long.

I answer the call for the audition. They shuffle me from one room to the next until I land in the director's office.

"Take off your clothes."

"What?" At first, I'm sure I misunderstand him. And then I wonder what the hell kind of place this is.

"If you're going to do this, you'll have to strip, you know."

Suspicion crests in my brain. "What kind of films are these?" At this point, I am so stupidly naïve, I have no idea what's going on.

"They didn't tell you?" he asked.

"No."

"Welcome to porn, baby." He chuckles.

"Porn? Oh, I can't possibly do that."

"You're desperate for money, right?"

I stare at the man. He doesn't look like someone I'd imagine would make porn movies. He looks like a grandfather.

"You can't make money close to this anywhere else for such little work."

"How little?"

"One or two days a week, at most. We're really not that sleazy either."

"How much?"

"Five thousand a week. To start."

Holy moly, that's a lot of money. I think about baby Jack and his need for a new heart. Not to mention I wouldn't have to search for daycare because I wouldn't be working that much.

"I know you need the money, right? Just take off your clothes so we don't waste any more of each other's time."

I make a quick decision and strip. The only man who's ever seen me naked was my foster dad. Even his sleazy friends never saw me completely naked.

"Turn around."

I do.

"Bend down and spread your legs. And don't balk at this. We do lots of close-ups."

I do. I despise every second of it for how dirty it makes me feel, but all I focus on is getting baby Jack a new heart and that maybe he'll survive as a result of this.

"Okay, you can stand up and dress. You'll have to wax. We require our actresses to have bare pussies. No hair at all. Have you ever acted before?"

No hair? "Never."

"Not a problem. Our actors aren't exactly known for their stellar acting ability." He says it so matter-of-factly, I'm getting past my shock factor.

"Yeah, I wouldn't have thought so."

"You can be a huge hit, you know, with that ass. And your tits are magnificent. Can we die your hair black?"

"Black is my natural color. I would prefer to keep it blond. Recognition purposes, you know."

"I'm okay with that. You're in if you want to look over the contract. You get a percentage of your sales too, so if your movies hit, you'll make more money. A lot more money."

I don't know if I should be happy or not. I take the contract and start to leave.

"Can you let me know by tomorrow?"

"I'm letting you know now. I'm signing. When do you want me back?"

He eyes me for a long moment and announces, "Welcome to the triple-X family, Lusty Rhoades."

Six months into my porn career—which turns out to be very lucrative—my beautiful baby Jack dies in my arms, struggling to take his final breath. The heart I had waited and prayed for never came. Jack never thrived, and my hope against all the odds, hope that things would turn around with his new heart, never happened. My sweet little guy never got his chance at life. For weeks, I could barely take a single breath of my own. It was like my soul had been stolen right out of me. And in many ways, it had been. When Jack's light was extinguished, everything around me felt lifeless and dimmed.

I bury him next to my mom. Baby Jack Summers. I figure they can keep each other company because they both struggled and fought their own battles, fights neither of them could win.

My purpose for living is gone. Everything I did, I did for baby Jack. I try everything I can, but nothing works. Things never seem to go my way after he's gone. Leaving Phoenix is my last option. I dye my hair back to its natural color, have my nose altered, get rid of the contacts, change my name to Midnight Drake, and move to LA. This is my clean break, my new beginning. But is it really?

I go through the motions, working as a waitress, until one day I answer a call for an actress in a B-rated movie. It's about a girl who loses a child to a congenital illness. I get the role, probably because I don't have to act one tiny bit.

My second acting career is born, only this time it's not in a dim warehouse, and I'm fully clothed. I'm not mainstream yet, but I'm going to work my ass off to get there. I'll do it for my baby Jack because I want to make him proud of his mother, the mother who never got to see him grow to become a man.

Chapter 31

HARRISON

THE DRIVE OUT TO FIND MIDNIGHT HAS ME THINKING ABOUT everything I should've done, should've said to her. All those fucking missed opportunities. Why the hell did I sit back and wait? Why did I not see perfection sitting in front of me? Why did I think she needed my fixing abilities? And how could I have been so damn stupid to put my male pride in the way? Now I know why when you rearrange the letters in male, you come up with lame. Men. We're nothing but a bunch of lame idiots. I swear to God, if anything has happened to her, I will kill the motherfucker who hurt her.

"What the hell, Harrison?"

Leland pulls me out of my thoughts.

"What?"

"You just crushed your sunglasses in your hand." I look down and sure enough, they're in pieces. "Good thing it wasn't your cell phone."

"Yeah. Good thing."

"What's got you so pissed off?" He glances at me quickly, then his eyes are back on the road.

"Nothing."

"Right. And that makes so much sense. We know she's okay, yeah?"

"We hope, Leland. We hope." My words are clipped. "Just drive, goddammit."

"Yes, sir."

"I don't know who I'm going to kick in the ass first. You, or her."

"Me? What did I do?"

"You let her leave when you were supposed to be keeping an eye on her."

"Okay, okay. I'm sorry. We're almost there. Call Rashid just to make sure she's still there."

"She's there or he would've called us."

We pull off the interstate and end up on a gravel road, way out in the middle of no-fucking-where.

"What the fuck was she thinking?" I slam my hand on the dash.

"Clearly, she wasn't."

"Jesus, F."

This gravel road winds around desert land until we pull up to a ramshackle house with two cars out front. A light can be seen through the front window.

I get in my bag, pulling out my gun, the extra mag, and add a handful of extra rounds.

"What the fuck are you expecting in there?" Leland asks.

"No idea, but I won't be caught off guard." I slip the gun into the waistband of my jeans and we're off.

Once we get to the house, I look inside the window and see things are clear to go in.

I knock, calling out her name to give her a heads-up. "Midnight, it's us. Let us in."

She flies out the door straight into my arms. Her body betrays the strength she tried to convey on the phone.

"Hey, it's cool. I'm here. We'll take care of things," I say. "Leland, go inside and see what's going on."

I hold Midnight for a few minutes. Then I usher her off the porch. "You've got to tell me everything."

"It's such a long story, Harrison."

I tip her chin up. Her cheek is swollen. That fucker hit her. Her lip is cut, and her eye looks like it might be cut, only it's too dark out here to tell.

"I'm not going anywhere."

"It started with this." She pulls a letter out of the back pocket of her jeans.

"Gummy bear, I can't read that out here. It's too dark. Can we go inside?"

"I don't want to."

I grab her hand, lacing our fingers together, and take her to the SUV. When we get in, I read the letter.

Dear Velvet,

I bet you thought you'd never hear from me. Guess what? I'm back. Truth is I never really left. I've been watching you for years. Yeah, that's right, Lusty. Didn't think I knew, did you? Oh, and Baby Jack Summers— knew about him too. I've had you followed for all this time. Started after you tipped off DCS and they came after us. After you ran away, I told them you ran off with some boy. They searched but then they got that little tip and came back here asking all kinds of questions. Threatened to press charges, but they couldn't prove anything. After that, I found you working in that motel. I watched you. For months. Then you disappeared. Until one day when I was watching porn, and who should pop up on my screen but Lusty Rhoades! I was proud to know I was the one who taught you everything you knew.

So that brings me to the reason for this letter. My lips won't speak a word about you IF you do exactly as I say. I want money. Cash. One million, to be exact. Now that you're a famous movie star, this should be a breeze for you. Bring it to Phoenix. Call me when you land—623-555-0955.

You might be wondering what will happen if you don't. Here's a

237

little sample of things to come. Come. Ha, ha. By the way, did you like
my friends in New York? I was told you had a great time. Just so you
know that porn ring of mine has brought in quite a lot of money for us.
Your contribution was a nice addition. See, I've always known where you
were.

Your loving Foster Father

"He sent me a thumb drive. On it were video clips. You remember how I told you he abused me? It was bad, Harrison. He physically and sexually abused me. For years. There were clips of me having sex with him. My face, not his. My body, not his. And then clips of some of my porn films. There was also a video of what happened in New York. It could ruin me. But that's not all."

"What else?" I hold her hand, stroking it with my thumb. I want to hold her for what that monster did to her. And then I want to march inside and cut off his dick. I also need to get in touch with Gino so he can call his NYPD contact. Our friend Trent lied to us and didn't tell us the whole truth when they took Midnight from the club. It was planned and stemmed from her foster father. But that can wait.

"When I was seventeen, I ran away from him. You already know that part, I believe. The main reason I did it was because I found out I was pregnant. If he ever figured that out, he would've killed me. He would've known the baby was his and that would've ended badly for me and the baby."

"What happened? Did you give the baby up? Or have an abortion?"

"Oh God, no. I had the baby. But he died when he was only seven months old." Then she breaks down and cries, clinging to me like a baby herself. Jesus, what do I say to that?

My arms pull her into my lap as I do my best to ease her broken heart.

"How old were you?"

"I'd just turned nineteen"—she sniffs between sobs— "when baby Jack died."

"So young. And you were alone?"

Her head bobs up and down. I run my hand down the length of her hair, onto her back, rubbing circles on it, remembering how my mom used to do the same for me.

"I'm so sorry that you had to go through all that by yourself." Her fingers dig into my arms. I wish I could take that pain away, but there's nothing more I can do than just be here for her.

"He sent pictures of baby Jack's tombstone. I never thought he knew about him. When I got here, he laughed about it. That's when I shot him."

"It's a good thing you're a bad shot. I've already called Misha. He'll be arrested for child molestation, abuse, and sexual assault. You don't have anything to worry about."

She leans back. "But I shot him, Harrison."

"Where did you get the gun?"

"It was his. When I got here he left the thing sitting on the counter."

"Well, you shot him in self-defense. Leland has probably called the police by now. Not to mention he tried to blackmail you. I'll be with you every step of the way. If I could, I'd kill the man and bury him myself, but would you want that on your conscience?"

Her head pivots from side to side. "I used to imagine ways I wanted to see him die. But I don't want to be a part of that."

"This way, you'll be charged, released, and when we go to court, you'll be free of all this. That man tortured you for years, Midnight."

I wrap her in my arms again and say, "I figured something out I want to tell you."

"What's that?"

"I'm an idiot."

"You are?"

"Yeah. Because you are the most important thing to me, and I let my stupid male pride get in the way."

"Oh, that."

"Yeah, that. So, you ready to go inside and get this shit over with?"

"Yeah."

We get out of the car and walk toward the house. When we walk through the door, I break out in roaring laughter. I don't even know what the guy's name is but he's lying on the floor, ass face up, with duct tape over his mouth and around his wrists and ankles. The funny part is she shot him in the ass. It reminds me of the story Weston told when his wife Special shot him in the ass.

"Jesus, you really are a bad shot."

"I know."

Leland is sitting in a kitchen chair, drinking a beer.

I take in the surroundings and there's one thing that puzzles me. "Midnight, how did you subdue him? I'm sure he was a little feistier than this."

"Oh, I hit him in the head. When I got here, he thought I'd have the cash, which I didn't. We started arguing and that's when I shot him with his own gun he'd left on the counter. He told me about how he came to LA and fired those shots at my place. His stupid mouth pissed me off so bad when he started in about baby Jack, I couldn't help it. Then after he grabbed his butt, he was whining worse than a baby. It was more than any woman could take. So, you see that frying pan right there?" She points to one sitting close to Leland.

"Yeah."

"I grabbed it and hit him on the side of his head. He went down like a stone."

Leland and I laugh. What's-his-name tries to say something, but with that duct tape over his mouth, we have no idea what it is.

"Hey, Leland, how about taking that tape off? Let's see what crybaby has to say."

Leland strips off the tape and the guy immediately starts threatening Midnight.

I bend over so he can see me and say, "I want you to take note of this. If you don't shut your mouth, I'm going to kick your face in. Do you understand me?"

That's pretty effective because he shuts up fast.

"You're going to be spending a long time behind bars. You do know it's illegal to molest and abuse your own foster child, don't you? I thought so. So, it would be in your best interest to keep your mouth shut."

Then, Midnight pipes in. "By the way, I recorded everything that was said tonight." She pulls her phone out of her pocket and hands it to me.

"Nice work, ace. You need a job?"

"I don't think so, but if I do, I know who to call."

Before the police show up, I mention to Midnight the deal with Trent. "Should we bring his name up to the police? Your foster father was the one who set that whole wheel in motion, after all."

"Isn't it too late for that?"

"No. Two years haven't passed. We can still get those guys."

"Then let's tell all."

The police show up, along with an ambulance, and everybody gives their statement. The paramedics want to take Midnight to the hospital, but she refuses. They examine her though, just to be on the safe side.

We go to the police station, and they decide, after a long night and listening to the audio, along with the videos and letter she provides, that no charges will be filed against Midnight at this time. She acted in self-defense when she shot that asshole. They will be in contact with NYPD regarding her rapists in New York. That ring is about to go public.

Her foster father, on the other hand, is charged with everything he deserves. After he's released from the hospital, he'll be held in custody until his arraignment. I hope he can afford a good lawyer, because he's going to need one.

The next morning, when the sun is just rising, Midnight and I take a drive. She directs me to a place she wants me to see. I make a stop along the way at a convenience store. When I come out, I have a bag that I won't let her open, and two large cups of coffee.

"Thanks. Why can't I open the bag?"

"Because. That's why."

"You're mean."

"No, I'm not."

She scoots over so she can lean against my shoulder. "I know."

I pull the car back onto the empty street and ten minutes later, we pull into the open gates of the cemetery. She tells me which way to go and when to stop.

"You ready?" I ask.

A long gust of air leaves her. "I guess."

I pull her hand to my lips and press my own to it. "I'll be right by your side."

The visit was her idea, but it's not going to be easy for her. She made a brief stop here when she arrived but didn't get out of her car, so in a sense, she hasn't been here since she left Phoenix all those years ago.

I open her door and help her out. Her hand grasps mine as she leads me toward the final resting place of the son who was stolen from her far too early in life.

Once there, it plows into me as I read his name. Baby Jack Summers. Tiny angels with wings surround it. No dates. Only his name. Last night, when we finally got to our hotel, she told me all the details about her son.

She falls to her knees as her fingers trace each of the letters, and then the tiny wings.

"Oh, Jack. If only things had been different. If only I had been stronger ... older ... wiser. Maybe you could've made it."

That isn't true, from everything I've read about pulmonary atresia. Nothing but a new heart could've saved baby Jack.

I put my arms on her and say, "Hey, it wasn't your fault. You did everything you could."

"No. I could've taken better care of him."

Pulling her back so I can hold her, I say, "No, that's not true. I've done my own research. And it wasn't anything you did. He needed a new heart. One that wasn't damaged. One that never came. It wasn't your fault. You need to let that go."

"I'll never be able to do that. He was my baby."

"Look at me."

Eyes so pained they practically slash through my own heart stare at me from beneath wet lashes. "You saw that he had everything he needed at the time, right?"

She nods.

"You made sure he had all his medicine and you gave it to him when you were supposed to, right?"

She nods again.

"He was fed and given a home. You kept him safe and loved him with everything you had. You were a great mother, Midnight. The best. Most people could never have accomplished what you did, given your circumstances. If Jack were here, as an adult, he would tell you the same. You sacrificed so much so he could survive. Don't take that away from yourself, or him."

"I should've gone to the doctor earlier. Maybe ..."

"They wouldn't have known. No one knows what causes it."

"Oh, Harrison, when he took that last breath as I held him, I wanted to die right along with him. I was alone without anyone to lean on and I didn't know what to do. But I tried ... everything I could," she says, stopping to look at the tombstone. "The choices I made—I answered an ad. I just needed the money so I could find my son a new heart, one that never came." She can't continue because her body is wracked with sobs, sobs that break my own heart as well as hers.

Her words crush me. To think she bore the weight of this for all these years fucking staggers me, not to mention she was only nineteen when he died. I think back to what I was doing then and I can't come close to imagining how she handled it all. And there I was, getting shitty about her doing porn when all she was worried about was her baby surviving.

I lift up her face. "You won't ever have to shoulder anything alone again, do you understand me? I'll be with you every step, by your side. Through good times and bad."

Reaching for the bag, I pull out the little stuffed bear I bought. I set it next to baby Jack's headstone. She smiles when she sees it.

"He loved to squeeze soft things and rub the satin edge of his blanket." A sad smile appears on her face. Then I pull out a bag of gummy bears and give them to Midnight. Her sad smile turns a bit happier when she sees them.

"Aww, thanks."

My last item is a yellow rose. I place that next to her mom's headstone.

"How'd you know she liked yellow roses?"

"I didn't. It was all they had in the store."

"How weird. Mom always said yellow roses meant joy and friendship and lavender ones meant love at first sight. She always said when she saw my eyes for the first time, she knew it to be true for sure because it was love at first sight for her."

"I'd have to agree." I hadn't meant to tell her this way, in a cemetery of all places. But the words spill from my mouth like water over a dam.

"What did you say?"

My arms circle her waist, and I draw her against me. "I'd say your mom was correct. The first time I looked into your stunning eyes, I was lost. I never found myself again. I'm in love with you, Midnight, Velvet, whatever you want me to call you.

You're my person, the one who sets me free, sets me on fire, makes me want to do crazy things with, but most importantly, spend the rest of my life with."

She throws her arms around my neck and kisses me. Not a long, passionate kiss, but a short, happy one. Then she steps back and takes my hand as we walk back to the car.

Chapter 32

MIDNIGHT

WHEN HARRISON AND I RETURNED TO LA, THE NEWS BROKE about FD and once again, I was in the melee. But this time Alta came to my rescue, my shining knight, to save the day. Their publicity team handled everything, and with Harrison's company in place, I came out again looking like a bigger star. Only no one will ever truly understand what it was like for me.

"How're you holding out?" Harrison asks one morning as he pulls me on top of him.

"I'm good. Or as good as I can be. It's still crazy. I never wanted anyone to know about this and now the whole world knows everything. Everyone is still begging for the real story. Interviews, a book deal—they'll probably want to make a Lifetime movie too."

"Sad as it is, people love sob stories. They say they want to empathize, but I think they just want the dirt."

I lift up and say, "Exactly. That's what makes me crazy."

"On another note, be prepared for tomorrow night." He's talking about the postproduction event that's being held.

"Oh, I know. My publicist says she's already got the lineup for me. I'll have tons of mics thrust into my face."

"I'm sure."

"She's supposed to be sending over all the requests for interviews today. Oh, and I hope you're ready. You may have to knock a few people out of the way." I use my pointer finger to dig into his chest. He grabs and kisses it.

Then he takes a chunk of my hair and tugs a little. "Why would I do that? You're a star, baby."

I plant a light kiss on his mouth. "You never know what someone will do." Then I click my fingers. "Did I tell you who Helen is going with?"

His brow furrows. "No, do I know him?"

I break out into a series of lighthearted giggles. He's going to die when I break this news to him. "Oh, you know him all right."

"Well, don't keep me in suspense. Who is it?"

"Holt Ward."

"The fuck it isn't!"

"Oh, the fuck it is."

He sits up so fast I roll off him like a marble. "You better get back in this bed if you know what's good for you, Mr. Kirkland."

He's out and pacing. Holt Ward is a dirty name around this house, which is why I've refrained from telling him that after we finished filming, the movie crew had a little get-together. Harrison wasn't around that day so Helen came with me. After that awful incident, Holt profusely apologized to me, over and over, for making such a fool of himself. He said he never intended to hurt me, and the kiss wasn't supposed to happen like that. He just got carried away. He went to therapy and isn't drinking anymore. Helen met Holt that night and they hit it off.

The truth is Helen saw something broken in him and is now on the path to fixing him. It's still hilarious to me, considering she knew about all the crazy shit he did to me. She gave him a hard time about it too. Their relationship isn't exactly smooth sailing, but it's not my business. They make the cutest couple and one thing is true—she takes zero shit from him.

"I cannot believe Helen would stoop so low."

"Hang on there, slick. You don't know what goes on between them and it's not any of your business."

He aims a pointed glare at me.

"Don't give me one of those looks either. I am not one of your employees."

His eyes immediately soften and he walks toward me. Then two strong arms reach for and pull me against his wall of a chest. "I only look at you one way, and that's with love. I adore you, Midnight Drake, and don't forget it. But back to Helen, I thought she ... that is, Misha told me she was on the other team."

"I think she plays for both sides these days. But I'd like to suggest that you get back in here and give me something to remind me that you adore me."

His lids drop and the corner of his mouth turns up. "Oh? And what type of reminder do you need?"

I get on my knees, and say, "I hope you don't have to ask. But if you come a little closer, I'll give you a hint."

He steps next to the bed and my hand slides over his cock, which hangs heavily between his muscular thighs. I take it in my hand and drop down so my tongue can tease him a little.

One thing I've learned about Harrison is he loves my hair. His hands furrow into it as he grabs it and pulls me close.

"I want more than you teasing me. Suck me, Midnight. The way you know I love."

I lift my gaze and see his mouth open a little as he bends his neck back. I engulf his cock with my mouth, taking him deep into my throat, as my hand finds his balls and massages them. A husky groan escapes him and that's all the encouragement I need. Speeding up my motion, I tongue and suck, until he's close. He'll let me know when to stop, and he does.

A large hand lands on my chest and pushes me backward until I hit the bed with a whoosh. My legs are spread and his mouth hits my pussy, with no time wasted. At this point, I'm filled with lust for him and all I can think of is his cock sliding in and out of me. But his tongue takes that away and I want to melt on him. Every nerve ending comes to life as his expert tongue fucks me to insanity. How many ways can a man lick a pussy? It's a question I can't answer but Harrison certainly can.

"Pussy a la Midnight. Should be an entrée."

"I'm sure that would go over well."

"I'd order it."

"Let me tell you what would be better. Kock a la Kirkland, with cock spelled with a K."

"Think we should open a restaurant?"

"No, but I do think you should fuck me."

I get a wicked grin for that comment but I also get what I requested. Harrison isn't stingy with his cock. He usually likes it from the back—doggy-style or reverse cowgirl. But not today. He slides in from the front, which I'm in the mood for, because I love to watch. He presses down on my pelvis, dropping a thumb to my clit, and commences to slide in and out, stretching me to the fullest. At first, he takes his time with long, lazy strokes. But when I buck against his hips with mine, he chuckles and gets my obvious hint.

"You in the mood to speed it up?"

"Yeah," I pant. He's so damn sexy, his corded muscles flexing as he moves. He's beauty and brawn, all wrapped together in a solid package.

He swivels his hips, slowly at first, then thrusts fast and hard against me. It's the best sensation, causing pleasure to radiate from everywhere because it hits his thumb every time, giving me a double whammy. I arch my back and grab his knees where they rest next to me, sinking my nails into his skin. This goes on, but not very long because I yell out number two orgasm, clenching his cock with my inner muscles as he moans out his own. He rests his weight on his arms and his mouth tugs my lower lip into his, where he nips and sucks it. Then he kisses me, sensually, completely, to the point where he owns my mouth. It's raw and sexy and my belly clenches with need.

"Your kisses make me wet."

"Are you greedy for more of me?"

"Yeah," I breathe.

"You'll have to wait a few, I'm afraid."

I kiss the corner of his mouth. "I love you more than anything. Pussy a la Midnight can wait."

He grins. Then he slides down my body and sucks one of my nipples into his mouth. It's stiff as steel and my breast feels so sensitive in his palm. He continues down until he gets to my new ink. It runs across my stomach, much like his. In fact, the same artist that did his did mine. Harrison wasn't exactly excited about it, but there was no stopping me when my mind was made up. His tongue outlines the letters as I watch.

"Do you still hate it?" I ask.

"I never hated it. I didn't want it to be a part of you because I don't happen to believe it's true."

It's the opposite of what his says. Mine says SCARRED.

"But I am scarred. And I'm a better person for it. And only because of you."

He licks the word again and hovers over me, cupping my breast.

"Scarred or not, you're mine. So what do you say, will you be mine forever? As in the legal kind of way? Marry me, Midnight. Make me the happiest man alive." He punctuates the request with a flicking of my nipple. "I can't live without this, without you."

I slide my hand into his hair. "Well, I was going to talk to you about that. When all that mess happened in Phoenix, I forgot about my pills and didn't take them for about a month. I'm a little bit pregnant."

He laughs. The man laughs.

He touches his forehead to mine. "How much is a little?"

"Um, around ten weeks. I counted back to Phoenix and

that's when I think it might have happened, but I'm not really sure."

His expression changes. "You're ten weeks pregnant and you didn't tell me?" He explodes off the bed and starts pacing.

"Jeez, I didn't really know for sure until the other day when I saw the stash of tampons at my apartment. I've been staying here and there aren't any in your bathroom. I honestly didn't think about it. Then it hit me and I had an *oh, fuck* moment."

"Christ. What did you do?"

"Went to the pharmacy and bought a pregnancy test. Then I went to Helen's and freaked the fuck out."

"And you didn't tell me? Why?"

"I was scared. Remember what happened to me last time? All those feelings came back and I just freaked. Helen talked me off the ledge."

"Helen. You went to her before the man you love and the one who loves you."

"Oh my God. You're letting your ego get in the way of everything."

"My ego. You let your fears—" He stops dead, then in two long strides, he's pulling me into his arms. "Jesus, I'm so sorry. You're right. It's not about my ego. And that jerkoff you just glimpsed won't be coming back out anymore. Forgive me?"

"Everyone deserves a freak-out now and again. I had mine."

"But not with you and a pregnancy. That was uncalled for. I should know better." He pauses. "So ... we're having a baby. Have you been to the doctor? Do we need to do anything special for you, as far as care?"

I know what he's asking, but I have no answers for him.

"I have an appointment next week. Harrison, this one's going to be fine. I have a good feeling about this."

"Does this mean you'll marry me?"

"I would've married you anyway."

"Before or after the baby?"

"Let's elope. I don't want a big wedding."

Chapter 33

HARRISON

THE FOLLOWING WEEK, WE GO TO THE DOCTOR. IT'S A beautiful thing to see your baby on the ultrasound. I never imagined the rush of emotions that hit me. Midnight is so gorgeous, lying there, a perfect smile lighting up her face. Heat radiates from my chest, making me weak. I grab the table she's on for support, gaining strength from her glow. If I'm like this now, how the hell will I withstand the delivery? I hope I'm not one of those pussies who passes out when it happens.

"Look here," the doctor says, pointing to the baby. You can hear the heart beating. I can't really tell what I'm looking at, though I know it's something alive.

Midnight starts to cry and then tells the doctor about baby Jack.

She pats her arm and says, "Midnight, we're going to do everything we can to make sure this one is healthy. What your first baby had is extremely rare. Understand? What I need for you to do is take good care of yourself. Eat properly and get plenty of rest. A pregnancy is only forty weeks. While that may seem long, it's not. Take time off from work if you can. Go back afterward. Sound good?"

"Yeah, it does."

It sounds good to me too, because I want to take her some-where for maybe a month.

We leave and she floats out to the car.

"I have a surprise. I know you want to elope. So I've made some arrangements, if they suit you."

"Yeah?"

"Yeah."

Then I shut up.

"Well?"

"Well, what?"

"The arrangements, silly."

"Guess you're gonna have to wait to find out."

She nails me in the arm with a fist. The girl has some power too.

"Aw, come on. You can do better than that."

"Really? How about this?"

Now she totally packs a punch. I give her the eye and we both get a good laugh. "I hope you didn't bruise my delicate skin."

I laugh as we drive home in the old Mustang with the top down.

Saturday morning, Helen and Holt show up with a breakfast of bagels and coffee. Midnight has no idea what's happening later today. I hope she doesn't kill me. Then Helen drags her off for a surprise Saturday at the spa. After they leave, everyone comes out of the woodwork and things start happening.

Mom and Dad cut their vacation short and flew in last night, so they arrive to lend a hand, along with Prescott, Vivi, Weston, and Special. My team from the office is here too. We get the terrace all fixed up for a wedding. The women and a wedding planner make it look extra special. At sunset, when the view is spectacular, we will be saying *I do*.

Lights are strung everywhere, with tables and chairs scattered around the pool. The caterers will arrive with food prepared immediately before we walk down for the ceremony, which will be on the beach. They can set up while we get married. The only guests will be those already mentioned. It's going to be a very small party, and I also invited a few people from the movie crew with the help of Holt. I have to admit, he's grown on me. Ever since he abandoned his crazy quest for Midnight, which he admitted was stupid in the first place and he was doing it for attention, we've become friends ... sort of. As long as he treats Helen well, I'm cool with the goofy fucker.

"This looks beautiful, Harrison," Mom says.

"Are you sure?"

"She's going to love it. The lavender roses with the touch of yellow are perfect."

I smile. I give Midnight lavender roses every week. She never knows what day they'll arrive, but they always do.

"It's her eyes, Mom. They remind me of them."

"She's a beauty. If she has a girl, you'll have your hands full."

Prescott overhears and says, "Yeah, I hope he does. I can only imagine it."

"Shut up, dude. Look at Vivi. I hope you have twin girls."

Prescott turns ashen. They decided to keep the sex of their baby a secret so they have no idea what they're having. We won't find out until our next visit.

"Oh God, my heart couldn't bear that." He hurries away to find his pregnant wife.

Weston overheard what I said and comes over. "That was brutal, man. He's not going to sleep for months."

"Yeah, he deserves it after all those months of manwhoring."

"Harrison," Mom chides. I forgot she was standing here.

"Oops. Sorry, Mom."

She walks away, shaking her head. Weston laughs. "Better get back to work."

I group some chairs together and take in the surroundings. Damn, I sure am thankful for these people.

"Hey, everyone. I just wanted to thank you all for helping me pull this off. I have no idea what I'm going to do when Helen brings her home from the spa, but I could never have gotten this far without all of you." I put my hand on my chest, pound it, then extend it out to them. "You are my people."

We finish setting up and everyone leaves with plenty of time to spare. The only problem is I'm a nervous wreck. I want this to be the most perfect night of her life. I want her to be surprised and thrilled with everything. If I blow this, it will be so disappointing.

Everyone is to arrive by six. Helen texts at four that they're on the way home.

When they arrived, Midnight complains about how sleepy she is.

Fuck. I never thought about her needing a nap. So I fix her a plate and bring it to her in bed.

"Mmm. Looks so good, but all that massaging and stuff made me too tired for that."

"Okay. Take a little nap."

She's out like a light. An hour later, I know she needs time to get ready. Helen picked out a beautiful dress for her and I want her to wear her hair down. Nothing fancy. I tiptoe into the room and she's snoring softly.

What the fuck should I do? In an hour, we need to walk down the steps and out to the beach to be pronounced man and wife.

I decide to run out and call Helen, my savior. In my haste, I trip over one of her sandals and go flying and bust my ass. Or more likely my nose. My curses have her jumping out of bed and running to my rescue.

"Are you okay? What happened?"

"I wasn't looking and tripped. Sorry."

"You gave me heart attack. Your nose is bleeding and you scraped your chin."

Exactly what I need. That'll look great for our wedding pictures.

"I'm fine." Maybe. "Hey, I was thinking that I'd love to walk on the beach and then go down to that cool restaurant. You up for that?"

She scrunches up her mouth. "Uh, yeah, I guess." Her tone is skeptical.

"You sure?"

She rubs her face a second. "I need a shower."

"Yeah, me too. You go first." I quickly usher her into the bathroom where she raises her brows. I leave before she can ask me anything. When I get to the kitchen, I dab my nose just to make sure there's no blood. But I'm sweating like a pig. It's five fifteen. I hope she's done showering. I move to the bathroom door. She opens it and I nearly fall on top of her.

"Jesus, Harrison. What the hell is wrong with you? You scared the shit out of me."

"Sorry. Bad timing."

I run inside, strip, and speed bathe. Then I run out and into my closet where I put on a white shirt and black dress pants.

When I walk out, she asks, "Where did this dress come from?" She's holding it up for me to see. It's the palest of lavender, so light it almost looks white.

"I bought it for you. I thought you could wear it tonight. Do you like it?"

It's backless with a halter neck and a sheer cover that over-lays a matching lace bottom. The cool thing about it is Helen showed me how the sheer thing detaches so she can wear it as a short dress again if she wants.

"Check it out." I show her.

"That's so cool. But don't you think it's a bit dressy for tonight?"

"Not at all. On you, it will be gorgeous."

"Okay." She's going with it, but she's not thrilled.

I have to help her with the hooks and zipper, but once it's on, she's in love with it.

"Oh gosh, this is amazing."

"Let me see."

I almost tell her she's the most beautiful bride in the world, but I stop myself. Her bouquet of lavender and yellow roses was a great pick for this.

When she's ready, I take her hand and we go out through the living room glass doors onto the terrace. Then we take the steps down that lead to the beach.

"We're not taking the car?" she asks.

"No, I thought we'd walk since it's almost sunset and it's such a nice day."

"Oh, Mr. Romantic tonight."

I lean over to kiss her. "I hope to be that man with you every night."

Once we hit the beach, there's a small outcropping of rock where everyone is waiting, and I've had an arbor placed there. The preacher waits for us with everyone else.

"Oh, look. Someone must be getting married tonight."

I stop and turn her to face me. "That someone is us." I raise her hand to my mouth.

"Wh–what?" Her mouth hangs open as her hand flies to her chest.

"You wanted to elope, and what better place than in our backyard?" When we get to the arbor, everyone gathers around us. She's in shock, and I pray it's the good kind. Helen takes her place next to Midnight, handing her the bouquet. Dad stands next to me and the preacher looks at the two of us.

"Are you two ready?"

"Yes, yes, I am," she says, her voice strong.

"Thank God," I say. "You had me worried there for a minute."

"At least I know why you were acting so bizarre in there."

The ceremony is brief, and afterward, we walk back to the pool area, where music starts playing and appetizers are served.

This is the first time Midnight is meeting all my friends, so once all the introductions are made the party is on. Mom is in her element.

"Not only am I finally getting a daughter, but I'm getting a grandbaby too. I couldn't be happier." She can't stop hugging my wife.

"Mom, you have to give me the opportunity to hug Midnight too."

"No, you'll have lots of time. I leave in the morning and won't be back for a while."

"Why are you leaving in the morning?" Midnight asks.

"They can stay, but you and I are going away for a month," I explain.

"We are? Where to?"

"You'll see." I give her an evil grin.

"You're awful."

"You won't be saying that tomorrow."

She slaps my ass. Too bad I have pants on.

Prescott and Weston join us. Prescott says, "Let's raise our glasses, brother. A toast."

"Oh no. Not you."

"Hey, man, I'm better, I swear."

Midnight looks at me for an answer. "He used to be the worst when it came to toasts. When Weston and Special got married, his toast was something about Weston's dick not falling off."

Midnight aims a finger at Prescott. "You definitely need help in the toast category."

Prescott holds his hands up in the air. "Harry, I swear, I'm good these days."

"Harry?" Midnight asks, laughing.

Pointing to Weston and Prescott, I say, "Midnight, meet

Westie and Scotty. Obviously I was Harry. Those were our Crestview nicknames. They've sort of stuck with us throughout the years."

"Aww, how cute."

Vivi comes up to us and says, "Don't let them fool you. Trouble, yes. Cute, no. They had all the girls dangling from their grubby fingers."

"I bet," Midnight says.

Special joins the group. "Are they telling Crestview stories again? Prescott, are you going to tell Midnight some of Harry's dirt?"

"Oh no, he's not," I say.

Prescott puts his hand in the air again, saying, "Hey, all I want to do is toast the newlyweds. Can you all believe we're respectably married people now?"

"Who said anything about being respectable?" Weston asks.

"Speak for yourself," I say.

"Okay, everyone, raise your glasses. To the newlyweds. May your lives be long and filled with love. Love each other more than any fight you will ever have, more than any struggle you will ever face, more than any distance that will ever lie between you, or any hurdle you will ever leap."

I look at Prescott. "That was solid, man. Thanks." We man-hug, and then I hug my other brother, Weston. It's a great night for all.

The women chat. Special tells Midnight about her son, Cody, and daughter, Elizabeth. "They stayed home with my grandmother, but I hope you two come for a visit soon. They would love to meet you."

"I'd love that, or bring them out to California. They would love Disneyland, I bet."

"Elizabeth may be a bit young, but Cody would go nuts over it," Special says.

I put my arm around my wife and add, "Maybe you could get Cody on the set to meet one of his superheroes."

"Yeah, if he comes when they're filming."

Special says it's a done deal.

Vivi claims Prescott won't go anywhere until their baby is ten years old. "I'm afraid I'm stuck. He's already such a freak about this baby. I'll have to come alone."

I wander back to where Prescott and Weston are and give him a hard time over Vivi's pregnancy. He's not dealing too well with it, according to her. Then I gaze over the group, and I can't believe what a lucky man I am.

After our guests leave and it's just the two of us, Midnight says, "I'm not sure how you pulled that off, but thank you. That was the most perfect wedding ever. Thank you for finding and fixing me. But most of all, thank you for loving me."

"Ah, I didn't think you could be fixed."

"I didn't think I could ... until I opened my heart to you."

And if that doesn't make me the happiest man alive, I don't know what does.

Chapter 34

MIDNIGHT

HARRISON WAKES ME UP AROUND NINE AND DRAGS ME INTO THE shower. This pregnancy is making me so tired all the time. He does a great job of washing my hair—and the rest of me. Then he makes sure I get a full breakfast before he hustles us off to the waiting plane. I still have no idea of where we're flying to our honeymoon.

Even when we land nine hours later, I know we're on an island, but which one?

We deplane to a beautiful Polynesian woman placing flowered leis around our necks and handing us glasses of some kind of pineapple and coconut concoctions. They are delicious.

"Welcome to Bora Bora," she says, smiling.

I squeal and hop into Harrison's arms. I've always wanted to visit Tahiti.

"Please tell me we're going to stay in one of those really cool bungalows over the water." My voice begs him to say yes.

"You'll just have to wait and see."

"You're such a tease."

He traces my cheekbone with a finger. "I know. But it'll be worth the wait."

A waiting car drives us to our home for the next two weeks.

I'm thrilled to see it's one of my dream tiki huts over the water. But this just isn't any tiki hut. This is a magical place, unlike anything I could ever have imagined. It has its own pool, its own private outdoor shower, and a bath that looks up at the stars. It's so romantic, but the best thing is it comes with our own personal maid and butler service.

"I'll be so spoiled, I won't know how to act when we leave."

"Get used to it because I'm going to spoil you every day."

I believe him, because he already has. I link my arms around his neck and say, "Well, this is going to be tough to top."

"I'll come up with something."

We swim in the turquoise water, and eat like royalty, but Harrison is a gentle lover every night.

"What happened to you?" I ask one afternoon.

"What do you mean?"

"You've changed. You treat me like I'm going to break."

He cradles me against him. "I'm not taking any chances until you're well into your fifth month."

"Why my fifth? The riskiest part is behind us."

"I don't care. I'm being extra cautious."

"I don't want cautious. I want abandon and desperation and I want you unhinged, uncontrolled. I want you telling me how much you need me and that you can't live without this kind of fucking, not treating me as though I'm going to break."

He flips me over so he's lying on top. His hair falls over his forehead and I brush it back.

"I do love you and can't live without you. But I also don't want anything to happen to this baby."

"It won't."

His hand moves between us as his mouth captures mine. He's not gentle now. This kiss is demanding, passionate, full of heat and desire, the kind I've wanted … needed. I'm wet for this and it only makes me wetter.

He rolls me to my side so we face each other and lines us up so he can slip inside. Long, slow, and steady is his new game, but I grip his ass, pulling him in.

"More," I pant.

He wraps his arm around me and complies. He hits me on every spot that makes me tingle, spreading delicious waves of pleasure everywhere.

"I can't hold out. You have to come. Come for me."

"Yeah." And I do. My orgasm contracts and he groans as the spasms hit me. When it passes, he touches us both where we join, feeling the slickness we've created.

"Was that more to your liking?" he asks.

"Much more. Please don't tell me you're going to be one of those worrywart dads."

"You know I will." He plays with a chunk of my hair. "After we get back and you go to the doctor, we'll find out what the sex is. I'll be walking on eggshells if it's a girl. I can't imagine how I'll be if she's a girl. All those penises I'll have to worry about."

"If it's a girl, the poor thing won't date until she's thirty with you as her dad."

He shudders. "Can we change the subject?"

I crawl on top of him, straddling him. "Aw, something you won't be able to fix, huh?"

"Not everything needs fixing, as you like to remind me."

The next day, we spend the afternoon snorkeling and have our dinner of fresh lobster brought to our room. We're lazing around when Harrison brings up the idea of a nanny.

"I don't know. I guess we'll need one if I'm going to be working."

"We'll start interviewing soon because we don't want to wait until the last minute."

"True, and God knows you'll have to make sure she doesn't

need any fixing." I wink at him. He picks me up and tosses me on the bed.

"Stop it." A playful glint hits his eyes and his fingers find my ribs as he tickles me.

"Noooo," I squeak. He knows exactly where to dig to get me going. But soon the tickles turn into something else and he's tweaking and sucking my nipples. I writhe and moan as his fingers find their way between my thighs, and my moans grow even louder.

"I love hearing you when we play," he says. "And I love fucking you. You are everything I've craved."

His mouth is almost touching mine so I reach for him and put my lips on his. Kissing Harrison is something I'll always love. He throws everything off balance but then turns it back to the way it was meant to be. Every kiss is the same, yet different. The beat of his heart, the throbbing of his pulse, the rush of his blood, is all conveyed through his kiss. Every time. It's what he doesn't say that's spoken using a kiss. It's a way to touch and feel his soul with that complex gesture.

As we kiss, he slides inside of me and rocks his hips against mine, back to being the gentle lover. Do I miss the way we used to fuck? Hell yeah. But this ... this is making love and there's a sense of closeness I've never had with another human being before. That displaces anything we used to do. We'll do it again after the baby comes. It'll be something to look forward to. But I'll treasure this forever.

He hooks an arm under my knee and rolls over, bringing me on top. Then he keeps up the rhythm until we both come. He likes for me to be able to lie on top of him. He's afraid of crushing me. It's funny really because I'd tell him if he did, but he still worries. A brief thought flashes through me.

"How's this going to work when I'm as big as a house?"

"You'll never be as big as a house. But you can be on top or we'll spoon, just like the book said."

"What book?" I ask.

"Oh, the one I got on pregnancy."

I raise myself up and stare. "You got a pregnancy book?"

"Well, yeah. Doesn't everyone?"

"I didn't."

"You can borrow mine when I'm done. Or wait, it's on my phone. Maybe not. I'll just buy you one of your own."

"Oh my God. My husband got a pregnancy book before I did."

"Yeah, so what?"

"Nothing." I should've known my fix-it dude would have answers to everything.

We stay in Bora Bora for two weeks and I know Harrison has other plans. But on the next to our last night, I lean over and ask, "Would you be terribly upset with me if I asked you to take me home after this?"

He's instantly on alert. "You want to skip the rest of the trip?"

"Yeah, but not for any other reason other than I want to sleep in our own bed."

"You're feeling okay?"

"Perfectly fine."

"Then home it'll be. I have to admit, I'm ready too."

When the plane touches down in LA, we both grin. "Welcome home, Mrs. Kirkland."

A week later, on a Saturday, we're sitting at home watching TV when the phone rings. It's the landline and that's completely weird. I answer it because Harrison is in the kitchen grabbing us something to drink.

"Hello?"

"Uh, Velvet?"

My belly hits the floor. No one, and I mean no one, calls me that. My spine tingles as the tiny hairs rise on the back of my neck.

"Who is this?"

Harrison hears and stomps over to me.

"This is Rusty, your, uh, foster brother."

"Rusty?" I'm so shocked to hear his voice.

"Yeah. It's me. I heard, uh, about everything that happened and I ... look, is there any way we can meet?"

"Where are you?"

"I'm here. In LA."

"Oh my God. You have to come over. To the house."

"Are you sure?"

"Yes. Can you come now?"

A weird laugh rumbles out of him. "Yeah. I can do that. I'll be there in about an hour."

When I hang up, Harrison explodes. "Are you crazy? He may be like his father."

"He's not. He never was."

"How do you know that?"

"I just do. You have to trust me."

He rubs his hair and walks around in a circle. Good thing we don't have carpet in here or there'd be a hole worn straight on through already.

An hour later, the doorbell rings. I fly to answer it, but Harrison's voice stops me. "Let me get that. Honest to God, you're gonna give me a fucking heart attack."

"It's fine. You'll see."

Pulling the door open with Harrison standing behind me, I gasp. Rusty is no longer the scrawny redheaded teenager that I remembered. In his place stands a tall, brawny, auburn-haired man. I stand gawking at him.

Hesitantly, he asks, "Velvet? Or Midnight, I guess it is now?"

I throw myself at him, hugging him. He hugs me back as I break down in tears. After a few minutes, Harrison clears his throat and asks, "Would you like to come in?"

"Oh, I'm sorry. Rusty, this is my husband, Harrison."

"Pleased to meet you, sir."

Harrison's brows arch. "Sir?" he asks. Harrison is only a few years older than Rusty.

Rusty chuckles. "It's tough to lose the military, you know."

We move inside and Rusty fills me in. Of all things, he's a Navy SEAL.

"Since I was no good at helping you when my dad was such a shit, I decided to be of help to others. It sort of snowballed, I guess."

"I'll say."

"I want you to know, Midnight, I called the police in Phoenix and told them I'd testify on your behalf. For the trial, if they needed me. He was a son of a bitch to you. Well, to all of us, but you got the worst of it."

"Whatever happened to your mom?"

"She died of liver disease. I guess alcohol was her way of dealing with him. She wasn't much of a mother to me, or to you, as far as that goes. Alcohol was her escape. I'll never touch the stuff."

Rusty and I catch up, Harrison patiently listening in and asking questions here and there. Several hours fly by and when he says he has to go, we exchange phone numbers and emails. He never knows where he'll be, but he's stationed down in Coronado, so maybe we can get together every so often. We promise to try, since neither of us has any blood relations.

After he leaves, Harrison says, "I like him. He's solid, you know?"

"Yeah. I'm glad things worked out for him."

"I'm glad they worked out for us too."

Epilogue

HARRISON

MIDNIGHT NEVER TURNS INTO A HOUSE. OKAY, MAYBE ONE OF those tiny houses that people are building these days. She claims she looks like she swallowed a huge watermelon. The kid is going to take after me, unfortunately.

It's November, and we're watching TV when she gets up to waddle into the kitchen for a glass of water. I'd gladly do it, but she claims sitting too long only adds to her aching back.

As she's standing there, she yelps like a puppy.

I'm there in a second. "What's wrong?"

She lifts up her shirt and her pants are wet.

"Did you pee?"

"My water just broke. I'd better shower so we can go to the hospital."

I help her to the bathroom and almost want to jump in with her.

Prescott and Vivi had their baby, a girl, and he claimed it was awful—the most nerve-wracking thing ever. I'm beginning to understand that now.

"Are you okay in there?"

"I'm fine."

About thirty seconds later, I ask, "How's it going?"

"Good."

Another thirty seconds pass and I can't take it anymore. "How long ..."

"Harrison, I have to rinse off. Jeez, give me a minute."

She finally comes out and her hair's wet. "You washed your hair?"

"Yeah. I wasn't sure when I'd be able to again."

"Okay, let me help you dry it."

"No, we're going with it wet. Did you call the doctor?"

"Was I supposed to?" She gives me the *you're a dumbass* look. Of course I was supposed to call. "Right, I'm calling now." We've had this thing rehearsed forever and now I'm failing miserably.

"You can call on the way. Did you grab my bag?"

"Your bag?"

"Yes, my bag for the hospital."

"Right. I'll get it now. Uh, where is it again?"

"In the closet, remember?"

I slap my forehead. "Right." I run to her closet and grab it. Then I run out to the car, only I leave her standing in the bedroom. I run back inside and she's smirking at me. Shit. "Let's go."

At least I'm together enough to usher her to the Mercedes and not the Mustang.

"Hang on."

"What?"

"I need to grab something." I jog to the Mustang and grab her bag out of the backseat where I tossed it. She rubs her temple.

I buckle up and we leave.

"Did you call the doctor?" she asks.

Shit. "I will now."

She grabs me by the shoulder and says, "Honey, take a deep breath. Now. For me."

I pause and do as she asks.

"Better?"

Nodding, I command the car to make the call to the doctor. When the answering service picks up, I say, "This is Harrison Kirkland and we're on the way to the hospital. We're having the baby." Then I hang up.

Midnight taps my arm.

"Yeah?"

"You do realize my last name is Drake."

She didn't change it because of her movie career. I'm not that big of an egomaniac, so I was cool with it.

"Yeah."

"The answering service has no idea who the patient is. I think I'd better handle this." She ends up calling. It works out much better that way.

Midnight is given a room and the nurse arrives. She's progressing well and eventually gets the epidural, which may help me as much as her. I'm doing my best to remain calm, but the truth is, I'm worse than a wreck. To see my wife, scared to death, groaning and writhing in pain, and not able to help her is the worst-case scenario for this fixer. I want to knock down the walls of this place. The nurses hate me. Not once, but several times I was down at their little station, demanding someone do something for her. They all assured me it was normal.

I finally grabbed one by the arm and got in her smug little face. "Listen to me. It may be normal for you, but the last time my wife had a baby, it was born with a congenital heart defect and ended up dying. This is traumatic for both of us, but especially her. Can't you do something?"

The smugness instantly disappears and is replaced with sympathy. "I'm so sorry. We'll have the doctor in there immediately."

The doctor shows up soon after and Midnight gets much better care after that. Our daughter finally announces her arrival into the world with one hell of a screech. They hand the baby over to us and Midnight has a loopy grin on her face.

"Guess she doesn't like it out here too much," she says.

"It's too bright for her. She wants to be all snug and cozy again." She's kicking her tiny legs out and crying again.

Then Midnight asks, "Is our baby ... is she okay?"

The doctor moves to the other side of Midnight from where I'm standing. "Yes, she is. Hear that cry? See how she's kicking her legs and how strong she is? And look how pink her skin is. She's healthy." The doctor takes a stethoscope and listens to the baby's heart. "She has a strong heartbeat too. Her Apgars are fine."

Midnight's smile brightens the room even further. A nurse comes over to wrap the little one in a blanket.

"Are you going to bathe her?" Midnight asks.

"Yeah, but we wanted to let you hold her awhile," the nurse says.

"Isn't she beautiful?" Midnight asks me.

"Looks exactly like her mother. Now we have to decide on her name."

"I want to go with your suggestion."

"And what if her eyes aren't lavender?" I ask.

"I still like it."

"Lavender Summer Kirkland."

She moves the blanket down to get a good look at the baby's face. "Are you sure it's not a goofy name? I don't want her going through life with a name like I did."

"There's the other option."

"You mean Harley?"

"Yeah. Harley Lavender Kirkland."

Midnight lets out a fierce laugh. "Helen would absolutely love that."

"And who's your best friend?"

"Helen."

"Let's do it. Harley, it is. I love the sound of that. Harley Kirkland."

The nurse comes over to take Harley to be weighed and measured.

Midnight grabs my arm and clamps down on Harley with the other. Her eyes dart around the room. "You can't take her."

"It's okay. They're going to bring her right back."

"No, you don't understand. The last time they took my baby, it was bad news." She's crying now and the nurse tries to take Harley again.

"You can't have my baby," Midnight cries. I'm trying to soothe her, but the nurse won't leave her alone.

"We only need to weigh and measure her. After we bathe her we'll bring her right back to you."

The doctor hears the commotion and comes over. "Here, let's get a quick weight and measurement now. I think the baby will be okay for a little while longer and then maybe Ms. Drake can go with you when you bathe her."

"How does that sound, Midnight? You want to bathe the baby with the nurse?" I ask.

"Yeah."

Another nurse moves in. "I have an idea. We'll bring everything to your room and bathe the baby there. How's that?"

Midnight is still drowsy so she nods. I take Harley and hand her to the nurse so she can weigh her. Maybe by tomorrow, Midnight will be over her panic.

The nurse hands Harley back and she rests on Midnight's chest until she falls asleep. About fifteen minutes later, she's crying and wanting to be fed.

The nurse, true to her word, brings in everything necessary to bathe Harley and Midnight happily watches them clean her up.

Harley doesn't have any issues with latching on. This is Midnight's first go-round with breastfeeding too. When she had baby Jack, she was so stressed out, she didn't produce enough milk at first so they had to supplement his feedings in the hospital with formula, and later she wasn't eating enough to keep up the demand so her milk dried up. That won't be the case this time.

I watch the two of them, and it's more than amazing to see how we created this tiny life. It steals my breath when I think about it.

All of a sudden, Harley lets out a wail.

"Guess she didn't like that."

"Like what?" I ask.

"Being switched to the other side."

Once she finds her food source again, she's a happy little thing. I marvel at them, the lovesick fool that I am. Midnight's lids droop with exhaustion. I'm amazed she's even still awake after giving birth. I'd be taking a twelve-hour nap. Pulling out my phone, I take some quick photos. She might want to kill me, but the two of them look absolutely beautiful.

Being as quiet as I can so I don't wake up the new mom, I bend down to see if Harley is asleep. Her eyes are slammed shut. This may be tricky, but I gently pick her up and cradle her to my own chest. She makes a tiny squeak, but that's it. I cover Midnight up with the blanket and sit down in the large recliner, laying the baby on my chest.

A few hours later, or I think it's that, a lusty cry awakens both Midnight and me. I jolt with the baby in my arms and realize where I am.

Midnight sits up in the bed and laughs. "We have a baby, and a loud one at that."

"She must take after her mother."

"Why do you say that?"

"Because I've heard you yell like that a time or two."

"Funny. Here, I'll take her. I bet she's hungry."

"Or maybe a dirty diaper?"

"Maybe. I'll let you handle that."

I'm instantly squeamish. "Me?"

"Yep. You need to get used to it. There'll be plenty of them."

Midnight gives me step-by-step instructions and it goes pretty well, until the diaper falls off when I'm done. She falls back on the bed in hysterics.

"It won't work."

"Make sure that Velcro stuff sticks, dummy."

"Shit."

"And don't curse around her."

"She's only a few hours old."

"We need to start now."

"You're right. I'll be better," I say.

There's a knock on the door and a cute elderly lady comes in dragging two carts behind her. They're loaded down with floral arrangements. "I have deliveries for you. Where shall I put them?"

"Wherever you can find room, I guess," I say.

I read Midnight all the cards. They're from everyone at the office, Mom and Dad, Weston and Special, and Prescott and Vivi.

"They're lovely."

"Not as lovely as you. I have something for you." I dig into the pocket of my jeans.

"What is it?"

"Close your eyes."

When she does, I hand take her hand and place the ring in her palm. When we got married, I only had a band for her. But today I'm giving her the diamond. It's a little backward, but what the hell.

"Harrison, it's beautiful."

"You like it?"

"I love it."

She slides the ring onto her finger. It's a round diamond but the band is what the jeweler called an eternity ring. I thought that was appropriate for us. "Since I didn't give you a diamond for our wedding, I thought now would be a good time."

"Thank you."

"Thank you for our daughter. She's the greatest gift of all."

"I'm glad you didn't give up on me and walk away when I was such a bitch to you."

"How could I? I was craving Midnight too much to do that." I lean down and press my lips to hers. It's always the same when I kiss her ... it's never enough and I'll always crave more.

Three Months Later

The cameras flash as we walk down the red carpet, my hand on Harrison's arm, and we stop every so often to pose and answer questions. I feel like a princess in my designer gown. Initially, I balked at wearing one, but Rita, and my new personal assistant, insisted. They said if I didn't, I would be a spectacle, and not in a good way.

When we finally make it into the theater, I'm ready to sit. Thank God I took Rita's advice about eating something before coming here.

"This is going to be a long night, filled with lots of talking and alcohol. If you don't eat, you'll regret it." Damn, she was right.

When we get to the front row, reserved for us, Helen is there, along with the crew from The Solution. Harrison's parents are present, Rusty (along with a date), and so are Weston and Special, and Prescott and Vivi. Holt and Helen are still together, believe it or not, in an on-again/off-again way.

Danny and Greg are floating on a cloud because the reviews for this movie are off the charts. Everyone says both Holt and I are shoe-ins for Oscar nominations. I won't hold my breath. I'm purely excited that the film is being thought of so highly. I have offers coming in right and left. My agent can barely keep up with everything.

We watch *Turned* and not a peep can be heard in the theater. In the final scene, when the letter is read, I hear people sobbing, and I'll admit, I'm one of them. When the credits roll, a thundering applause breaks out. Harrison pulls me to my feet and swings me around in the air. Then Holt does the same, followed by Danny and Greg.

"I knew you had it. I saw that spark from the start," Danny says.

Harrison pulls me close and whispers, "So did I. So did I, Midnight."

The End

Thank you so much for reading **Craving Midnight**. I hope you loved Midnight and Harrison. You can read more about The Men of Crestview in **Chasing Vivi** and **A Special Obsession**. You can also read Rusty's story in **I'll Be Waiting**, a novella.

If you want to stay up to date on the latest from me, please consider subscribing to my newsletter **here** or join my reader group on Facebook and become a hellion in **Hargrove's Hangout**.

I'LL BE WAITING
Lilou

Fighting for my country cost me part of my leg and my career.

Putting my life back together wasn't easy, but I did it.

Only I would never be the same.

I was broken, damaged, scarred.

And always would be.

But then I met *him*.

He was perfect in every sense of the word ...

Something I clearly was not.

Why is it the things you want the most are those you don't think you can ever have?

Rusty

When I saw her I knew she was mine.

There was one only thing standing in my way ... *her*.

But nothing was going to stop me, not even my ugly past.

I'd learned early on that the most important battles are the ones worth fighting... and there are some things worth waiting a lifetime for.

One Click **I'll Be Waiting** here.

A SPECIAL OBSESSION

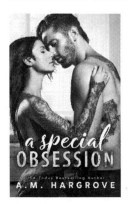

Rule Number One: Never let anyone get too close...

There was no way I would **ever** break that rule.

Even when the gorgeous **Weston Wyndham** woke up in my apartment. Even when he walked into my kitchen without a shirt and exposed those ridiculously sexy abs of his.

Not a chance. Especially after the arrogant ass started ordering me around.

In my house.

If he thought he could do that, just because he was a rich boy, then he'd better think again.

I was far too wise for that. I'd learned the hard way what those rich bad boys were all about.

Weston Wyndham was off limits.

End of story.

Only he had different ideas. Because for some reason, he kept showing up, pestering me.

But I had a very deep secret to guard.

If I wasn't careful, letting him in could spell disaster.

One Click **A Special Obsession here.**

CHASING VIVI

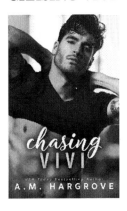

Prescott Beckham always got what he wanted … with one exception.

Ten years ago I was nothing but a highly functioning brain to the gorgeous Prescott Beckham.

We were classmates at Crestview Academy and all he saw in me was a way to get his homework done.

Now? He is Manhattan's wealthiest bachelor and is relentless in his pursuit of me.

The man refuses to take no for an answer.

Just because he can control everyone else in his life, he thinks he can strong arm me too.

I have some important information for Mr. Beckham.

I've changed. I am not the same person I was ten years ago.

So if he wants to keep this up, I only have one thing to say to that.

Game on.

One Click **Chasing Vivi** now!

About The Author

A.M. Hargrove

READER, WRITER, DARK CHOCOLATE LOVER, ICE CREAM Worshipper, Coffee Drinker, Lover of Grey Goose (and an extra dirty martini), Puppy Lover, and if you're ever around me for more than five minutes, you'll find out I'm a talker.

A.M. Hargrove divides her time between the mountains of North Carolina and the upstate of South Carolina where she pursues her dream career of writing. If she could change anything in the world, she would make chocolate and ice cream a part of the USDA food groups. Annie writes romance in several genres, including adult, new adult, and young adult. Her books usually include lots of suspense and thrills and she sometimes ventures into the paranormal, sci-fi and fantasy blend.

If you would like to hear more about what's going on in my world, please subscribe to my mailing list at
http://bit.ly/AMNLWP
You can also join my private reader group—Hargrove's

Hangout & Hellions— on Facebook if you're up to some shenanigans!
Please **stalk** me. I'll love you forever if you do. Seriously.

www.amhargrove.com
Twitter @amhargrove1
www.facebook.com/amhargroveauthor
www.facebook.com/anne.m.hargrove
www.goodreads.com/amhargrove1
Instagram: amhargroveauthor
Pinterest: amhargrove1
annie@amhargrove.com

For Other Books by A.M. Hargrove visit
https://amhargrove.com/book/
Or
https://smarturl.it/RLs

Adult Novels
The West Sisters Stand Alone Novels:
One Indecent Night
One Shameless Night - September 2019
One Blissful Night (TBD)

The West Brothers Stand Alone Novels:
From Ashes to Flames
From Ice to Flames
From Smoke to Flames

Stand Alones
Secret Nights
For The Love of English
For The Love of My Sexy Geek
I'll Be Waiting

The Men of Crestview Stand Alone Novels:
A Special Obsession
Chasing Vivi
Craving Midnight

The Edge Series Stand Alone Novels:
Edge of Disaster
Shattered Edge
Kissing Fire

The Tragic Duet Stand Alone Novels:
Tragically Flawed, Tragic 1
Tragic Desires, Tragic 2

The Hart Brothers Series:
Freeing Her, Book 1
Freeing Him, Book 2
Kestrel, Book 3
The Fall and Rise of Kade Hart
The Hart Brothers Series Boxset
Sabin, A Seven Novel
A Hart Brothers Novel Spin-off

YA/NA Clean Romance
The Guardians of Vesturon Series:
Survival
Resurrection
Determinant
reEmergent

Co-Authored Books
Cruel & Beautiful:
Cruel and Beautiful
A Mess of a Man
One Wrong Choice

A. M. HARGROVE

A Beautiful Sin

The Wilde Players Dirty Romance Series:
Sidelined
Fastball
Hooked

Worth Every Risk—
A Wilde Players Spin-Off

Other Books

For Other Books by A.M. Hargrove visit
https://smarturl.it/RLs
or
https://amhargrove.com/book/

Adult Novels
The West Sisters Stand Alone Novels:
One Indecent Night
One Shameless Night
One Blissful Night (TBD)

The West Brothers Stand Alone Novels:
From Ashes to Flames
From Ice to Flames
From Smoke to Flames

Stand Alones
Secret Nights
For The Love of English
For The Love of My Sexy Geek
I'll Be Waiting

The Men of Crestview Stand Alone Novels:
A Special Obsession
Chasing Vivi
Craving Midnight

The Edge Series Stand Alone Novels:
Edge of Disaster
Shattered Edge
Kissing Fire

The Tragic Duct Stand Alone Novels:
Tragically Flawed, Tragic 1
Tragic Desires, Tragic 2

The Hart Brothers Series:
Freeing Her, Book 1
Freeing Him, Book 2
Kestrel, Book 3
The Fall and Rise of Kade Hart
The Hart Brothers Series Boxset
Sabin, A Seven Novel
A Hart Brothers Novel Spin-off

YA/NA Clean Romance
The Guardians of Vesturon Series:
Survival
Resurrection
Determinant
reEmergent

Co-Authored Books
Cruel & Beautiful:
Cruel and Beautiful
A Mess of a Man
One Wrong Choice

Craving Midnight

A Beautiful Sin

The Wilde Players Dirty Romance Series:
Sidelined
Fastball
Hooked

Worth Every Risk—
A Wilde Players Spin-Off

Made in the USA
Las Vegas, NV
19 September 2021